He Never Forgot How to Love

Larry W. Plummer

BLACK ROSE
writing™

ISBN: 978-1-61296-922-0
PUBLISHED BY BLACK ROSE WRITING
www.blackrosewriting.com

Printed in the United States of America
Suggested Retail Price (SRP) $18.95

He Never Forgot How to Love is printed in Garamond Pro

For my Mom, the real "Momma Rose." This novel would not have lived through the third chapter without her unconditional love and support.

He Never Forgot
How to Love

Prologue

I twisted the hell out of Borgelt's ear and dodged the wild swing of his fist. It was the only way I could wake him, and the surest way to bring that smirk across his face.

"You're lucky I missed, Marshall."

"You're lucky I didn't kiss you on the cheek," I threatened.

"Yeah, then I wouldn't have missed," Borgelt promised.

"It's time to change the watch, Les," I stated the obvious.

Les shook like a wet dog to fight off the chill. "What time is it, Jake?"

"A couple hours before dawn."

Les pulled the clip out of his M16 to inspect its contents. "Is it still 1969? I could swear we've been here for three years on this all-expense-paid vacation to Vietnam."

"Yeah, Les, it's April 19, 1969 and it's a couple hours before dawn."

Les ejected the round from the chamber and looked down the barrel to ensure it was clear. "Yeah, you already said that."

"I was born a couple hours before dawn, Les."

Les shoved the clip back into his rifle and paused to listen.

"In twelve hours, it will be my birthday in Kansas, Les."

Les loaded a round in the chamber and patted me on the shoulder. "Damn, Jake, I should have baked you a cake."

Then he patted his weapon and ambled a few yards away. He leveled his rifle and began a sweep of the jungle.

I sat on the chilly, damp ground, pulled my poncho over me, and placed my life in Les Borgelt's hands.

I propped the M60 machine gun like a tent pole, and listened to the patter of rain on the poncho. Sleep came quickly, and so did the dreams. I drifted across 8,000 miles and back ten years. For two precious hours, I would not be in a war zone. I would not be hungry or cold or afraid. For two precious hours, it was my ninth birthday.

It was a Sunday. But Sundays and birthdays began the same as any other day on the farm.

Chapter 1

"Don't let the sun catch you sleepin', Jake."

I sat straight up at the sound of Daddy's wake-up call and planted my feet on the floor. The cold hardwood startled me awake.

I talked to myself to resist falling back into the warm envelope of the pillow. "Gotta keep moving. Gotta keep moving. Cows to milk, chickens to feed, hogs to slop."

I dressed against the pre-dawn chill, rambled down the stairs and stepped outside to breathe in the cool moist air.

It was the early spring of 1959 and the fields around Hays, Kansas were laden with the dew left behind by the crisp nightly wind across the prairie.

I began as always in the barn. I pressed my head and shoulders firmly against the cow as I milked and absorbed her alleviating warmth.

I held my breath as I poured the slop into the hog trough, and slowly sighed in relief as the bucket became lighter and lighter.

Each handful of chicken feed I tossed in the yard carried a multitude of dreams on the wind.

I washed up at the pump head and lumbered in to the kitchen table for breakfast. All those distant dreams and all my dreary labors melted away at the smell of Momma's biscuits and gravy. I could have lived in that moment forever.

When the last bite of biscuit sopped the plate clean of gravy, Momma instructed, "Hurry and get dressed for church."

I dressed in the latest clothes Momma had found in a yard sale. Everything was a bit too big, allowing for a few months of wear for a growing boy.

The shirt would never be pure white again, but the pants had no holes or patches and the shoes were clean.

Momma always carried a comb in her purse so she could try to tame my cowlick at the church entrance.

Daddy, Momma, Sister Josie and I would take our places in our usual pew and listen to a sermon that would peel the enamel right off your teeth. I figured the idea was to scare you into believing. After all, Daddy always said to fear nothing but God.

Walking home from church, Josie and I would often race ahead of Momma and Daddy. But on this Sunday, we straggled behind, shoving each other from side to side and calling each other names under our breath so Momma wouldn't hear.

It was the eternal battle of love between a bossy older brother and a dumb little sister. I could never shake that redheaded nuisance from tagging along wherever I went. But the truth was that Josie was always there any time I needed — I need her.

I could always count on Daddy for strength, encouragement, and an occasional good whuppin'. Momma was there for tender, loving care, and an occasional good whuppin'.

After a whuppin', Josie would come to sit by me. I would hide my face and Josie would stroke my hair — and just be there.

Josie helped me bury old Blondie and cried the tears I couldn't find. She laughed until she fell down the day I ripped my pants on the barbed wire, running from the neighbor's bull. I swore she pushed me into the creek one day, but it didn't matter after she jumped in behind me with a shriek of joy.

All the splashing and dunking washed away all fear of God. God is love and Josie is love.

As soon as we got out of our church clothes, Daddy grabbed the axe to go get a young fryer hen and Momma started peeling potatoes for that blue-ribbon potato salad acclaimed at the Ellis County Fair.

Josie and I started a batch of homemade ice cream. We took turns sitting on the freezer bucket while the other turned the crank, and Josie relished a few pieces of the salty ice swirling under the blanket.

It was more than a couple hours before we were eating, but the Kings of England have never eaten better. Nothing compares to the smell of fried chicken wafting through the outdoor breeze, and Sundays were perfect for stuffing yourself until there was no room for dessert.

There would be plenty of time for cake and ice cream after a blissful nap under the oak tree. Daddy played his fiddle, while Momma hummed along and held my head in her lap. I kept my eyes open just long enough to see Josie swaying to and fro, with her arms outstretched and her face to the sky.

Dusk settled over the farm, and the mosquitos started to bite. I woke to find myself alone under the tree. I followed the sound of Daddy's fiddle coming from inside the house. Climbing the back steps, I caught the glow of birthday candles reflecting in the window. There is no warmer glow this side of Heaven.

Nine candles to blow out. Devil's food cake with double Dutch chocolate frosting. Homemade ice cream. A brand-new fishing pole with the latest spin cast reel. Life could not get any better. But it did.

There was no school for Mrs. Marshall's little boy Jake on Monday morning. I finished my chores early and ran to find Daddy in the barn.

The sun was still hidden when Daddy and I headed down the path to the pond. Momma met us on the way with a thermos of hot broth, and Josie handed me a can of freshly dug worms.

I hope I said thank you. I can't recall. But they must have seen it in my eyes.

Daddy and I sat quietly on the bank of the pond and watched the sun slowly ascend into its rightful place. Silence was a time-honored rule of fishing. The intent was to not scare the fish away. But I think the real purpose was to not miss a single sight, sound or smell of nature.

I was sure I smelled the fish lurking below the surface. My heart beat a little faster each time I saw a ripple near my line, and the early morning songbirds filled our ears with their chorus.

Daddy began to speak in low tones. "Jake, you'll have to figure out most things in life as you go along. But there are a few things you need to know now."

I lowered my fishing pole and turned my head slightly toward Daddy, just to assure him that I was listening. This had to be important for Daddy to break the code of silence.

"Always take care of your family, Jake, especially your Momma and your Sis. Work hard and never give up. Never take unfair advantage of another man, and never let another man take unfair advantage of you. Remember who created you, Son. And remember your way home."

Daddy slowly reeled his line in a couple of feet and then gave me a glance.

I cranked my reel enough to make sure the line was taut and answered, "I'll remember, Daddy."

Chapter 2

"Jake, we're moving out, Jake." Tommy knew to announce himself before touching me when I was sleeping under a poncho with a loaded weapon.

I woke from my precious dreams and threw off the poncho. I felt the early Vietnam jungle air permeate my damp uniform, and a quick shiver made my voice break. "Where are we heading, Tommy?"

I don't know why I asked that. I was heading wherever Tommy went. He was our squad leader, but to me, he was so much more. He was the rock I had attached myself to and the reason I had been able to keep it together the past eight months.

I was the only one allowed to call him Tommy. But in front of the other guys, I called him Sergeant Weeks, and he called me Private Marshall. In one more month, Tommy and I would both be rotating back to the States. I couldn't wait to take Tommy fishing back home and to have him taste Momma's chicken.

"Well, Jake, my boy, I'm going to go get some chow. You coming with me?"

That got me to my feet. I hadn't had anything more than a few soggy crackers for the last two days.

Tommy grinned at the incredulous look on my face, pointed over my shoulder and said, "Chow is two klics that way. We have about an hour to get to the drop site, and you're taking point."

I understood completely and folded up my poncho. A helicopter was going to deliver our C-Rations to our doorstep, but we had to get to the doorstep in time. If you aren't popping smoke at the drop site when the chopper arrives, they can't hang around waiting to be shot out of the sky. And they're certainly not going to drop any rations for the Viet Cong, "Charlie," to get ahold of.

Tommy wanted me to set the pace, because he knew I was not going to miss out on a meal. In his thick Brooklyn accent, Tommy told me to swap the

M60 machine gun for Johnson's rifle and "Start humpin', Farm Boy."

Most guys would trade anything to not be out on point, but I saw the advantages of leading the way. You never got whipped in the face with a branch brushed aside by the guy in front of you, and you got to choose the path. I always got to choose the path when Daddy and I went hunting, because Daddy was wise enough to walk behind a nine-year-old carrying a loaded weapon.

With the map stuffed in my shirt, the compass hanging from my neck, and rifle at the ready, I waited for Tommy's signal. Tommy used a few signals of his own invention and I knew them all. Once he had positioned all ten of us, he removed his helmet and swept it from his left to his right in a swooping bow, as if to say, "After you."

The hunt was on in that ever-present disparity between being the hunter and the hunted. All thoughts of home, of yesterday, or of tomorrow had to be tucked away to focus mind, body and spirit on that next perilous step.

Fear was both friend and foe, but could never be allowed to be the master. Knowing that we were on Charlie's turf kept my head and eyes swiveling back and forth and my ears tuned to every sound of the jungle. Charlie had such an extensive network of underground tunnels that he could appear virtually out of nowhere.

Every few minutes, I heard Tommy's unique call behind me. It was a sound from deep in his throat that was impossible to describe. It was a low tone that wouldn't carry too far. It was unlike any sound I'd heard from man or animal. It was the sound of Tommy alone.

Tommy and I took another look at the map, the compass and the time. Tommy sent me off again with that confirming pat on the back. Tommy took a vigilant stance on one knee as he watched to ensure that everyone behind was accounted for.

I halted once again at Tommy's call, and he said, "Good job, Jake. Our drop site is a small clearing just ahead. Find yourself a good spot in eye-shot of the clearing while I get the rest of the perimeter secured. We'll rendezvous fifty meters to the west of the clearing."

I crawled through the undergrowth until a ray of sunlight made me squint my eyes. I crouched in a spot where I could survey the clearing and waited.

I heard the familiar Whop-Whop-Whop of the chopper blades in the distance and saw the purple smoke rising above the trees. The Whop-Whop-Whop grew louder, which always made my heart beat a little harder. It was the sound of power and the promise of relief. It was the lifeline between strife and deliverance.

As soon as our rations hit the ground, the chopper was gone in a flash. Sanchez and Borgelt ran out to grab the bundle and started dragging it to the rendezvous point.

Fifty meters into the brush, Tommy posted security, as Sanchez opened the cartons, making sure they were upside-down.

Each individual box of C-Rations was labeled on top as to what was inside. To avoid the delays of picking and choosing, the cartons were always opened upside-down.

One of the favorite C-Ration meals was spaghetti and meat sauce, while the most dreaded was ham and lima beans. The beans were so hard, we joked that they should be fired from mortars at the enemy.

One by one, we each came in to grab a couple boxes and returned to our position. We wouldn't be eating, however, until we had walked a couple of hours farther from the clearing where we had popped the smoke.

Johnson was out on point for this trek and I had the M60 back. The weight of the machine gun was worth the feeling of confidence I had in its awesome effectiveness. But adding the weight of a metal box of ammo reminded me of trying to carry two buckets of milk from the barn without spilling a drop.

The two-hour walk made the weight seem to double, and I remembered how each bale of hay bucked onto the wagon was heavier than the last.

Tommy picked our spot to rest and posted security in two-man teams. One man of each pair would eat while the other kept watch.

Tommy positioned himself near me and offered, "I'll take the first watch. You just save me a piece of your Momma's fried chicken."

I leaned back against a tree and took a big gulp of water from my canteen. "Oh, I wish, Tommy. Today is my nineteenth birthday."

"Well I'll be damned, Farm Boy. Who would've thought we'd live to see that?"

It was easier to joke about death. It seemed to somehow keep the thought of death at bay.

I poured a little water on the back of my neck. That splash of water brought back the memory of washing up at the pump head after chores.

I looked at the label on the C-Rations and called to Tommy. "Well happy birthday to me."

I held up the box of rations — and a bullet pierced right through the ham and lima beans.

In one resounding thud, all bellies hit the ground, and a barrage of small arms fire shredded the jungle above our heads. The deafening roar was obviously more firepower than our small squad could return.

A confused muddle of thoughts raced through my mind. "Where did these guys come from? I can't even lift my head to set up the gun. Where's Tommy?"

There is no greater chaos than when you are trapped between the rumbling earth beneath you and a torrent of death above. Your hands cannot block the thunderous tumult from your ears, and your mind is rendered catatonic. The slightest wrong move is certain death and there is no right move.

Tommy stood straight up so all could see him and waved his arm in the opposite direction of fire. That was his signal that our only hope of survival was to run.

I pawed the ground until I felt the cold steel of the M60. I straightened out the belt of ammo trailing from the gun and sent up one last prayer.

The only way to remove a loose tooth is to yank quick and hard. The only way to jump into the freezing depths is to GO!

I vaulted to my feet with the M60, spraying every last round in the belt. I hoped that Charlie would put his head down long enough for us to start the run for our lives.

All my senses blurred as the old friend fear made me dig each stride from within. I kept my eyes fixed forward, not daring to look back. My head was pounding as I fought for one more breath and one more stride.

I snagged my foot and sailed headlong into the brush. I felt the concussion of a grenade and heard the whistling of the shrapnel whizzing over me. I started to crawl without a coherent thought. "Gotta keep moving. Cows to milk, chickens to feed…"

I froze when I felt a hand on the ground. There was something in that touch that made the world stop. It was a surreal passage from disbelief to realization — that's all it was, a hand.

I stared at the hand and my eyes filled with the first tears I had shed in Vietnam. I was looking at Tommy's class ring. I shut my eyes tight, peeled Tommy's ring from his finger and clasped it in my hand.

I whimpered, with my fist between my teeth and felt the barrel of an AK47 rifle against my head.

I waited for the bullet. I waited for the darkness. Faces from home flashed through my mind. Screams of pain filled the battlefield.

I wanted that bullet. I wanted that darkness. I wanted the screams to stop. I wanted the nightmare to end. "PLEASE, PULL THE TRIGGER!"

One by one, sporadic gunshots silenced the screams, but my bullet never came. My life was not spared. My death was denied.

I was stripped of my gear and my pockets were emptied, but I didn't care. A rope was noosed around my neck and cinched up tight, but I didn't care. Charlie reached to find what was clenched in my fist, and then I cared.

I gripped Tommy's ring so hard, my nails pierced my skin. "NO! NO! PULL THE TRIGGER, MOTHERF--KER! NO!"

I lost that battle to a rifle butt in the face. I lost the last piece of Tommy, and there was nothing left to care about.

Half led and half drug through the jungle, bound and leashed, the gun smoke stuck in my throat and stung my eyes. A rifle butt incessantly pounded on my back, pushing me to pick up the pace. I stumbled and fell more than a few times, and the only reason to get up again was to stop the kicks to my ribs.

Each step was a step further into degradation. Each breath was a breath I didn't want. Each thought was riddled with guilt. I didn't want to live. I just had to.

I watched the sun trek from east to west and counted each step. First to the northeast, and then due north. We walked miles by day and more by night.

51,045 steps northeast and 64,523 steps north and I was tied to a tree for the night. A scrap of food was shoved in my mouth. I chewed, I tasted the disgusting morsel, and I hated.

Each day was more of the same and always to the north. Each night was worse, and I hated more.

I had counted over 300,000 steps when Charlie put the plastic bag over my head. He cinched it tight around my throat and I didn't care. The bag stuck to my face and cut off my air, but I didn't fight it. The sight of hell on earth began to blur. The smell of death and my own stench faded. The sound of my own breath ceased, and I was grateful.

Charlie ripped the plastic bag off my head and pissed in my face. I gasped and sputtered, and I was cheated of death once more.

"OH, GOD, HELP ME! I WANT TO DIE!"

"OH, GOD, FORGIVE ME! I WANT TO KILL!"

Rage kept me going after that. A new mission formed in my mind. It was the foulest of purpose, but it was all I cared to live for. I had to kill just one Charlie.

I memorized every face of Charlie. I studied every weapon and every movement he made. I sneered and relished the fact that Charlie was staying farther and farther away from the stench of my soiled trousers. If I ever got just one hand free, it would be his last smell.

Perhaps Charlie noticed my sneers. Perhaps he saw his own death in my eyes. He cinched the rope tighter around the tree that night. His boot to my chin made me spit blood. His boot to my ribs made me pant and struggle for another breath of hate.

I willed myself to sleep, grinding my teeth. Charlie got to live one more day, but maybe tomorrow...

A hand placed over my mouth jolted me awake. I cringed and struggled against a force I could not see. It was time to fight. It was finally time to die. If only I had one hand free.

My vision cleared and the moonlight revealed the gentlest pair of eyes. He was just a boy, like me. He was just a soldier who had seen enough of war. He was a brother who could bear no more.

I was the one bound and helpless, but Young Charlie's eyes begged for mercy. He relaxed his hand from my mouth and smiled. He opened his other hand, and a faint glimmer of light reflected off Tommy's ring.

My mouth flew open, and Young Charlie closed it with his hand. He nodded and I nodded back. He withdrew his hand and slipped the ring into my pocket.

Young Charlie thumped my chest and pointed southeast. He thumped again and pointed. I nodded faster. It was faster than a nod of understanding. It was the rapid nod of "YES! THANK YOU! YES!"

Young Charlie circled the tree and cut my bonds. I spun around and looked, but my Friend Charlie had vanished into the bush.

I turned to the southeast and went into a crouch. Freedom is a scary thing, so easily taken away.

I started moving slowly, picking my way through the jungle. I hoped that I was the only one who could hear my heart pounding.

The farther I went, the more erect I became and the quicker my feet advanced. Faster and faster, I progressed in a straight line until I had accelerated into a dead run. The plan was simple now. I had to cover as much ground as possible before daylight and find a place to hide.

My pace slowed, but never ceased as the night rushed by. The dense flora whipping my face only confirmed that I was being swallowed up into the concealment of the jungle.

I felt the temperature drop, and I knew that I was in a race against the revealing rays of dawn. I was driven by the will that exists somewhere between heart and mind, with a singular thought, "Remember your way home, Son."

At the first hint of daylight, I collapsed in a hollow, covered by the cold, damp brush, and my body heaved into numbness. I curled into a ball and drifted into oblivion. I mouthed the words, "If I should die before I wake, I pray the Lord my soul to take."

I was absent, as the next day passed without me. Wars raged on. Battles were won and battles were lost. People lived and people died. But I lay dormant.

It was my sweat from the late afternoon sun that made me stir. I writhed against that groggy, intolerable state that one tries to ignore but cannot deny. As each bit of remembrance awakened in my mind, I uttered a weak moan. I shot straight up and stifled a scream.

I looked wildly about for the ghouls that had filled my nightmares and I strained for a grip on reality. My first clear thought was of the docile eyes of my friend, Charlie.

God does not grant wishes. He answers prayers. I did not die as I had prayed. I did not kill as I had wished. God chose life for me and my friend, Charlie.

I reached into my pocket and felt Tommy's ring encircle my finger. It was like the pinch that tells you this is not a dream. I pulled the ring out into the light and slid it onto my finger.

I saw Tommy. He was pointing home. I felt him. He was patting me on the back. I heard him, "We'll be right behind you."

Tommy was there. He was scanning the floor of the jungle with me, looking for shadows to determine my bearings. He was watching as I drew in the dirt to formulate my plan.

Let's see. We were here when the C-Rations were dropped. We were there when all hell broke loose. 51,000 steps northeast, divided by two is about 25 klics. 250,000 steps north are about 125 klics. That would mean friendly territory is 200 to 300 klics southeast.

"Is that right, Tommy?" I turned the ring on my finger and Tommy agreed.

I can go maybe one klic per hour in this brush. I should have five or six hours of darkness to travel each night. 300 klics divided by six...

"OH, MY GOD!"

The math was irrefutable. Two months of walking and crawling lay ahead for this already beaten and starved body.

Is it possible? Am I up to it? "Start humpin', Farm Boy" was the answer.

Dark clouds preceded the sunset and sent down their refreshing drops. I lay on my back, with my mouth wide open and drowned in gulps.

"I'm going to do this," I said to myself. "Stick with me, Tommy, and try to keep up."

Darkness descended and I took my first steps toward home. My head was on a swivel and my senses were peaked.

I heard sounds I had never noticed before. I saw the silhouettes of small animals scurrying to hide, just like me. I felt their panic and I smelled the fear of freedom too easily lost.

I met my goal before first light. I was 12,000 steps closer to home. I hid, I slept and I dreamed.

I was at the regional track meet of my senior year. I had spent too much gas fighting for second position in the mile run. I was ready to drop, and there were a hundred yards to go.

I saw Daddy near the finish line, whooping and leaping. Momma was screaming and pounding on Daddy. Josie was running along the sidelines yelling at me, "That bull's right behind you, Jake. RUN!"

The other guy had the speed and the endurance, and he knew it. Victory would be his. He had no doubt. All I had was my family to run home to.

They told me I had won when I collapsed in their arms. But all I knew was that I had made it home.

I kept that dream in my mind as I plodded through the endless jungle. I felt my body wither a little more each day. Bugs, berries and leaves passed through my intestines, some faster than others. A snake in the grass was no match for my teeth. I can't say that it tasted just like chicken, because I had never eaten a raw chicken.

I travelled by night and slept by day. I lapped every drop of rain I could catch and I walked. Survival of the fittest was the name of the game, and I knew I was losing.

I woke on the nineteenth day in a pile of dung, but it didn't smell any worse than me. I tied another knot in the vine to mark the day and raised my feeble frame upright.

I scanned the jungle and reached for Tommy's — "TOMMY'S RING! IT'S GONE!"

The ring had slipped off my bony finger and I dropped to my knees. I scratched and searched all around me, swatting at the flies flitting around my head. It was the flies that pointed me toward that small round depression in the dung.

They were crawling in and out of that fresh hole, in search of the sweet treasure beneath.

I plunged my hand deep in the shit and felt it. The ring was in my grasp once more. I shoved the ring in my pocket, covered in the gooey sweet stench, and Tommy was with me again.

I sat in the filth and watched the flies. A worm wiggled to the surface and I held back a laugh. Josie's voice echoed in my head. "I bet you can't eat one."

I dug with both hands. I pawed my way into the crust of the earth and a bounty of worms wiggled and squirmed. I imagined Josie's freckles cringing together as I swallowed each and every worm.

Josie never left my mind after the nineteenth day. I couldn't shake her. She was always tagging along, and she would just not shut up.

I came upon the edge of a clearing and motioned to Josie. "Keep your head down, Dummy, and shut up."

I worked my way around the clearing, looking back to check on Josie. I halted at the west edge of the clearing and signaled Josie to advance.

Josie was at my side in a heartbeat and I ordered, "Stay here, Dummy."

I took five more steps, and tumbled headfirst into a stream. I came up gasping and looking for Josie. As sure as the angels live among us, Josie was there. She was floating down stream, with her arms outstretched and her face to the sky.

I waded and floated down that stream night after night. There weren't enough bugs or berries or snakes, but there was always Josie. My body wasted away and hope dwindled, but I kept following Josie.

My face never left the ground as I dragged myself out of the stream and into the brush. I tied the thirty-seventh knot in the vine and knew that it would be the last. I would not make it back to the stream that night. I just knew. I had fought the good fight. I had finished the race. Josie would have to go on without me.

I had remembered my way home, but I wasn't going to make it. There was only one thing left to remember, the One who created me.

My fingers trembled as I tapped out the rhythm of the tune invading my head. *"Just a closer walk with Thee…"*

It was Momma's voice singing that hymn. It was Daddy's fiddle that carried the tune. The music grew louder, just out of my reach.

I inched along the ground, following the melodic call. I crawled into my past and I crawled toward my destiny. The brush parted and gave way to the rising sun over a lush green field.

Daddy's bow was blazing across the strings in the middle of that field. Josie was prancing and twirling and her red hair was sailing in the breeze. Momma was sitting in the grass, beckoning me to her arms.

I grabbed at the clumps of grass and pulled myself toward Momma. I made it. I made it all the way. I laid my head on Momma's lap, and I was home.

I never gave up and I never forgot. I let go and I remembered.

The last thing I remembered was hearing that familiar Whop-Whop-Whop.

Chapter 3

I woke from a lifetime worth of dreams in a Naval Hospital bed on the island of Guam. An angel was watching over me and tending to the tubes of fluids trickling into my body.

She leaned over me and said, "It's about time you woke up, Cowboy. I'm Cassie."

Her eyes were too irresistible to escape, and her smile was too genuine to be more than a dream. I reached up to touch that vision, but my hand quivered and strayed. Cassie clasped my hand and I was sure that heaven is real.

"You're on Guam, and we're going to get you home," she promised. "Just rest easy, and let me know when I can get you some real food."

I pulled her hand closer and begged, "Now, please."

She pressed my hand against her face and ensured, "You've got it, Cowboy, as soon as the doctor takes a look at you."

Cassie coaxed my hand onto my chest and lingered until my grip relaxed. She looked back before she left the ward to give me a wink of assurance that I would see her again.

Doctor Mackenzie addled my brain with examination notes and lab results. My pulse quickened and my breathing shortened into exasperated breaths.

The doctor laid his charts aside and spoke in words a farm boy could grasp. "You have no significant organ damage that we can't turn around. This young body will heal, and you'll be as good as new."

I disagreed. "I'll never be new again, Doc. But that's ok. I'll probably never own a new car. But that's ok. Just fill the tank and check the oil. I'll settle for being a good used car."

"How about we clean the windshield too," the doctor chuckled.

"I'd appreciate that, Doc. Can I see Cassie now?"

The doctor wagged his head. "You boys all want to see Cassie."

"Doctor?" the major interrupted. "We need to talk to your patient."

Doctor Mackenzie turned to face the major and kept me hidden behind his back. "And you are?"

"I'm Major Halverson and this is Lieutenant Montgomery. We're with the Military Intelligence unit and we have to ask your patient some questions."

The doctor placed his hand on the major's chest and backed him up a few feet. "This boy has been through a living hell. You need to let him rest."

"We have our orders, Doctor," the major pushed back. "I could get the General on the phone."

The doctor drilled a fiery look at the major. "Very well, Major. You have your orders. But if you endanger my patient's recovery, I will have your ass."

Doctor Mackenzie turned back to me. "I don't know your name, son. You didn't have any dog tags."

"Jake Marshall," I introduced.

The doctor shook my hand and leveled, "I'm going to go look for Cassie, Jake. You let me know if these guys give you any trouble."

The doctor shot one more warning glare at the major and stepped away.

"So, your name is Jake Marshall," the major confirmed. The lieutenant scribbled on his pad.

"It's actually John Alan Marshall, after my grandfather. How did I get here?"

"What is your rank, Marshall?"

"Private First Class. How did I get here?"

And your serial number, Private?" The lieutenant insisted.

"5 – 1 – 2… HOW DID I GET HERE?"

My shout echoed through the ward and the officers frantically looked around for the doctor that would have their ass.

"You were spotted by a reconnaissance flight," the major revealed. "They picked you up just south of the DMZ."

I pressed my head deep into the pillow. "South of the demilitarized zone," I repeated. "Oh, God!" I praised. "I really did make it home."

"Yes, well, let's continue, Private," the major pressed on. "What unit were you with?"

"3rd Battalion, 187th Infantry," I was proud to declare.

The questions came faster and harder. "Where was your unit operating last? When and how did you get separated from your unit? What date was it?"

The questions swirled in my head and the answers churned in my gut. I knew where we were when I heard those screams. I knew how I got separated from life and sent to hell. I knew the date of my own birthday. And I heard Tommy's voice, "Well I'll be damned, farm boy. Who would have thought we'd live to see that?"

"CASSIE!" I screamed. I lashed out and sent the lieutenant's pad and pen sailing across the ward.

"Whoa, son," the major tried to calm. "It's ok. Take it easy."

"CASSIE!" I screamed.

Cassie pushed the major out of her way and grabbed my hand. "I'm here, Cowboy. I'm here."

I was inhaling more than exhaling, trying to catch my breath.

Cassie threw a piercing glare at the officers and they retreated for the day.

"I see trees of green, red roses too…"

Cassie sang and my breathing slowed.

"I see them bloom for me and you…"

My heart stilled and my mind floated.

"And I think to myself, what a wonderful world."

My eyes drooped and I drifted away.

"I see skies of blue and clouds of white…"

Cassie stayed with me until the sun set. She laid her head on my chest and she was still there when the sun rose again.

I woke first and watched her breathe. Breathing is the gift most taken for granted, until it's taken away. It is so little understood because we don't have to think about it. But I watched every breath Cassie took and understood a little more.

Breath is given to us, but it is not ours to give away. It is ours to share, and I shared every breath.

Cassie stirred and woke with a start. "Oh, my gosh! I've got to call my Mom. She's got to be worried sick."

Cassie raced away and the guy in the bed next to me rose onto his elbow. "You're one lucky bastard," he grinned. "What's your secret with women?"

I laced my fingers behind my head and gloated, "You have to breathe with them, brother."

Cassie was back in two shakes, carrying a big bowl of Jell-O. The Jell-O jiggled as she waltzed through the ward.

Voices echoed and competed all through the room. "Good morning, Cassie!"

"Good morning, guys."

Cassie stopped at Adam's bed and reached in her apron pocket. "Got a letter from home for you, Handsome."

Adam had no hands, but he had a smile.

"I'll be back to read that letter to you, Handsome."

The Jell-O jiggled a few feet more. "Surgery today, Skip. You ready to get that knee working again?"

"I'm ready if you'll be there, Cassie."

"I'll wheel you out of here and I'll wheel you back, Sweetie."

The Jell-O jiggled from bed to bed, until Cassie set it on the stand next to me.

"Jonesy!" Cassie scolded the guy leaning on his elbow next door.

"The doctor told you to lie still and let that lung heal. Now you lie down and just breathe easy."

Jonesy laid back and had his moment of breathing with Cassie.

Cassie picked up the bowl and scooped a spoonful of Jell-O. "What's your name, Cowboy?"

I lusted for that spoonful. "Jake," I craved.

I had earned one spoonful of heaven. I let it melt in my mouth as it should. I let it slide down my throat and I lusted for more.

The next spoonful was held farther away. "Jake what?"

I would answer anything for that next bite. "Marshall."

The next spoonful hadn't yet left the bowl. "Tell me about your girlfriend, Josie."

"MY WHAT?"

The spoonful swayed back and forth and taunted me. "I heard you call her name in your sleep."

"Oh, Josie's just my dumb sister!"

The spoonfuls kept coming after that. Cassie had heard all she needed to know for now.

Cassie left, as I knew she must. She had promises to keep. Each soldier in each bed had a wish to be granted. Cassie read the letters and fluffed the pillows. She held a straw to the thirsty mouth. She held the hand of a frightened soul. And every now and again she gave me another wink.

"She's a looker, isn't she?" the captain surprised me. I saw the cross on his lapel and the solace in his eyes.

"I'm Chaplain Ensley."

"I'm Jake, Sir."

"Please, call me anything but Sir. How about Brother Bob?"

"I can always use another brother, Bob."

Brother Bob and I prayed and we talked. I told him about how badly I had wanted to kill, and Bob talked about forgiveness. I told him about the friends I lost, and Bob talked about eternal life. I told him about my Friend Charlie, and Bob said, "Thy Will Be Done."

"I see your ride coming, Jake."

Cassie rolled a wheelchair next to my bed. "Hi, Brother Bob," she greeted. "Could you find us some more bibles? These guys keep walking off with them when they check out," she chuckled.

"That's music to my ears," Bob smiled.

"Jake has an appointment with Doctor Albertson," Cassie announced.

"That's our local shrink," Jonesy tipped off.

"Jonesy!" Cassie scolded. "You know he doesn't like to be called that."

"So, they think I'm crazy?" I ventured.

Jonesy coughed a laugh. "Everybody that ends up in this place has reason to be a little nuts."

I threw my legs over the side of the bed. "I think I can walk. I'd like to stretch my legs."

"The wheelchair is hospital regulation," Cassie insisted.

I slipped off the bed and landed on legs of Jell-O. I wobbled and swayed and then sank into the wheelchair.

Cassie put the slippers on my feet and teased, "Now that you've stretched your legs, here we go."

She pushed the chair through the corridor and leaned over to speak softly. "Doctor Albertson's a good psychiatrist, and he's also a very good listener. The crazy ones are the guys who don't talk to him."

She wheeled me into the private office and introduced me.

The doctor began with a handshake, and I already liked him. "I'm Major Albertson, but while you're in this room, I'm just Al. Thank you, Cassie."

Cassie helped me onto the couch and whispered, "Talk." She stepped out of the office and closed the door.

Al sat in his overstuffed chair and tossed a tennis ball at me. I made a good catch and I liked him more.

"Are you a tennis player, Al?"

"Nah, I never cared for the game, mostly because I stunk at it."

"My first laugh in months spewed out of me."

"I'm a golfer, Jake." Al grabbed another tennis ball and began to squeeze. "This does wonders for my grip on the club."

It was as contagious as a yawn and I began to squeeze.

Al closed his eyes and breathed in rhythm with his squeeze. "It also helps me picture in my mind making that perfect sweet swing. Try it, Jake."

Al opened his eyes to watch my breathing slow and my grip grow stronger.

"What would be a perfect thing for you to visualize, Jake?"

"Oh, that's easy, Al. It would be the first light of day reflecting off the pond."

Behind my eyelids, I saw my heaven on earth. I stood only four foot five and Daddy was watching me swing my rod around, sending my bait across the water.

My eyes flew open. "Wow! That really works, Al. I made the perfect cast."

"Don't stop now, Jake. Close your eyes. Breathe and squeeze. Where is this pond?"

I closed my eyes and found that picture again, and I squeezed. "The pond is on our farm back in Kansas."

"I've never been to Kansas. Take me for a walk around the farm, Jake. Tell me what I see."

"It's summer. You can almost see the heat waves in the air, but there's a nice breeze. Do you smell that, Al?"

"What do I smell, Jake?"

"You smell everything. You smell the breeze off the wheat field and the earth under your feet. You smell the fish under the surface of the pond. Even the occasional whiff of manure smells sweet now."

"I smell it, Jake. Tell me about the happy times."

I scooted lower on the couch and laid my head back on Momma's lap. "My ninth birthday. You should have been there, Al. Everything was perfect. Everything was — wonderful."

"You can go back there anytime, Jake. You can see any and all birthdays."

I crushed the tennis ball and panted and writhed on the couch.

Al grabbed my shoulders. "Breathe, Jake, squeeze. Where are we, Jake?"

"The jungle — I can't breathe, Al!"

"Squeeze and breathe, Jake. Squeeze and breathe." Al sat next to me on the couch and wrapped his arms around me. "I've got you, Buddy. Is this your birthday?"

"Yes! Yes! Get your head down, Al, don't move! No — no — we've got to run, Al. Tommy says to run. I can't get up, Al! HELP ME, AL, HELP ME!"

Al lifted me to my feet, but I collapsed and took us both to the floor. I curled up into a ball and Al kept his arms around me.

"Their gone, Al."

"Who's gone, Jake?"

"Tommy," I panted. "Borgelt — Sanchez — Cooper — all of them. EVERBODY'S DEAD!"

"Let's get out of here, Jake. Breathe and squeeze. Take us back to the farm, Jake. Breathe and squeeze. Take us home."

I squeezed hard and I breathed hard. I ran miles and miles through my mind and Al ran with me. I ran out of breath and I ran out of squeeze.

"We have a long way to go, Jake, but we're going to make it. We're going to make it."

Al helped me back onto the couch and we rocked. We rocked until the end of the hour, and there was a knock on the door.

I relaxed and dropped the tennis ball. "Cassie?"

Al smiled and shook his head, and opened the door. "You're just what the doctor ordered, Cassie."

He led Cassie to the couch. "Have a seat and keep Jake company while I go get us some coffee."

Cassie sat and ran her fingers through my sweaty hair and Al left the room.

"Well I guess you talked, Cowboy. I could hear you down the hall."

I looked at her and her smile was contagious too. "Yeah, well, sorry about that."

Cassie leaned back and pulled my head onto her shoulder. And she sang.

We had our coffee with Al. We shared a tear or two and we shared a laugh or two. I was hoisted back into the wheelchair and Al put the tennis ball in my hand. "Cassie, make us an appointment for tomorrow. Jake and I have some more walking to do."

Cassie was still humming her sweet tune as she wheeled me down the hall. I closed my eyes and squeezed.

A Navy Yeoman blocked our way and brought us to a halt. "I've got them on hold, Cassie. Bring him down now."

Cassie pushed faster and the yeoman cleared the way. "Where are we going, Cassie? Isn't there a speed limit in here?"

"Just hang on, Cowboy!"

We spun around the corner and turned into a room full of electronics. The yeoman grabbed the telephone receiver and reported, "I've got him."

He handed me the receiver and said, "Say hello."

I hesitated, but Cassie nodded, "Yes."

"Hello?"

"Where have you been, Fathead?"

"JOSIE!" I screamed.

Cassie kissed her finger and planted it on my forehead. "Talk, Cowboy."

Cassie and the yeoman left the room and I talked. I talked, I listened and I loved. Momma's voice was full of tears, and Daddy's voice held them back. And Josie's voice stroked my hair.

Cassie wheeled me back to bed, and tucked in the sheet. She dipped the spoon into the bowl of tapioca. "Now, tell me about Josie."

"No," I refused. "Not until you tell me your last name."

"Johnson, Cowboy. Cassie Johnson."

I got my tapioca and Cassie got to know Josie, and Momma, and Daddy.

Cassie took me on many rides down the halls. Al walked with me many a mile through my memories. Each day, I felt a little closer to home and each day, my legs grew stronger.

Cassie helped me graduate from Jell-O to tapioca and to oatmeal. Then we walked.

Cassie walked me to the bathroom and I was done with bedpans. She walked me to the cafeteria, and I graduated to beef vegetable soup.

I was wielding my own spoon now, and it was time for Cassie to talk.

"Have you always lived on Guam, Cassie?"

"Oh, no. I'm a Texas girl from Fort Worth."

Cassie crumbled a couple crackers in her soup. "My dad works at the Naval Fire Station here. I love the island, but it's still not home."

"What's your middle name, Cassie?"

"You first, Cowboy."

"Actually, I'm John Alan, named after my grandfather, but I can't remember when I wasn't called Jake. Your turn."

"Cassandra."

"Cassandra? As in Cassie? Ok, what's your first name?"

Cassie looked up from her soup without raising her head. "Melanie Cassandra Johnson. But don't you dare ever call me…"

"Ok, ok, I've got it, Cassie."

Cassie kept her warning glare fixed on me and chewed her soggy crackers.

"Any brothers or sisters?" I probed further.

Cassie stopped chewing and let her spoon sink in the soup. She couldn't look at me and she could barely utter the words. "I, uh — had a little sister."

I reached for her hand and shuddered to ask, "Had?"

Cassie was done eating. "Can we walk?"

We walked to the court yard and claimed a bench. Cassie drew in the fragrance of the tropical flowers, and I watched and waited.

"I had a little sister for two days. She was so tiny — so frail."

I was afraid to say the wrong thing or to say the right thing wrong. So, I just listened.

"I got to hold her for a few minutes." Cassie stood and walked over to the plumeria.

She rubbed a petal and sniffed the fresh burst of perfume. "Maybe it would have been easier if I had never touched her."

I walked over and chanced a stroke of Cassie's hair. "No, it wouldn't have been easier. The slightest touch is worth all the pain."

Cassie reached behind her and wrapped my arms around her waist. I breathed and squeezed. "What was her name?"

Cassie picked a blossom and held it to my nose. "Gretchen."

"Aren't we a pair?" Cassie squeaked.

We headed back to the ward and I never let go.

Chapter 4

Cassie had finished her rounds the next morning and she was watching the rapid movements behind my eyelids.

A small box, wrapped in a bow was resting on my chest, rising and falling with the pace of my dreams.

Jonesy could stand no more. "Wake up and open the box for God's sake!"

I rubbed the sleep from my eyes and looked at Jonesy. "Who is this girl, Jonesy?"

I learned that Cassie knew how to throw a punch, and my shoulder would remind me for days.

"Open it!" Cassie demanded.

Jonesy laughed and coughed and I rubbed my shoulder. I untied the bow and reached in the box.

I felt that perfect golden circle, and I felt Tommy with me again.

A simple neck chain trailed from Tommy's ring, and Cassie bubbled, "We got it all shined up for you."

"Oh — geez — oh — I thought I lost this in the jungle." I clenched my fist around the ring and Cassie saw the tear trying to escape my eye.

"I thought we could hang it around your neck until we fatten-up your fingers," Cassie proposed.

"This isn't my ring," I choked.

I looked over at Jonesy, and he was ready to cry. He knew why a guy would carry a brother's class ring.

Cassie looked at Jonesy's tears and back at mine. "Are you ok, Cowboy? I'm sorry if I…"

"It's ok, Cassie. You didn't do anything wrong. You've given me more than you know. You gave me the last piece of my best friend."

Cassie cupped her hand over her mouth and shuddered.

"What was his name?" Jonesy asked.

"Sergeant Thomas Weeks."

Cassie became ashen-white and gasped a long deep breath. She backed away and turned to run.

"Cassie?"

But no one and nothing stood in Cassie's way as she crashed through the swinging door.

"CASSIE! Oh, my God! Jonesy, what do I do?"

"Tell me about this Sgt. Weeks, brother," Jonesy urged.

I collapsed into the pillow and stared at the ceiling. "He was the best," I began.

"He was a soldier's soldier. He was a leader of men. He was a friend you could count on."

Jonesy listened and nodded and responded. "Yeah, brother." "I get it." "I know what you mean, brother."

Cassie came racing through the door, pushing a wheelchair, hell bent for leather. The fella in the wheelchair was bandaged from head to toe and was hanging on for dear life.

Cassie parked the chair at the side of my bed and gyrated with excitement.

Her mummified passenger strained to lean forward and peer through the gauze. "It was ham and lima beans wasn't it Farm Boy?"

"Tommy?" "Tommy?"

I leapt from the bed and fell to my knees. A hush came over the ward. I crawled on my knees to the wheelchair and lifted myself closer to those eyes, to that voice. I reached out with my hand that trembled for every soldier who had lost hope.

"What took you so long getting back, Marshall?"

"TOMMY!"

The ward erupted in cheers. Bedpans clanged and windows rattled. Victory rang out in the ward that day, and hope was alive again in the collective tears of many. I wept more than ever before or since., and I didn't care to stop.

I lifted my head from Tommy's lap and opened my hand. Tommy took the ring from my palm, raised it to his eyes, and asked, "Who would have thought we'd live to see this again?"

Tommy looped the chain around my neck and the ring hung over my heart. "If I ever need this, I'll know where to find it."

Tommy and I were bunked side-by-side that very day. All the doctors concurred, but I knew that Cassie was the one who made it happen. Cassie made herself scarce and let Tommy and me be Tommy and me, but she kept a watchful eye. Tommy and I slept little and talked constantly.

"What about all the guys, Tommy? Were they, uh – were their bodies…?"

Cassie stopped by to check on us, just as Tommy answered, "Yes, all their bodies were taken home."

Cassie backed up and started to leave.

"You don't have to go, Cassie," Tommy consoled.

I reached out for Cassie's hand. "I'd like you to stay. I was about to ask Tommy how the hell he got out of there alive."

"Well, Jake, it was a matter of taking enough shrapnel, losing enough blood and looking dead enough. The fire-fight was spotted from the air and the chopper boys got to me just in time. But not in time for the other guys."

Tommy insisted, "Let's get out of here."

Cassie and I got Tommy into the wheelchair and he added, "Bring my cigarettes."

We found our spot in the courtyard and I lit Tommy's cigarette.

"We've all got to die of something," Tommy quipped.

Tommy took a couple of long drags off the cigarette and asked, "How the hell did you make it damn near 300 klics to the DMZ?"

I squeezed Cassie's hand. "You might want to pass on hearing this part."

"Oh no, Cowboy. You've taken me this far. You're not getting rid of me now."

So, I told my tale of rifle butts and boots to my gut. I told about plastic bags and piss in my face. I talked of hate and the need to kill. I talked about my young friend, Charlie, and the need to live. I recounted each step, each bug and worm. And I described how Josie floated downstream, with her arms outstretched and her face to the sky.

I couldn't have told my story so completely to Doctor Al or Brother Bob. Only to Tommy and Cassie could I reveal everything. Our stories were ours alone, and we three found a world together that war couldn't touch.

Tommy had the advantage of gauze and tape to hide his tears, and he mustered the courage to break the news.

"I'll be moving on tomorrow, kids. They're shipping me to the Army hospital in Hawaii. There are a few more pieces of shrapnel they need to take out and I have a lot of work to do to get out of this chair. But someday, we'll rendezvous on that farm of yours, Jake."

Another day, another week, or another month with Tommy would not have been enough for me, and tomorrow came too soon.

Tommy was packed and ready to leave when Cassie came to wheel him out. As in all good-byes, there was so much to say, but so little could be said.

There were several calls from the beds we passed, as we made our way through the hospital ward. "Give 'em hell, Weeks." "See you around, brother."

Some guys simply raised whatever limb they could in a farewell salutation.

I worried about Tommy facing the coming challenges alone, and I wished that I could go out on point and clear a path for him. But Tommy would always be my rock, and I knew I would see him again.

Now it was only Cassie and me, but that was enough. Cassie tended to everyone on the ward, but it was noticed that I got the most tending.

"You're one lucky S.O.B."

"What makes you so special?"

I delighted in all the grumbling. I was having the spaghetti and meat sauce, and everyone else drew the ham and lima beans.

Six days a week, Cassie and I smelled the plumeria. Six days a week I fell hopelessly in love.

It was only 15 days and 32 minutes after Tommy had gone that I sat at the window and watched the sun come up. I didn't expect to see Cassie that morning. It was her day off.

I looked down at my orders. I was shipping out tomorrow. I held my ticket home in my hand and I wanted to tear it up.

The fields of Kansas were beckoning, but what about Cassie? A family of arms were waiting to embrace me, but then there was Cassie. So many months of dreams were within my grasp, but everything I needed was right here. But I had always done what I had to do, and I would again.

I was on my third cup of coffee when I saw Cassie coming up the walk. I was waiting at the door when Cassie entered the ward.

"What are you doing here today?"

Cassie shrugged an answer, "Oh, I didn't have anything else going on today. What are you hiding behind your back?"

I handed over my travel orders and watched for the slightest reaction. But I saw no reaction. Her face was as steady as a seasoned poker player. She simply folded the paper, and then looked up.

"You want to go for a ride, Cowboy? Get dressed and I'll get you a day pass to get out of here."

I had never dressed faster and I met Cassie at the door. She led me to the parking lot and stopped at a little Ford Falcon that had maybe ten square inches of paint left on it. She proudly introduced, "Meet Mildred."

Cassie drove Mildred around the entire island of Guam, pointing at the hills and waving to the ocean. The wind ripped through the open windows of the car, fluttered her auburn hair and highlighted the sun-drenched tints.

We stopped to play at Talofofo Falls, and left with our clothes soaked and clinging to our bodies. We walked barefoot on the beach and let the wet sand squish between our toes. For the first time, we held hands without any pretense or excuse. It was just us and the tide.

We were drawn by the sound of music and strolled into a small village. People dashed out of their homes and pulled us into a celebration of life.

"FIESTA! EAT! DRINK! DANCE!"

And we ate. And we drank. And we danced as if tomorrow didn't exist.

But tomorrow was only a few hours away when we arrived back at the hospital. I had danced fast and loved hard and I was shot. I had spent more than my body was ready to give, but my heart wanted more.

I was leaning on Cassie for support as we walked across the lawn. The automatic lawn sprinklers turned on and caught us in a magical mist of rapture. We looked at each other and laughed in our dwindling minutes together.

The kiss was inevitable, and nothing like I had imagined it might be. It captured my heart and conquered the depths of my soul.

Cassie drove me to the airfield the next day, and the air was stifling with dread. Love is a scary thing and even scarier to express. It sticks in your throat like a lump that you can't swallow and can't spit out. All you can do is choke.

"You're going to write to me, aren't you, Cowboy?" Cassie quaked as we waited for the last boarding call.

"You bet, Cassie. I'm gonna…" I grabbed that girl in my arms and shook with tears.

"I'm going to write. I'm going to remember. I'm going to – to love you."

I hope, for your sake, that you know the kind of kiss we shared. It was the kiss that everyone should have at least once in their life. It was the kiss that would never end, even after the lips parted.

Cassie broke the kiss by touching my lips with her finger, and turned to run back to Mildred.

I buckled my seatbelt in the plane and looked out the window at the sun peeking over the horizon. I opened my notebook and began to write, "Dear Cassie."

Chapter 5

A hundred thoughts passed through my mind for every sentence I wrote to Cassie. But each sentence said more than I could dare to speak. The words began to flow only when I decided to stop thinking and start feeling.

I was oblivious to the world around me, until the plane touched down in Hawaii and made my pen scribble across the page.

There was barely enough time to catch the flight to Seattle. I boarded with all the people wearing brightly colored clothes, tapping their toes to the music plugged into their ears, and looking as if they didn't have a care in the world.

The lady next to me on the plane was leafing through a magazine and paused to look at pictures of armed American soldiers, standing near Vietnamese peasants who were crying over their dead.

As secretive as her glances were, it was obvious that she was aware of the glint from the brass on my uniform and the shine on my shoes. She crumpled the magazine back into the seat pouch and tried to ignore the reality of the war that I represented.

The fella on the other side of me gave me a light jab with his elbow and advised, "Hey, buddy. Trust me. If you have any civilian clothes in that duffle bag, you should go to the bathroom and get out of that uniform."

His warning lingered in the back of my mind, as I tried to return to the sanctuary of my letter to Cassie. I wrote about the times that Borgelt saved my butt, and the times that Sanchez lightened my load. I wrote about all the things that made me proud to wear this mantle of brotherhood. There was nothing that would make me relinquish the honor embodied in my uniform.

I was the last person to leave the airplane when we landed in Seattle. The fella beside me departed with one last jab, "I tried to tell you, brother."

I gave my shoes one last quick buff, squared my hat on my head, proudly marched off the plane, and set foot back on the North American continent. I looked East, toward home. It was only two thousand miles away. I would walk that far if I had to, and I knew I could.

It was three hours until my next flight departed for Kansas City. I took a seat facing the panoramic windows of the airport terminal and soaked in the magnificent backdrop of pine trees and the sky that stretched all the way to Kansas. After more than nine months in the jungle and after battling all the demons hell had to offer, I was almost home.

I smiled and nodded at folks passing by, but nothing was returned. Conversations ceased and whispers followed. "Just keep walking." "He might be high on something."

My attention was diverted to a little boy with his head in his momma's lap, exhausted from the rigors of travel. I was fascinated, watching the innocence in that little face, and following the rise and fall of his shoulders as he breathed in and out. I shared the warmth of that mother's lap and lost myself in the security of that little boy's youth. This was worth fighting for and worth living for.

I looked up to meet the mother's eyes and saw a scowl of distrust. The mother snatched her child from his slumber and scurried away.

The air became thick in my nostrils, and I broke out in a sweat from all the searing glares. This was not the home that I had left and I did not feel welcome. This was hostile territory that reeked with the scorn of an enemy camp, and I was struck again with the disturbing urge to FIGHT, RUN, or HIDE. I had to get out of there.

I lifted my duffle bag onto my shoulder and headed for the nearest exit. Panic was nipping at my heels and my phantom fears pursued me out the door. I sucked in a desperate breath of fresh air, and choked back the impulse to vomit. I frantically hailed a cab and dove into the back seat.

"Where to, young fella?" came the greeting from the cab driver.

"I just want to ride around for a while, if that's ok," I answered. "I have to be back here in a couple hours for my flight."

The driver was happy to start the meter and drive away. He sported a few days' growth of whiskers, masking the wrinkles in his face, and seemed very comfortable behind the wheel of his yellow chariot. We cruised the streets without the slightest sense of urgency, and I searched for any sight of the America I had known.

The driver rolled his window down and asked, "Do you mind if I smoke?"

I rolled my window down and answered, "Not at all."

The driver lit his non-filtered Camel cigarette and sucked in a deep drag. He released the smoke in a billowing cloud that swept slowly out the window and he asked, "Are you just gettin' back from Vietnam?"

"Yes, sir," was all I cared to answer.

"How bad was it over there, Sonny?" the driver probed.

I resisted against his inquiry and simply responded, "Pretty bad, sir."

"Well," the driver drawled, "I'm a veteran too."

I dropped my guard enough to hear more. "Is that so, sir?"

"Yep, World War II." He slapped his hand emphatically on the steering wheel and boasted, "Now that was a real war!"

My guard was back up as I challenged, "A real war, sir?"

The driver raised his hand in conviction and gloated, "Yeah, you know, they never declared war in Vietnam. It was just what they call a conflict."

I now knew the meaning of the phrase, "My blood began to boil." It begins in the face, where all bodily heat collects and makes the scalp throb. Every muscle contracts against the pressing need to lash out. I knew of the heroism that defines a veteran of any war, and would not deny this man his share. But I could not allow the sacrifice of my brothers to be sloughed off in obscurity.

I slung one last comment. "I don't know the difference between a conflict and a real war, sir. All I can tell you about Vietnam is that there's a whole lot of real dying going on."

There was nothing more to be said in the next tense moments, apart from the driver's accepting bid, "Welcome home, son."

The American flag was furling its steadfast stripes as we neared an expanse of green, manicured lawn. I grabbed the back of the driver's seat and insisted, "Pull over here!"

I handed the driver a tip and a request, "Wait a few minutes for me, please."

The driver nodded in gratitude and lit another cigarette.

The soft grass invited my shoes to tread on its blanket of peace, and sent up its fragrance of home. The breeze wrapped around my spirit and lifted my eyes to the stars of Old Glory. My fingertips automatically rose to my brow in my sharpest salute. I was a statue, both humble and proud, as I thought about all the lives that were taken and all the lives that were given in the name of that flag.

I fell on my weakened knees and bent down to kiss the ground. When I raised my head from my reverence, I saw sandals and blue jeans.

I stood to face the most unkempt head of hair, bound in a red, white and blue bandana. Through his cocky grin, the young man uttered, "What the hell you doin', Baby Killer?"

I wagged my head back and forth in a warning not to proceed. My eyes swerved from left to right, and I saw a group of similarly dressed rivals encircling me, adorned with their "love beads" and their symbols of protest. I heard the spit from the challenger in front of me and looked down at his saliva dribbling over my shoes. My hat was knocked from my head and I watched it tumble to the grass.

I felt the same rage I had felt with Charlie pissing in my face. I set my jaw and clenched my fists. I shot a glare of loathing and a snarl of vengeance at my adversary. He took a wary step back and I stepped forward. I was a heartbeat away from unleashing all my hate and all my fury, when I felt a gentle tug on my jacket.

I looked down and saw a little girl with hair the same shade of red as Josie's. She was looking up at me in a serene appeal, and I knelt in front of her. I was absorbed in those enchanting green eyes, and she gave me the sweetest hug in the world.

She picked up my hat, placed it on my head, and whispered in my ear, "God bless America – and you too."

She left as quickly as she had appeared, and all that remained was a peaceful truce. I walked back to the cab in dazed enlightenment and climbed into the back seat. The driver looked at me in gaping awe, and I said, "God bless America."

I was immune to the glares and whispers as my flight took off for Kansas City. One small girl with enormous love had quieted my heart and redeemed my hope. Home was only hours away and love was within my grasp.

I didn't sleep, but I dreamed. I dreamed of home and I dreamed of Cassie. The two were inseparable now, and there was no going back and no going forward without them.

Kansas was so recognizable from the air. The unfamiliar observer may have seen 60,000 square miles of flat wasteland, but I could almost feel the varying textures of the gently rolling hills. From the different shades of green, yellow and brown, I could form a pretty good guess as to whether I was looking at soy beans or wheat.

Daddy always said that his favorite thing about Kansas was that as far as the eye could see and beyond, every field and every grove of trees was producing life-giving food.

Many a time I would see Daddy sitting silently by the garden in the cool of the evening. Daddy said that if you were quiet enough, you could hear the new sprouts of vegetables breaking through the surface of the earth. Sometimes Daddy would invite me to sit with him, and he would say, "Shh. Listen to the garden growing."

At long last, we landed in Kansas City, and I made my way from the airplane to the bus ticket counter. I laid my money on the counter and said, "I need a one-way ticket to Hays, Kansas please."

The ticket agent leaned forward on his elbows with piercing eyes and said, "There will be no ticket for you today, young fella. The only way you're getting to Hays is to turn around and walk away. Go ahead, turn around!"

I squared off with equal resolve and prepared for yet another confrontation. I was too close to home to back down now and pointed my finger in defiance. The man didn't flinch. He only smiled as he looked behind me.

I instinctively turned to face — "Josie! Momma! Daddy!"

Desperate hugs and unfettered emotions were accompanied by a pandemonium of cheers and applause that would have drowned out any marching band. I still lived, love still lived, and I was home.

Daddy sat alone in the front seat of the car as he drove us home. Momma and Josie sat on either side of me in the back seat. I don't think Daddy minded, because I could see the glint of his eye in the rearview mirror.

I refused to answer all the rapid-fire questions. I told them I wasn't going to say anything until they told me all the news from home, and I made the gesture of zipping my lips.

Josie was not to be outdone and proceeded to tell me that she had a baby that she named after me. Momma shouted, "Josie! Stop that!"

My belly was aching from laughter by the time we arrived home. The sun was just beginning to set, giving a soothing calm to all the so familiar sights. The mail box still bore the name MARSHALL, with the "R" backwards, just as Josie had painted it. The oak tree had a couple years more growth, but still looked smaller than I remembered. The kitchen light was on, as it always was, and the house still smelled exactly as I remembered.

Momma headed straight to the coffee pot to start a brew, and Daddy pulled my chair out from the table. The chair fit my bottom like an old shoe, and I glided my fingertips over the faint ripples of wood grain on the table top. I closed my eyes and traced my finger over the initials I had carved on the edge of the table and remembered the whuppin' that was now well worth it.

Momma started pulling food out of the refrigerator and shoving it under my nose. It was a little of this and a little of that, until I was surrounded with delectable treats. I didn't even get scolded for talking with my mouth full. "Isn't anybody else going to eat?"

Josie giggled, "You're just so skinny, Jake."

I picked out a long strand of cabbage from the coleslaw and dangled it above my face. "Well, Sis, that's what happens when you're living on worms."

I watched Josie's face cringe as I wiggled the juicy morsel into my mouth.

All the faces of my dreams were fixed on me. I filled my belly with the tastes of home and my heart was filled with the endless joy of family. I wiped my mouth with the napkin more often than I needed, just to catch a stray tear on my cheek. One tear would come from happiness, and another tear would come from not having my nine brothers at my side.

I even saw Daddy whisk away a tear as he asked, "How long do we have you here, Son?"

"I'm taking the full thirty days," I asserted. "Then I'll be spending the last few months before my discharge at Fort Ord, California. And oh, I have to get new stripes sewn on to my uniform. I'm now a Specialist 4."

Momma's hand on my arm grew heavier, and then twitched as she recovered her drooping eyes from their cry for sleep. Momma conceded, "Well, we've all had a big day. Maybe I should call it a night so I can have a big breakfast ready for my boy."

I walked Momma to the stairs and she wrapped her arms tightly around my neck, trying to recapture the hundreds of hugs she had missed. I smelled the cozy comfort of her hair, and twisted one of her natural waves around my finger.

Her muffled voice assured, "You're safe now, baby. You're safe. Are you OK?"

I withdrew enough to look directly into Momma's strikingly blue eyes. I wondered how she could see my face, when her eyes seemed to penetrate straight to my soul. I answered with the same sincerity I had always shown when she asked me if I had remembered to brush my teeth. "Yes, Momma. I'm finer than frog hair."

That brought Momma's smile, which always began in her eyes and traveled to her crinkled nose, and she puckered her lips for a goodnight kiss.

Daddy was waiting for me at the back door, and lit the lantern when I entered the room. I willingly followed him out into the night and matched his quiet stroll toward the pond. I followed his lead as he stopped along the path to gather a handful of small stones.

Daddy extinguished the lantern and we sat watching the moonlight reflecting off the pond. Our stones skipping across the surface made the light dance, and the stones disappeared in the darkness with their plop, plop, plop. We shared our bond through nature and our treasured communication that could be felt but not heard.

After Daddy had thrown his last stone, he dusted his hands and started to nervously shuffle his feet. In his uneasiness, he scooted a little closer to me, and he cautiously spoke. "You don't have to say a thing, Jake, but if you want to talk about anything, I'll listen."

At that moment, I became nine years old again. I buried my head between my knees and blubbered, "They hurt me, Daddy."

Daddy wrapped his arms around me, as he tried to crush the pain and shield me from the world. I could feel his heaving sobs, and returned his embrace.

"But I'm OK, Daddy. I heard you — I heard you telling me to remember my way home — and I made it! I remembered who created me, Daddy, and He never let me down."

There were no more words spoken that evening. The lantern was forgotten, as Daddy and I huddled together, and our feet searched the dark path back to the house. Daddy didn't even say goodnight. He just gave me one more firm pat of relief and climbed the stairs.

I sat on my bed, looking at all my childhood mementoes, and let them play in my mind. I looked out the window at the moon and saw Cassie. I turned on the bed lamp and wrote a couple more lines to Cassie. I asked her to look at the moon, and to count three stars to the right. That would be the star that I was looking at right now.

I switched off the light, sank my head into the folds of my pillow and thought, "I'm sure Daddy would just adore Cassie, and Momma would wrap her heart around her. Oh, and Cassie just has to meet my dumb sister."

Josie quietly opened the door and came to sit on the side of my bed. She ever-so-gently stroked my hair — and was just there.

Waking before dawn came as naturally as ever. I got dressed and danced a little jig down to the kitchen. Momma asked, "Do you want a cup of coffee, Honey?"

"No thanks, Momma. I've got to start my chores."

Momma smiled sweetly and said, "Josie's already on it. She's been doing your chores ever since you left."

"I gotta go, Momma!"

I raced out the back door and found Josie throwing feed out for the chickens. She was dressed in overalls, with that red hair tied up and stuffed under a straw hat.

I grabbed the bag of feed from her and flung it all at once across the yard. Then I grabbed her and strangled her in a bear hug.

Josie was panting for air when she asked, "Have you lost your mind, Dummy?"

I laughed and said, "That was from a girl named Cassie."

Josie and I did the chores together, as I told her all about Cassie and Mildred and about Tommy. All the while, Josie grinned from ear to ear and occasionally let out that cackling laugh of hers.

We washed up at the pump head, and Josie just couldn't resist splashing me until I was dripping wet.

We all gathered around the kitchen table, and Momma piled more eggs and bacon on my plate than I had ever seen. Josie broke into a sing-song voice and said, "Jakey's got a girlfriend."

I threw a slice of toast at Josie and Momma shouted, "Stop that young man, and start talking."

As I regaled everyone with everything I treasured about Cassie, I saw a peaceful calm come over Momma and Daddy's faces. I think it soothed their hearts to know that I had come home from that cruel and pointless war with the gift that conquers all. I didn't have to confess that I was in love, they knew.

Years' worth of love was packed into the next thirty days. It was the love of work and play. It was the love of old times and new times. It was the love of laughter and tears that ended too soon.

I packed my duffle bag once again, while Momma packed a lunch for the trip to Kansas City. Daddy checked the oil and water in the car, and Josie was pouring over a family picture album.

Daddy stepped in the house and commanded, "Got to get going."

I asked everyone to go out to the car and give me a minute to take one last look around the house. When everyone had left, I reached into my duffle bag and pulled out three gifts to leave on the kitchen table.

I left a souvenir for Josie that said, "Guam, Where America's Day Begins." For Momma, I left a picture of Cassie and me. And for Daddy, I left a can of ham and lima beans.

Goodbyes never become easier, no matter how many times you practice.

Waiting at the boarding gate for my flight, Daddy shifted from one foot to the other, while Momma straightened my tie. Josie stood at the window, watching the planes take off and land.

I held off saying goodbye until the last moment, hoping to find the right words. There are no right words.

Daddy gave me that strong handshake that he had taught me to give, but that wasn't enough for me. I threw myself into Daddy's chest and whispered in his ear, "I'll remember, Daddy."

Momma almost fell into my arms and squeezed the back of my neck. I implored, "Just keep the kitchen light on for me, Momma."

Josie and I swayed to and fro as we hugged, and I lifted her off the floor. Josie handed me a picture of herself she had taken out of that family album and said, "Send this with your next letter to Cassie."

I couldn't look back on my way to board the airplane. I shoved my duffle bag into the storage compartment and got buckled into my seat. I grabbed a magazine and held it to my face. The shivering magazine betrayed the tears I was trying to conceal. It was the best cry I had ever had.

Chapter 6

It was September of 1969 when I dipped my bare feet in the Pacific Ocean again. Behind me were the fields of home and I would miss another harvest. In front of me was that far away war that promised no end.

Tomorrow I would report for duty at Fort Ord, California. For now, I watched the sun set, knowing at that moment that the same sun hung in tomorrow's afternoon sky over Cassie. Her today was my tomorrow.

I stood in front of Captain Abrams desk the next morning and saluted.

"Specialist Marshall reporting for duty, Sir."

The Captain finished signing the morning report, and then returned my salute.

"At ease, Specialist, and welcome. Have you secured your quarters yet?"

"Yes, Sir. I haven't unpacked my duffle bag, but I found my bunk."

"Well," the Captain directed, "Take a couple of days to get settled in and then we'll put you to work. Are you fit and able?"

"Absolutely, Sir. Just point me in the right direction. But I have a question, Sir."

"Shoot," the Captain invited.

"I understand this is a basic training post." I explained. "But I heard we were in peace talks with the North Vietnamese. I passed by the battalion barracks, and it looks like we're still training a lot of troops."

"Yes, we are," the Captain agreed. "The peace talks are a long way from settling anything. And just this year, the war has escalated, and we've stepped up the bombing. There's no telling when this thing will ever end. Have a seat, Specialist."

The Captain looked at me with authority and concern.

"I see in your file that you've had a rough go of it. Most men would have a hell of a time coming back from what you've been through."

"Yes, Sir," I confided. "But I've had a lot of help."

"I'm thinking about assigning you to teach Survival, Escape and Evasion techniques," the Captain advised. "Escaped P.O.W.'s are few and far between, and your experience would be invaluable to the training program. I just need to know whether you could handle the — uh — well..."

"I appreciate your concern, Sir," I interjected. "You're wondering if I can handle dredging up the memories and reliving my experience."

"That's right, Specialist, and it would be fine if you wanted the think on it for a while. I need you to be sure."

The Captain had to wait only a moment for my answer.

"I've done enough thinking over the last few months, Sir. I know that I can't run or hide from what happened, and this may be the best way to put my experience to good use. The Army teaches two basic things, how to kill, and how to not be killed. Given that choice, I would rather teach survival."

"Very well," the Captain acknowledged. "In two days, you will be reporting to Sergeant Washington, and he'll guide you through the training program."

The Captain excused me with a salute, and I left his office, proud of my decision and scared to death.

Sergeant Washington had the poise of a man who had spent two tours in Vietnam. It was an air of confidence that comes from having seen death, faced death, and imagined nothing worse. It was an aura of acceptance, yet distance. He had a job and a duty that could no longer allow him the luxury of a close friend.

"I'd like to call you Marshall, and you can call me Washington," the Sergeant proposed. "The Captain wants you to just tag along and learn for a while. But if you have something to offer, speak up."

"You've got it, brother," I returned.

"Washington!" the Sergeant corrected.

That was the last time I called him anything else.

"These are kids we're training," Washington went on. "But we have to train them like men. We can't kill 'em, and we don't want any ambulances or stitches. But we have to make it real. We have to teach them the one thing that may bring them home alive."

I nodded in agreement, and I thought back to my own training. It didn't seem real then, but it was now. This was where I needed to be.

I watched some of the best training the world has to offer, and paid close attention to the faces of the young troops. They were intrigued, watching the instructors' demonstrations for snaring an animal, and spell-bound watching an animal being butchered in the name of survival. But they were bored, listening to tips on navigating by the sun and stars, and inattentive to the precautions for surviving captivity. Overall, the trainees displayed the interest of watching water boil in a chemistry class.

The troops were gathered in the P.O.W. training compound, and treated with only a taste of hell. They were bounced off walls and thrown to the ground. They were interrogated without mercy and listened to filthy insults about their mothers and their country. To some of the trainees, it was a rude awakening, and to some, it was their worst nightmare. To others, it was a joke.

Washington had a group of trainees assembled in the compound, with their heads hung in submission, except for one.

Washington thumped me on the shoulder and said, "We've got a laugher, Marshall."

It was easy to spot the youngster who was so amused with the training, by his smirk of total disregard. He was a stout young man who had probably clashed shoulder pads with many a linebacker, and perhaps had never lost a fight. He displayed the arrogance of one who had not yet met his match, and doubted he ever would.

I squared off nose-to-nose with him and asked, "You think this is funny?"

"Ah, come on, man," he spitefully argued. "You know this shit isn't real."

With a boot hooked behind his leg, I took him to his knees, and with my knee to his chin, I put him on his back. I pinned his arms to the ground under my knees and gripped the jugular in his neck.

"This shit wasn't real until it happened!" I yelled in his face. "You'll never lose a fight until it happens! You'll never die until it happens!"

The young recruit struggled and gasped, and the color started to leave his face.

"The only thing the enemy wants more than to kill you is to watch you suffer! Learn it! Believe it! And pray that it never happens!"

I abruptly stood and shouted, "Everybody on your knees, NOW!"

The instantaneous obedience of all the troops told me that my message was understood.

Half an hour later, Washington found me, feverishly pounding my fist against a wall. He resisted the temptation to touch me and simply said, "Damn, Jake. That was a good piece of training out there."

"MARSHALL!" I corrected.

Washington and I forged a bond of trust and respect, but not friendship.

"There is no greater love than to lay down one's life for a friend." We would each willingly make the ultimate sacrifice for the other, but we could not afford the pain of losing another friend.

Each day of training, I waged my own private war. The objective was to teach. The mission was to one day get these boys back to their mothers. The battle was with my own demons. Each day, I gave a piece of myself, only to get it back in my letters to Cassie.

Dearest Cassie,
I see you in the mirror, when I'm looking for myself.
I hear you in the stillness, when I'm listening for the answer.
I smell you in every breath, when I'm inhaling life.
I taste you on my tongue, when I lick the tears from my lips.
I feel you in my heart, when I'm reaching for the stars.
LOVE, Jake

The sun never caught me sleeping at Fort Ord. I stepped out into the early morning fog and began to run. There is nothing but strength in running. You can't hurt anyone, and you can't change anyone but yourself. Anger gives way to fatigue and makes room for peace. Fear falls away and hope emerges. Muscles build and a better tomorrow beckons.

The tragedy of life comes in moments when you think that all is lost and you can't go on. I had been there. The victory of life is felt each moment in which your dreams are fulfilled. I had been there. The joy of life happens when you embrace the tragedies and the victories as the sum of your life and choose to go on. I ran until I was no longer running away. I was chasing that better tomorrow.

I only occasionally left the post to tour the surrounding area. Once you've seen one beach, you've seen them all, and none of them had Cassie there. I felt closest to Cassie sitting in a diner, ordering oatmeal and Jell-O.

I sat in a diner well into the night, gazing out the window at the brilliant sky.

The waitress stopped by and apologized, "I'm sorry, Sir, but we're closing up now."

"Oh," I exclaimed. "Wait a second."

While I rummaged in my pocket for a tip, the waitress asked, "What have you been staring at all this time, handsome?"

I could feel the blush in my face as I sheepishly answered, "To tell the truth, I was looking at the third star to the right of the moon."

"Ah!" the waitress realized. "I'm guessing someone else is looking at it too."

I surrendered and confessed, "Yeah, she's thousands of miles away." I patted the seat beside me and added, "And she's right here."

The waitress daubed a tear from her cheek and leaned over the table.

"The La Fonda is open for a couple more hours. It's a piano bar three blocks down."

"What's a piano bar?" I asked.

"It's just a lounge with a piano player that will play anything you want," she informed. "Why don't you go sing a song for that lucky girl?"

"But I'm not twenty-one yet," I admitted.

"I think you'll pass," she assured. "Don't order a drink. Just look for Mary Lou."

I paused at the door to look back at the waitress. With a flick of her hand she insisted, "Go!"

The La Fonda was a quiet respite, with subdued lighting and mellow tones being played on the piano in the corner. Couples, young and old, shared drinks and laughs and longing eyes.

I took a seat at the half-circle bar surrounding the piano, and watched the graceful fingers gliding over the keys. The elegant lady at the piano swayed in rapture, as she intoned the music of love. Her maturity of years painted a picture of what love had been and what love could be.

She opened her eyes, after her flirtation with passion, and cast her smile on me.

"Hello, I'm Mary Lou."

I was so entranced by her ageless beauty and charm, that I could barely form the words, "Hello — I'm Jake."

Mary Lou slid the microphone across the bar and asked, "What would you like to sing?"

I didn't blush; I turned pale white and stammered, "I couldn't — I've never sung in front of anyone — ever."

"Sing to me, honey," she coaxed. "Just to me."

I don't know how or why, but Mary Lou started to play the love song that had been stuck in my head all day. She closed her eyes and repeated, "Just sing to me, honey."

I flowed with Mary Lou's gentle sway and stumbled meekly into the song.

"Close your eyes, honey, and feel," she inspired.

I closed my eyes and felt for Cassie's touch. My voice didn't matter anymore. The words were there and Cassie was there. The music from the piano swelled and I followed. I was carried away to a place I had never known and to a height I had never reached. I drew in all the breath I could and soared into the last line of the song.

I could hear Cassie harmonizing with me in a voice as clear as if she was right next to me. We held on to the last note until breath faded away.

Amidst the generous applause of the crowd in the lounge, I could feel Cassie's hand on my shoulder. I reached to steal a phantom touch of her hand — of her — her hand! "CASSIE!"

The crowd erupted in cheers as I turned to grab, to caress, to forever hold my Cassie. I had no plan to ever let go, until we heard Mary Lou's, "Hmm, Hmm."

"Oh, Cassie, this is Mary…"

Cassie slid right in with, "Hi, Aunt Mary."

Cassie and Aunt Mary gleamed at each other, as I stood dumb as a post and happy as a lark. Mary Lou retrieved her purse and bid the crowd goodnight.

"I don't think I'll wait up for you, Cassie." She winked, and walked out in her exquisite style.

I exploded in reckless excitement.

"When did you get here? How long are you here for? What are you going to…"?

"Whoa, Cowboy, take a breath! I just dropped my bags off at Aunt Mary's. My Dad retired, and he and Mom are heading back to Fort Worth. I'll be staying with Aunt Mary for a week, and then heading to Texas. As I recall, you owe me a tour."

The tour began immediately, as we strolled along the wharf and down onto the beach. We found paradise in what were once mere sand and waves, and the third star to the right of the moon shined only on us. Every word written in our letters was confirmed with an embrace, and every thought between the lines was expressed with a kiss.

For seven fleeting days, we stole every possible moment, and lived each one to the fullest. We sampled every flavor and smell together. We pointed and gazed together. We listened to each other's heart, and touched each other's soul. The world could have ended in a cosmic flash, but we would remain — together.

The day before Cassie's departure, she met me at the post hospital. She wanted to spend the day visiting every single ward. I strained to lift her suitcase out of the cab and bellowed, "What's in this thing?"

Cassie wrinkled her brow and declared, "The only thing that I love more than you. And don't you dare look."

It was a challenge to keep up with her, as I lugged that suitcase through the corridors. Cassie greeted the first wounded soldier we met with the same exuberant cheer she had given me. Her smile and her touch had the grace and power to transform lives.

I was ordered and I obeyed. I opened the suitcase and picked out the first box of chocolate-covered cherries. Soldier after soldier, and box after box, the suitcase lightened and hearts took flight. It is a scientifically verifiable fact that it is impossible to despair with a chocolate-covered cherry in your mouth. If there were no workable fingers, Cassie fed the chocolates and I wrote the letters.

Our last visit was with the purest of hearts, named, Eddie. I had never met anyone so happy to be alive, and so ready to love. Eddie laughed us into stitches with every corny joke he knew, and delighted in the love he saw between Cassie and me.

"Would you write a letter for me?" Eddie beseeched.

"Let's see," I suggested. "Dear Mom and Dad?"

"Yeah," Eddie affirmed. "And say…"

Guess what. I'll be home for Christmas! How about that? And I'm going to bring my friend, Frank. You're going to love him. He has a great sense of humor, and he's going to love your turkey stuffing, Mom.

He's going to need a wheelchair and lots of drinking straws — the bendy type. And we're going to have to help feed him and such, but — he has no place else to go. Mom — Dad — Frank saved my life twice. And now he needs me. He needs you.

LOVE, Eddie

It was the hardest thing I had ever done to finish writing Eddie's words through the blur of my tears. It was Eddie who needed the bendy straws. It was Eddie who had no arms or legs.

I don't know who leaned on whom the most, as Cassie and I left the hospital. We were in the grips of something bigger than us, and it was part of us.

The cocoa was too hot to drink, but it warmed our hands as we waited for Cassie's flight to Texas. I had known the anguish of ripping myself away and leaving all that mattered behind. Now I sat in torment, helpless to stem the march of time until Cassie would walk away.

"I guess it's back to writing letters, huh?" I moaned.

Cassie raised her coy eyes over the cup of cocoa and replied, "Some of your letters get pretty steamy."

I cowered in embarrassment, as if the whole world was reading my mind.

"I'll see you in the spring, the day after my discharge."

The final boarding call was inevitable, but still a riveting shock. Cassie wiped away the cocoa that I had sloshed on my hand and pressed a note into my palm. A hug, a kiss, and one last glimpse were all that I would possess until we met again.

I folded into a chair and opened Cassie's note.

Dearest Jake,
When you look in the mirror, see us.
When you listen in the stillness, hear our song.
When you breathe in a smell, draw me in.
When you taste a tear, save it for me.
When you feel me in your heart, I am yours.
LOVE, Cassie

Two weeks after Cassie had gone; I was called into Captain Abram's office.
"Sit down, Jake."

The Captain was allowed to call me anything he wanted, but I was astounded to hear him call me Jake.

The Captain handed me a large envelope and informed, "We received this from the hospital, addressed to you."

I kept my eyes fixed on the Captain as I opened the envelope. He burned his fingers as he crushed out his cigar, but he didn't wince. The air was heavy with grief as I extracted the letter, stained with the colors of chocolate and cherry.

My Dearest Boy Eddie,

We are so excited! Everyone is coming for Christmas, just to see you. I'm so busy planning and decorating. It's going to be the best Christmas ever! I've got your room made up just as you left it, and I'm going to stuff you fuller than the turkey.

Oh, you have some apologizing to do, Son. Your girlfriend, Betty, is kind of peeved that you haven't written her.

About your friend, Frank, I don't know, Honey. With your father's health and all, I just don't know. Maybe I can ask around about any help there might be, but I don't think we can handle caring for an invalid around here. I'll just have to let you know.

Anyway, I'm counting the days until my little boy knocks on the door.

Love, Mom

The Captain saw and heard the letter rumpling in my hand and disclosed, "Eddie bit through his tongue and bled to death last night. His body will be shipped back home, but his arms and legs are…"

I bounded out of the chair, and the Captain heard the bones snap, as I smashed my hand on his desk.

"HIS ARMS AND LEGS ARE IN VI-ET-FU*****-NAM!"

There are dark places in this life, from which there is no return. The door you stumbled through is forever closed, and it can take a lifetime to find the door that opens to the light.

Eddie died in that darkness and the world was diminished. I cursed the darkness and I cursed the world. I cursed all of humanity that had failed to carry a brother who had lost so much and loved so much.

There are so many Eddies among us, and too few arms reaching out. I begged in prayer, and I pledged an oath. My arms and my legs now belonged to the next Eddie I found.

I made the excruciating phone call to Cassie. No letter could describe, and no letter could console. I had to hear her voice. Pain must flow out in tears, and there is no telling how long those tears will flow. Heartache must be shared, when it is too great to bear alone. Eddie would always be a part of us, and only time would turn the burning loss into a treasured glow.

Chapter 7

The longest of my winters slowly morphed into spring. I had my discharge papers in one pocket, and my plane ticket in another. My destination was the only choice I could make. I was headed to the Dallas-Fort Worth Airport. My uniform was packed away in the past, and I was dressed in the garb of my future. Blue jeans, a western shirt, and Cassie were all I needed.

The miles trudged by in their tedious time, and patience was not a virtue that I could claim. I counted minutes and I counted hours. I added dreams and subtracted sorrows. My heart was racing and my soul was in flight.

The plane ultimately sank into its descent from the sky and lifted my spirit to the heavens. The wheels gripped the runway, halting my headlong dash to the finish line. I strained against the seatbelt, until I broke free from my bonds and ran.

I snatched Cassie off her feet in a dizzy spin of ecstasy. I danced deliriously in the clouds until I was brought back to earth by the voice of Cassie's mom, "Excuse me."

Cassie sputtered, "Oh, Jake, this is my Mom and Dad."

There was no mistaking the hug of a mother and the strong handshake of a dad. This was what I knew of family. If you were loved by one, you were loved by all.

Mr. Johnson was the first person I ever heard say, "Welcome home, soldier."

Cassie and I were swaddled by the spring air blowing through the backseat of the car, and gently rocked by the rumbling lull of the road. Mr. and Mrs. Johnson listened to the silence of young love. Mrs. scooted closer and laid her head on Mr.'s shoulder in happy reminiscence.

The engine came to rest in the driveway and Mr. Johnson softly stroked a smile onto his bride's face.

"Welcome to our little piece of heaven, Jake."

"Oh, Dad," Cassie bubbled, "I want to show Jake around."

The seasoned love birds understood and strolled arm in arm into the house.

Cassie and I dodged from hiding place to hiding place. From the horse stalls to the pecan trees. From the creek bank to the tire swing. A kiss here, an embrace there, and a cry in between. We rollicked in a world where dreams have faces and love can be touched, until the porch light signaled us home.

We stepped into the kitchen with our hair in a muss, and an undeniable glaze over our eyes. A faint smirk lit up Mrs. Johnson's face, and Mr. Johnson shoved a coffee mug in my hand.

I stammered a thank you and made a feeble attempt to distract.

"How much ground do you have here, Mr. Johnson? It felt like we walked around five acres or so."

Mr. Johnson sprawled and relaxed at the kitchen table and took his time answering.

"Just under five acres. Have a seat, Jake."

I felt so secure and welcome as Cassie escorted me to a chair and wrapped her arms around my neck. Then, SHE LEFT! She bounded out of the room and left me in a witless tremor.

"Where's she — where's Cassie going?"

"She'll be right back, Jake," Mrs. Johnson soothed. "Cassie has told us so much about you."

Mrs. Johnson reached across the table to caress my hand. "Now you're real."

Cassie returned with a stack of family picture albums. She was wearing the broadest smile I had ever seen, as she opened the cover of the first book of treasures.

We perused through pictures of Cassie from pigtails to prom dresses. Even the black and white photos danced in a colorful display of all that lived in Cassie.

My jaw genuinely dropped at the sight of a stunning young woman pictured in glowing radiance. Cassie emitted a quick giggle and pointed to her blushing mom.

"Mr. Johnson," I wowed. "How did you manage to catch a beauty like this?"

Mr. Johnson shot back, "Just turn the page, sonny boy."

On the next page was a picture of Cassie's dad, with his western hat and boots, standing tall next to his quarter horse.

I looked at Cassie and said, "Oh, I get it."

Cassie nodded and revealed, "Yep, Cowboy."

Next was a picture of a newborn child, beautiful in her frailness.

"Is this you, Cassie?" I unwittingly asked.

"No," Cassie moaned.

Mrs. Johnson intervened and salvaged a tear from Cassie's cheek. "That's my Gretchen, on the day she died."

The picture blurred in my eyes and the somber stillness sent a shiver down my spine. I weakly spoke through a sob, "I'm so, so sorry..."

Mr. Johnson leveled the anguish of love unforgotten and said, "Those were two awful and wonderful days, Jake. But all the love we have for our two daughters is sitting right beside you."

Mr. and Mrs. Johnson clasped their hands in satisfied triumph as they watched me hug the fullness of Cassie and Gretchen.

"It's your turn, Jake," Mrs. Johnson directed. "I want to hear about Josie."

With the common bond of family, we swapped stories, shared precious memories, and learned each other's hearts. Through those wee hours of the morning, there was not one thing wrong in the world.

Cassie and I packed everything we could into the next few days. Cassie showed me all the cherished spots of her childhood, until I knew the way home from anyplace in Fort Worth. We laughed more than we cried, but we cried harder than we laughed. The laughter was for what we had and what promised to come. The tears were for what had been and what never came. All things were possible together and unimaginable apart.

The last night of my visit, Mr. Johnson had beaten me eleven straight times, but I challenged him to one last game of checkers.

"I'm betting you a million dollars on this game, old man."

The old man countered, "You don't have the million dollars you already owe me, whippersnapper."

The board was set and the battle lines were drawn. The old man made the first casual move and said, "You must be anxious to get home to your family."

I was not distracted. I carefully weighed my options and responded to his move.

"Yes I am. Your move now."

The old man made a bold move and asked, "You got your plane tickets?"

I captured my first piece from the board and announced, "Cassie is driving me to Kansas."

The old man ruthlessly returned to capture two of my pieces.

"Is that so?"

The conversation drifted away and the battle forged on. Each time I gained an inch, the old man pushed me back two. It was the same scenario as the last eleven losses, and as the old man dealt the final devastating blow, he commanded, "Have my daughter home by midnight, give or take a couple weeks."

I watched the folks waving in the rear-view mirror, as Cassie hung half way out the window, shouting and flailing her arms. I grabbed the waistband of Cassie's britches and pulled her back in so I wouldn't lose her on the sharp turn to the left. She was whimpering softly as she cleared her tangled hair from her face. She dried her wind-streaked tears on my shoulder and snuggled in a tranquil doze.

We took turns driving straight through, stopping only at gas stations and diners. We sang song after song, and we pointed and awed at sights that would have escaped our separate eyes.

I laid my head in Cassie's lap as she drove, and studied each blink, each breath, and each wind-blown strand of hair. When she glanced down, I closed my eyes in secret admiration, disclosing my contentment only through an irrepressible smile.

I drove the last few miles of my favorite route home. Cassie spotted the Marshall mailbox and shrieked as if I might miss it.

"There it is, Cowboy! Right there! We're here! We're here!"

Before the engine had quieted, Josie was next to Cassie's door, dancing as if she had to go pee. I asked Cassie, "Are you ready for this?"

Cassie chuckled and resolved, "Oh, Yeah!"

The two girls hugged like twins who had been separated at birth, and their screams split the air.

I walked on, with my hands over my ears, to find shelter in Momma and Daddy's arms.

"I want you to meet Cassie, if Josie ever lets her go."

Momma was the first to pry Cassie loose and pull her against her heart.

"Come here, you beautiful girl."

Daddy was careful to not be too bold, and offered his hand. Cassie threw all her love at Daddy and choked his neck. Daddy squeezed out a few raspy words.

"I just might steal this girl away from you, Jake."

It was another late night, as Cassie took her turn at fielding a frenzy of questions around the kitchen table. Nothing was too personal and nothing was withheld. Thoughts and memories were freely spoken and feelings were freely shared.

I could scarcely see Cassie's eyes bulge over the family picture albums Josie stacked high. The girls zipped through the pages, in a race to view every image and picture every moment. Cassie oohed at every photo of Momma and Daddy. She aahed at every snapshot of Josie. And Cassie giggled in unison with Josie at every picture of the little boy, Jake.

Daddy moaned and Momma stroked behind his ear.

"I've got to hit the sack." Daddy rose from his chair and gave me that wink. It was the wink that said, "You're one lucky young man."

Cassie gleamed as she asked, "What time do we get up for chores?"

"I'll get us up in time," Josie answered as she grasped Cassie's hand. "Come see my room. We're going to be bunkees."

That left Momma and me standing in the middle of the kitchen. Momma led me to the closet and pulled out an extra blanket. "Make sure Cassie gets tucked in tight, Honey."

I rolled my eyes and remarked, "If I can get between her and Josie."

Momma stilled my face with her tender fingers and said, "The last time you were home, you told me you were just fine. Now I know why."

I lay on my bed in a struggle of purpose. I needed sleep so I could seize every moment of the morrow. But sleep would rob me of the moments of today. I held those moments in my mind and hoped they would live a while longer in my dreams.

There was a slight creak of the door and a shadow passed my bed. Cassie knelt at the window and rested her elbows on the sill. She smiled at the sound of my bedsprings and sighed as I wrapped my arms around her.

"I couldn't sleep, Cowboy."

"Me neither."

"I absolutely love your family, Jake."

I squeezed a little tighter. "I knew you would. And I knew they would love you."

"This family, this home is what brought you out of the jungle, isn't it?"

We swayed back and forth, with our heads together. "Yes. Every day I walked, I was walking back to here, to them."

I turned Cassie's face and kissed her tear. "When I got to Fort Ord, I learned to run again. And every day I ran, I was running back to you."

Cassie looked out and pointed at the moon. She counted with her finger, one, two, three stars to the right.

"I think I can sleep now, Cowboy." And that was our goodnight.

I was shaken awake the next morning by Cassie and Josie, sitting on each side of my bed. In the dim light, I saw Josie in her overalls and straw hat. I looked over at Cassie, in her overalls and straw hat. I pulled the pillow over my face to muffle an exaggerated yell, "THIS IS TOO MUCH!"

Josie announced, "Cassie and I are doing all the morning chores, even Daddy's."

Cassie chimed in, "And your Daddy is going to teach you how to play the fiddle!"

I pulled the covers over my head and just hid.

It was easier for Daddy to show me how to birth a calf than it was for him to teach me the fiddle. I worked hard at learning how to position my fingers for all the notes. I learned how to tune the strings and tighten the bow. Still, the screech from the bow sent the chickens off in a flutter, and I was applauded by Josie howling at the moon and Cassie doubled over in laughter.

Daddy and I shared many a cup of coffee before dawn, as the girls skipped through the chores. Momma was humming over the stove, and I was wincing at the touch of my fiddle-blistered fingers.

"Those will turn into a musician's callouses soon enough, son," Daddy advised. "You're starting to find the notes, but there's something wrong."

I saw the concern in Daddy's composure. He was talking beyond music.

"I've seen love in your eyes when you look at Cassie. I've seen joy in your step as you walk to the pond. But I hear a darkness in the notes you play. Something is wrong."

All the walls I had erected and all the pretenses I had hidden behind could not conceal my pain from Daddy.

"Momma, would you come sit with us?"

Daddy's and my eyes were locked in shaking anticipation until Momma calmed the troubled waters with the stroke of her hand.

"I need to tell you about Eddie," I submitted.

Momma and Daddy listened with their hearts as I told about Eddie. About his arms and legs. And about the chocolate-covered cherries. They held their breath as they heard about his letter, and wept a deluge for the boy who never made it home.

"I cursed and I swore everything I have and everything I am to the next

Eddie I find. But that doesn't mean anything unless I know how to help. Unless I know what to do."

"There are so many Eddies out there," I went on. "Some have legs but lost their arms. Some have arms but lost their heart. And some just lost their way home."

"If you ever find another Eddie," Momma sternly affirmed, "You bring him here."

Daddy solemnly agreed, "This will be any and every Eddie's home."

I slammed a kiss on Momma's cheek, hugged the daylights out of Daddy, and grabbed the fiddle. I drew the bow across the string in my first note of hope. Daddy smiled at the sound of light.

I was playing the same song, as Cassie and I sat on the bank of the pond. It was the song that must have been written for Eddie and us.

Cassie skipped stones across the water. I played and sang.

"The road is long – with many a winding turn…"

"You're getting better with that fiddle, Jake."

"That leads us to who knows where…"

"This is for Eddie," I devoted.
"OH, JAKE!" Cassie wept.

"But I'm strong – strong enough to carry him…"

"I've got plans, Cassie. We're bound to find another Eddie someday. This is for him too."

"He ain't heavy, he's my brother."

Cassie joined in and the song was complete.

"So, on we go – his welfare is my concern. No burden is he to bear. We'll get there."

Cassie and I were lost in song and found together.

"For I know – he would not encumber me. He ain't heavy, he's my brother."

Cassie and I laid back together, cried together, and believed together.

"Tell me your plans, Jake."

I rested the fiddle on the ground and laced my fingers behind my head. "The next Eddie we meet is going to find a home here."

Cassie lay close to me and gazed into the same dream. "I like the sound of 'We'."

"Daddy and Momma will give all their love, but we're going to need money."

"We," Cassie reiterated. "What are we going to do?"

I sat up and threw a stone across the water and into the night. "Well, a friend of Daddy's is retiring and trying to sell his semi-truck."

Cassie was excited. "There's good money to be made if you own your own truck."

"That's right, and I have enough saved up from my time overseas to make a pretty good down payment. I wouldn't mind travelling the country for a while and making some money in the process. Maybe I'll even find a couple of Eddie's along the way."

Cassie instantly noted that the 'We' had left the dialogue.

"What happened to 'We'? What about – us?"

"Well, Cassie, I would love for you to come along with me on the road, but…"

"But what?" Cassie groped.

I hung my head and dragged out a response. "But Momma would never stand for it."

Cassie sprayed her remaining stones across the water in an exasperated multitude of plop, plop, plops.

"Unless…" I teased a little further.

Cassie clenched her fist and drew back her arm. "Unless what?"

I could feel my shoulder hurting already. I had to talk fast.

"Marry me, Cassie. I have seen us in the mirror, and that's all I want. I've heard our song, and that's all I need. I can't draw a breath without the scent of you. I can't taste today or tomorrow without you. My heart belongs to you, and my life is in your hands."

Cassie's fist stopped only an inch from my nose. "You just saved your ass, buddy."

Cassie unclenched her fist and pressed her hand against my chest. "I'll trade you hearts. You hold mine and I'll hold yours."

I took that as a yes. We shared a kiss and hearts were exchanged. Promises were made and a new life began.

"There's just one thing I need first, Cowboy."

"Anything!" I swore.

"I need you to ask my Dad for his blessing."

"Oh, My God!" I recoiled. "Anything but that!"

Cassie drew her fist back into striking position again.

"OK! OK! What's twelve more losses at checkers?"

Chapter 8

The next morning's breakfast was unusually solemn and quiet, until the dishes clattered in the sink. They clattered in response to the sound of Cassie clicking the latch on her suitcase.

"Are you sure you can't stay a few more days?" Momma hoped.

Cassie regretted, "I'm sorry, but I have to get back home to start school."

Only I knew the name of the school where Cassie would be learning to drive a truck. It would be our secret until I had taken my beating at checkers.

Daddy cleared his throat and said, "I'd better check the oil and water in your car, Cassie."

I handed Josie my handkerchief and Cassie took her by the hand for a last walk around the barnyard. Momma made a few sandwiches for Cassie's trip, and wiped her eyes on her apron. I packed the bags in the car and saw Daddy blowing his nose on the oil rag.

I held fast to our secret. That's how Cassie wanted it. She wanted her Dad to be the first to hear, and that is how she would have it.

No happy news would have made it easier to watch Cassie leave. The simple fact was that no one could resist loving Cassie.

I climbed the stairs toward bed that night and stopped at Josie's door. I was the one stroking her hair, and Josie was the one with her face in the pillow. I stayed until she had exhausted the last tear.

I didn't get my bed lamp switched off before I fell asleep. I dropped my notebook on the floor with only a few words that began, "Dear Cassie."

I bought that semi-truck and started my license training. Daddy's friend taught me everything about his old truck. He taught me how to listen to it purr when everything was humming together. He taught me to listen for its moans when the harmony wasn't right. I learned that the load had to be my first and last thought. Get that load to its destination on time, and all the rest falls into place.

My days were packed from before dawn and beyond nightfall. Chores came first. School came next. There were fields to be cultivated and crops to be planted. Then came the labor of love over pistons, fuel lines, and wheel bearings. Daddy and I blackened our hands under the lamp that some fool decided to call a "trouble light." Trouble had no chance against Daddy and me and the purr of the engine.

Cassie's name pervaded every conversation around the kitchen table. I read each of Cassie's letters out loud, leaving out the parts meant only for me.

The Vietnam War raged on as we finished the harvest of 1970, and I was only months away from my twenty-first birthday. Who would have thought I would live to see that? I carried Eddie on every walk through the fields, and smelled Cassie's hair in every breeze. All that had past had brought me to now. All that lay ahead was mine, Cassie's and Eddie's.

We had put the finishing touches on the truck, and Daddy suggested, "Maybe you should take this baby out for a good road test."

"Yeah, Daddy. I was thinking about seeing if this rig could make it to Fort Worth and back."

Daddy smirked and agreed, "That would be a good test run."

I was packing my things in the truck when Josie stopped by to give me a huge bear hug. "Give that to Cassie."

She dashed off to start her chores and I went back in the house to have one more cup of coffee with Momma and Daddy.

Momma had a bag full of food for me to take along and a thermos of hot broth. "Do you have enough clean underwear, Honey?"

Daddy added, "You got all your maps and enough money?"

I didn't answer. I just hugged them until they said, "Give Cassie our love."

By the time I crossed the line into Oklahoma, I had sung every song that Cassie and I had shared. In between songs, I rehearsed in my head what I might say to Cassie's Dad to win her hand.

I pulled off the highway at a truck stop and downed the last sip of broth. As soon as I had switched the engine off, Josie poked her head out of the sleeper compartment and asked, "Are we there yet?"

"What — When — How — Josie! Do Momma and Daddy know you're here, Josie?"

Josie sheepishly admitted, "Well, I did leave them a note. And don't worry about the chores. Mike is going to help out while I'm gone."

"Mike!" I shouted. "You mean that kid I backed against the wall for pinching your butt?"

"Yes, that Mike," Josie replied. "But I wouldn't advise you to take him on again. He's a pretty big boy now."

I buried my head in my hands and shook my head in disbelief. I gathered my thoughts and then chanted, "Josie's got a boyfriend."

Josie slugged me on the shoulder, planted her straw hat on her head, and insisted, "Let's go eat."

We had a hearty trucker's breakfast, but not until I dialed up Momma and Daddy and had Josie take her lumps over the phone.

I tried to show the disgruntled disapproval of a big brother, but the truth was that this trip would become nothing short of life-changing. There were no parents around to break up our arguments. We could fight until we found a truce. There were no parents to hear our private conversations. We could say thank you for the times we were there for each other, and no thank you for the times we were not.

Raindrops on the windshield brought out a few sad memories, while the glare of the sun transported us back to the happiest of times. Josie and I found contentment with the life we had shared.

It was no use trying to keep Josie from blowing the horn the last half mile before we arrived at the Johnsons'. Now it was Cassie who was doing the pee-pee dance, waiting for us to climb out of the truck.

"Oh, thank you, Cowboy, for bringing Josie along!" Of course, I took all the credit for the idea.

Mother Johnson came running. "JOSIE!" And Father Johnson came swaggering behind.

I let Josie captivate the Johnsons with her irresistible charms, while Cassie and I rushed head-long to catch up for an absence too long.

Josie had bounced through more miles than she had ever travelled. She rollicked and romped and loved more than most hearts could hold. Dinner and laughter took their toll, and Josie's eyes drooped, with a smile stuck on her face.

With a wink in my direction and a hold on Josie's hand, Cassie bid us goodnight, and led her bunkee off to bed.

That wink left the ball in my court and the game rested on my shoulders. Now was the time to face my fears and declare my heart. I began in broken words.

"Mr. and Mrs. Johnson, Cassie and I — I was hoping to ask you — I would love to…"

Mrs. Johnson turned away and giggled. Mr. Johnson began to set up the checkerboard.

I panted in the desperation of defeat and grappled for mercy. "Just hear me out, please. I love…"

Mrs. Johnson set a glass of ice before me and asked, "Bourbon or Scotch?"

"Bourbon," I instinctively replied.

Mr. Johnson rubbed his eyes and said, "You want to marry my daughter, don't you?"

"Yes sir, I do."

Mr. Johnson sat on his side of the checkerboard and said, "It's your move."

Mrs. Johnson poured my drink and poured a little extra for Mr. "Watch your left flank, Jake," she advised, and kissed my forehead goodnight.

I sweated through that game of checkers, watching Mr. Johnson's every facial expression, but he just stared at the board. There were no bravados or verbal distractions. This was the ultimate game for the ultimate prize. I would work beyond a lifetime to pay the two million dollars I owed, if only I could win Cassie's hand.

I played boldly and threw chance to the wind. I took my losses and came back to fight some more. It was the longest game we had ever played and our glasses were empty. I fumbled awkwardly as I picked up my king and captured Mr. Johnson's last checker. I sighed in relief and quaked in fear.

Mr. Johnson leaned back in his chair. He took a long deep breath, and said, "Call me Dad."

I will never know whether Dad let me win that checker game. I only know that he gave me the greatest gift he had to offer.

I woke Cassie just before dawn with my finger pressed against her lips and whispered, "It's time to tell Josie."

Josie was still rubbing the sleep from her eyes, as we walked her down to the creek out back. Cassie stopped along the way to pick some wildflowers to stick in Josie's hair, and then grabbed my hand to race to the creek.

Cassie and I were watching the creek bubble its way to the south when Josie walked up behind us. Josie placed her hand on Cassie's back, placed her other hand on my back, and PUSHED!

Cassie and I tumbled into the crisp, frigid water and came up gasping and grasping for each other. We saw Josie doing her little victory dance and beaming with joy. I scolded Josie harshly and demanded, "Give us a hand to get out of here."

Josie crossed her arms in refusal and said, "I'm not about to trust you, Brother. But I would trust a sister-in-law."

Cassie and I sank deeper in the water and I whispered in her ear. Cassie threw her arms in the air and yelled, "Yes, Cowboy, YES!"

We watched Josie twirl, with her hair sailing in the breeze. Cassie reached up to join hands with her new sister, and PULLED!

The three of us splashed and dunked until there wasn't a breath left between us. Cassie and I held each other close as we watched Josie float downstream, with her arms outstretched and her face to the sky.

Three drowned rats sat around the table in bathrobes, eating stacks of pancakes. Cassie caught her Dad's eye and asked, "Were you surprised, Dad?"

Dad refuted, "Are you kidding? I knew as soon as you enrolled in that truck driving school."

Cassie's Mom challenged by saying, "I knew as soon as you came home from Kansas. Nothing else puts a smile like that on a young woman's face."

Josie licked the syrup from her lips and asked, "What's the wedding date?"

"July 15," I answered.

Josie's eyes bulged. "We've got to get moving. I've got some great ideas. We could have the reception down by the creek. It would be like a picnic."

I cut Josie off immediately. "You're not getting me anywhere near that creek again, Sis."

Cassie added, "And Josie, I kind of have my heart set on having the reception under a certain oak tree, if that's OK with Mom and Dad."

Dad laid his hand on Cassie's and answered, "Like I could ever say no to you. Besides, a couple of retired folks like us could stand some traveling."

"Cassie and I already called Momma and Daddy," I confided.

Josie's eyes fluttered in panic as I continued, "I have to head back to Kansas, so you better get packed, Josie."

Josie dropped her fork and shielded her eyes. She gasped in trembling breaths, trying to hold back the tide.

"Unless you want to stay here a while longer with Cassie," I offered.

Josie pranced and squealed. She twirled and hugged. She even planted a little peck on my cheek. It was only a peck, but it was everything beyond love.

It was the easiest of all my goodbyes. Mom pressed her cheek to mine and said, "See you in July."

Dad skipped past the handshake and gave me a quick manly hug, then started kicking the tires on the truck.

Josie teased, "I almost wish I was going with you. Nah — not really."

I resisted as Josie pushed me toward the truck. "Hold on, Josie! I have one more goodbye coming."

Everyone tried to appear as if they were looking away as I gave Cassie the kiss that would linger until July.

Chapter 9

Not a moment was wasted of the next few, priceless months. It was just Momma, Daddy and me. I worked hard, and Daddy matched my every push and every pull. We labored together and we played together. Life was hard but loving was easy.

Momma taught me how to cook and how to sew. She taught me how to add flavor to life, and how to clothe it in love. She taught me that a woman's work would make a man out of me.

Josie's boyfriend, Mike, continued to show up to help. He was as strong as Josie had described, and as willing of a worker as I had ever seen. He had a playful side, and could pin my shoulders to the ground in under a minute. We worked, we sweated, we wrestled, and we became friends.

One unforgettable morning, as Daddy and I were slopping the hogs, Mike had just finished feeding the chickens and was heading back to the barn. He stopped behind me and pulled the empty feed bag over my head in play.

I spun around in a flash of terror and rage and grabbed that Viet Cong soldier by the throat. I was on top of Mike, swinging wildly at his face and screaming, "BORGELT! SANCHEZ!"

A bucket of hog slop in the face disrupted my rampage, and Daddy ripped the bag off my head. "JAKE! IT'S DADDY! STOP!"

My face gyrated in Daddy's hands as I muttered, "Anderson, Kowalski."

I felt Daddy's words reverberating as he clutched me to his chest. "You're home, Son. I've got you. I've got you."

I gripped Daddy's arm and felt my bloody hand against my face. Mike rose into my view, with the same blood streaming down his face. "Oh, my God! Mike! Did I do that, Daddy? Oh, my God!"

Daddy half-carried me on the walk to the pond for the talk that would never be finished. "You have some more stories to tell, Son, and I'm going to listen."

Mike limped behind, wiping the sweat and blood from his face, "It's ok, brother. Are you ok?"

I recounted memories that defiled the peace and tranquility the bank of the pond had always offered. Memories were fresh and wounds were raw. The devil had not let go of me, but neither did Daddy. "Tell me more, Jake. Tell me more."

I remembered things I thought I had forgotten, and I cried tears that could no longer be held back. Daddy flinched for each blow of the rifle butt on my back, and set his jaw to absorb every ounce of my pain. The comrades I mourned became sons that Daddy had lost.

Mike was speechless, as he dipped his hands in the pond and rubbed them over his face. He listened in horror and he grunted in rage. His anger built beyond control and he slammed his fist into the dirt.

"Damn it, Jake! If only I could have been there with you. I would have…"

"No, Mike!" I shouted. "None of us should have been there! That's the whole problem! It was all a — it was such a — it was just a waste!"

I was out of words and too exhausted to cry any more. I watched the early morning light flickering on the pond and pulled on the chain around my neck. I turned Tommy's ring over and over in my fingers, and Daddy said, "Let's go call him, Son."

"Weeks here."

"Tommy, you old war horse."

"Jake, you dumb ground-pounding bush-beater. Where are you?"

"I'm back in Kansas, Tommy. I'm trying to learn how to be a civilian again."

"Jake," Tommy responded in a suddenly serious tone. "You are an American citizen, and you are a veteran. But you will never be a civilian again. How's Cassie?"

"Cassie?" I evaded. "Who's Cassie?"

"Give me a break, Farm Boy. I may have lost a few pieces over there, but I still have two good eyes."

"Well, Tommy, since you asked, I need a best man."

"Whoo-hoo!" Tommy sang out. "You don't waste any time."

"So how about it, Tommy? Can you be here on July 15?"

The silence was unnerving and I begged for a response. "Are you there, Tommy?"

"Look, Buddy," Tommy ached. "I would be honored — but — I don't know if I can make that. I have a couple more operations to go, and I'm still working on standing up. I just don't..."

"Hey, don't sweat it, Tommy. You'll be my best man where ever you are. Are they treating you ok at the hospital?"

"Oh man," Tommy moaned. "You know what's wrong with this country? Male nurses! You got Cassie and I get Jeffrey."

I laughed, but it was not the laugh that Tommy remembered.

"Hey, Jake, how long since you cleaned your rifle?"

"Cleaned my what? What are you talking about?"

"You know that if you don't keep your rifle clean, it's going to jam and misfire on you. Break that weapon down, Jake. Talk to me."

I was the weapon that needed to be broken down, and Tommy was the oil to clean it. Over a thousand miles apart, Tommy and I sat under the same poncho and shivered in the same rain. I told Tommy about the day's events, about the terror and the rage, and about Mike's bloody face.

"I'm scared, Tommy."

"You've been scared before, Jake. That's what kept you sharp. That's what kept you alive."

"But what about Cassie?" I cried. "How can I marry her when — how can I trust myself — what if I..."

"Listen, Jake, and listen good. I guarantee you that Cassie knows what she's getting into. One night before you arrived on Guam, Cassie was reading a letter from home to me. She took a step backwards and bumped into the bed next to mine. The guy in that bed went berserk, and it took two guys to get him to let go of Cassie's neck. She knows, Jake."

"Oh, man, Tommy! I didn't know. But still, I can't..."

"There's something else she knows, Jake. She met a lot of guys in that hospital, and she knows when she's met a good man. Marry that girl, Jake, and don't look back."

I listened to Tommy's words that had never let me down. I listened to the sage advice of Daddy that had never proved wrong. I listened to Momma's heartbeat in the arms that would never let me go. And I listened to my own heart that had no place else to go but to Cassie.

July 15, 1971 took me by surprise. Only weeks ago, I was broken down for cleaning and I was still reassembling the parts. I sat in the family's usual church pew, pondering all the things I didn't understand.

Why did I make it home, while so many others didn't? How did I get so lucky to find Cassie? And how do you tie this darned bowtie?

The Maid of Honor touched me on the shoulder and offered, "Let me help you with that."

I asked, "Aren't you supposed to be helping Cassie get ready?"

Josie whipped that bowtie into perfect shape and answered, "She sent me out to make sure you were really here."

Half a dozen wildflowers in Josie's hair made me take notice of how beautiful she really was, how beautiful she had always been.

Mike walked up behind Josie, gave her a quick pinch on the butt, and reeled from the sharp slap to his face.

Josie stomped away with the faintest little giggle, and Mike shrugged his shoulders. "What did I do?"

I shook my head and mumbled, "My best man, huh? I should have just put a tuxedo on one of the hogs."

Mike cackled, "Your father-in-law wants to see you outside."

I found Mr. Johnson sitting on a bench, with the checkerboard all set up. I grinned, and all the tension flowed out of me.

"You let me win that last game, didn't you?"

Dad's eyes never left the checker board. "The only thing I let you do was have my daughter. Sit down, Jake."

I sat on the bench in cautious respect. "Whose move is it?"

"It's your move, Son, and it's Cassie's move. I just want to say that it's not always going to be a bed of roses. I know my daughter, Jake. She's going to give you some grief. And I imagine you'll be a total jerk now and again yourself."

I reached for a checker and Dad grabbed my wrist. "Look at this checkerboard. Think about all the giving and taking that goes into it. It's not about who wins or loses. What's important is that you keep setting the board up again, putting all the pieces back into place for the next round. With a little bit of luck and a lot of hard work, someday you'll know who won."

From inside the church came the sound of the organist warming up. Dad slid his hand from my wrist to my palm and placed Cassie's care in my hand. "I have a little girl to walk down the aisle."

Momma met me at the church entrance and ran a comb through my hair one more time. I escorted Momma through those hallowed doors, and scanned the sanctuary with the eyes of a point man clearing the path. I smiled at Cassie's family on one side, and my family on the other. Momma was watching Josie direct the bridesmaids into their proper places, and Daddy was waiting to take

Momma from my arm.

The groomsmen were clustered in a circle like school boys watching a game of marbles. The circle opened, and Mike smiled, with his arms filled with "TOMMY!"

I latched on to Tommy. I felt everything that mattered and feared nothing. His dress blue uniform hid so many wounds, but as long as I held on, I feared nothing that walks.

"Check your six o'clock, Jake," Tommy intoned.

The organ blared as I turned to watch a fantasy unfold. Seeing is believing, unless this was a dream. Beauty is only skin-deep, unless it touches your heart. Mr. Johnson was bringing the light of his life to illuminate mine.

Cassie put her hand in mine, and we became more. More than fate or destiny. It was the will of the Almighty. And it was another moment I could have lived in forever.

Rice and flowers and music sealed the day that had just begun. The Marshalls and the Johnsons were ready to party.

Daddy and Tommy were sitting under the oak tree, clinking their beer bottles together, and toasting everything.

"To the newlyweds, HERE — HERE!"

"To Love, YEAH!"

"To Life, OH YEAH."

"To America. HELL YEAH!"

"To Ham and Lima Beans, CHEERS!"

Cassie's Dad was staring at the checkerboard, while Mike scratched his head in bewilderment. The moms were swishing flies away from the food and talking and laughing about whatever moms talk and laugh about. Cassie and Josie were taking turns sitting on the ice cream freezer and turning the crank. Kids were running everywhere. Some were chasing chickens through the yard, while others were splashing and shrieking around the pump head.

I sat next to Tommy, and Daddy stood to excuse himself.

"You don't have to go, Daddy."

"Yes, I do, Jake. I've had a couple of beers and I need to go NOW!"

"Well, Jake, I finally made it to the rendezvous point," Tommy quipped.

"I never doubted for a minute, Tommy."

Tommy handed me a beer and invited, "Whenever you and Cassie pass through New York, look for me at the YMCA. I already gave the address to your Daddy."

"The YMCA?" I asked.

"Yeah," Tommy explained. "I can't walk yet, but I can swim. And someday, I figure I'll teach some other boys how to swim. Hey, Jake, do you remember when you sank in the swamp and the M60 drug you to the bottom?"

"HA! Oh, yeah, I remember. Borgelt had to drag my sorry butt out of there!"

My voice broke half way through a belly laugh, and the lines of joy drooped from my face. By the grace of God and the selfless actions of my fallen brothers, I sat with a cold beer in my hand.

Tommy reached over and thumped my chest, right over my heart, and said, "Keep 'em alive, Jake. Keep 'em alive."

Tommy gave me a little wink and said, "Watch this."

Tommy grunted and groaned as he steadily lifted himself out of the wheelchair.

I jumped up to grab him, but he held his hand up in a halt. "Just let me hang onto your shoulder, Jake."

In his commanding voice, Tommy called everyone. "Gather around people. Come on. On the double. I can't stand here all day."

All eyes were fixed on Tommy as he spoke. "I'm a man of few words. I only say what I think needs to be heard. So, you folks listen, and you listen good. They don't come any better than this couple we married off today. I would march through hell with Jake. As a matter of fact, I did. And I would give the rest of this bum arm for a woman like Cassie. These two are each absolutely unbeatable, and now that they are together, a whole lot of people are going to see what strength, courage and love look like. I am honored that they both passed my way. Raise your glasses to Jake and Cassie!"

The cheers and applause were soon accompanied by Daddy ripping over the strings of his fiddle. Cassie, Josie, Mike and I joined hands and circled and danced in a carousel of life. With each spin of the circle, I saw Tommy nodding in time to the music and patting his hand over his heart.

The sun rested on the horizon and the mosquitos started to bite. The guests were departing with warm wishes and the food was being cleared away. I found Daddy checking the oil and water on the semi and I pulled him tight into my arms.

"You're going to be fine, Son."

"I know, Daddy."

"Just remember, Son…"

"I know, Daddy."

Daddy sauntered down toward the pond, putting a few stones in his pocket along the way.

Momma strolled out to the truck, clutching an extra blanket.

"You can never have too many blankets," she sniffed.

I wrapped that blanket around both of us, and we swayed to Momma's favorite lullaby.

I wrapped Cassie in that same blanket as I stole her from her parents' arms.

Cassie and I looked in the sleeper compartment of the semi, but Josie wasn't there. She wasn't in the chicken coop, and she wasn't in the barn. We found her in her room, with her face buried in her pillow. Cassie and I sat on her bed, stroked her hair, and cried her to sleep.

Cassie climbed behind the wheel of the semi and fired up the engine. I climbed into the passenger seat, opened the map, and pointed south toward Wichita.

Cassie drove slowly and quietly away from the farm house. After mile one, we were breathing in rhythm. After mile two, we were laughing in concert. After mile three, I looked at Cassie and said, "PUNCH IT!"

Cassie threw her head back and laughed, "YOU'VE GOT IT, COWBOY!"

Chapter 10

The truck eased across the dark prairie, with its soothing rumble. Cassie gripped the steering wheel like an old friend and swayed to the tunes on the radio. I slumped in the seat, put my feet on the dashboard, and stared at her in contentment.

"I see you undressing me with your eyes, Jake Marshall. Don't you think that I'm one of those easy Kansas girls you can have for a shiny ring and a flashy truck. You're going to have to buy me dinner."

"Good Lord, you're a hard woman. Your dad warned me you'd ride me hard and put me away wet."

"You ain't seen nothing yet, Cowboy. I'm going to ride you until I've got you broken in good."

"Yee — Haw!" I laughed so hard I choked, and I rolled down the window for a breath of air. I caught a whiff of Cassie's perfume and breathed it in until I could inhale no more. Then out gushed, "Get us to a motel, NOW!"

Cassie roared and pressed the accelerator down a little further.

We fueled up at a truck stop just outside of Wichita and had a light supper. With more future than past, we talked and snuggled and dreamed.

"I guess this is going to be our dining room," I mused.

Cassie played along. "Yeah, and we need to get a table cloth and some new curtains."

Cassie picked up her napkin to wipe the French dressing from my lip, and I wiped the Italian from hers. "And now shall we move into the living room?"

I took Cassie by the hand and led her over to the juke box. I put my coin in and we both reached for the same button. We danced to that same song that had brought a bar full of people to their feet.

The joking was over. This was serious. Long denied passions could now run free and sacred promises could be kept.

"And now shall we move into the bedroom?" I suggested.

I picked Cassie up to carry her into the motel room, but she grabbed the doorway and brought me to a halt. "Aren't you forgetting something?"

I backed up a few feet and Cassie pointed to the third star to the right of the moon.

We had been married less than twenty-four hours when we closed the doors on our first truck load and raced toward the sun. We put a lot of miles behind us that first day. We said hello and goodbye to Oklahoma before lunch. We put the sun behind us as we wound through Arkansas.

I was driving when we entered Tennessee, and Cassie was perusing the map.

"Oh, Jake! Let's go see Graceland! We don't have to stop, just drive by."

I started singing Elvis songs as Cassie closed her eyes for a nap. The miles slipped by, and the sun tantalizingly touched the horizon behind us. I serenaded that face that I first saw leaning over me in the hospital. I recalled the touch of that face that glistened in the mist of the lawn sprinklers. I cherished those lips that said, "I Do."

Cassie woke from her slumber and pulled herself up straight in the seat. She looked out the windshield at the highway signs, and yelped in panic. She grabbed the map to confirm and screamed, "You missed the exit for Graceland, JAKE!"

"Ah Gee, Cassie. I'll turn around."

"No!" Cassie retorted. "It's forty miles behind us. Just — you just — DRIVE!"

That was the last word Cassie spoke the rest of the way through Tennessee. I wished that she would slug me and keep yelling at me. Then maybe we'd be half-way through our first fight. But this wasn't a fight. It was a just punishment for an act of stupidity and a small fracture in a perfect honeymoon.

I pulled into a truck stop just before crossing the state line. We methodically went about our routine of filling the tanks, checking the pressure in the tires, and cleaning the windshield, all without a word. After I had paid for the fuel, I saw that Cassie had already taken her place behind the wheel of the truck.

I took a walk around the gift shop, hoping to find an appropriate peace offering. Hoping to find the words to apologize, to mend, and to recapture her heart.

I climbed shamefully into the passenger seat and pleaded, "Cassie, I just want to say – Open Wide."

The light and the laughter came back to Cassie's face as she looked at my outstretched hand and squealed, "CHOCOLATE-COVERED CHERRIES!"

The old adage was reaffirmed. We did not go to bed angry that night, and the honeymoon continued.

We pulled into Atlanta hours before our drop-off time, and found a cozy breakfast spot. Our appetites were unrestrained and our eyes were bigger than our stomachs.

We tackled piles of pancakes and eggs, bacon and sausage, and don't forget the ham. We had two kinds of juice, tall glasses of milk, and please leave the bottle.

Blame it on love, blame it on passion. We were attacking life together, and there were no limits, except for the undeniable size of our stomachs.

Our gorging slowed and Cassie tried to sneak some of her pancakes onto my plate.

"What are you looking at, Jake?"

I brought my eyes back to Cassie and nodded to a table across the way. There sat a young man, loading as much jelly and jam as possible on his single order of toast. Only water would wash down his marginal meal, and he stole an occasional glance at our half-eaten feast.

With no pause or deliberation, Cassie dashed over to grab his order of toast and brought it back to our table. The young man irresistibly followed, and I ordered another plate.

We communicated only in smiles, as the young man graciously and voraciously consumed everything we had to offer.

"Where are you from, and where are you headed, Soldier?" I ventured.

"Sailor," was the answer. "How did you know I was a veteran?"

"The same way you know I'm a veteran, brother."

Cassie reached to fill his glass with milk. "We're Cassie and Jake. Did you just get home?"

"I'm Zeke. Honored to meet you. I got home a couple months ago."

"But you didn't say where you're from," I pressed.

"Augusta," was all Zeke revealed.

Cassie and I sipped our coffee and let Zeke have his fill. Zeke ate and ate, then laid down his fork and washed down the last bite of ham. Our satisfied nods and curious smiles deserved a story.

"Ok, here's my story. I headed straight to the recruiters' office the day after high school graduation. My dad was proud, my mom was scared, and my girlfriend promised to be true."

Zeke paused to hail the waitress, "Could I get some coffee, please?"

The waitress cleared the dishes and poured the steaming brew. Cassie planted her elbows on the table and peered at Zeke through the steam.

"Well, I spent nine months at sea, writing letters to Susan every day, but I only got letters back for six months. The last letter was postmarked Atlanta."

Cassie reached to soothe the not-yet-healed lacerations on Zeke's hands. "You found her, didn't you, Zeke?"

"Yeah," Zeke floundered. "I found her — and the guy she was with." Zeke withdrew his hands, wrapped them around the warm coffee mug, and concealed his tears in the steam.

"What happened, brother?" I emboldened Zeke.

"This guy and I — we uh — things got a little — ah hell. I spent thirty days in jail for assault and paid almost every dime I had in fines. Now I'm hitch-hiking home so my mom can stop being scared. But what am I going to tell her?"

Cassie wiped Zeke's tears and lifted his chin. "You tell her how much you missed her."

There were no words to console for what might have been, and no advice for what might still be. Zeke needed to go home.

"Cassie and I are going to be passing through Augusta. But you're going to have to earn your ticket home, Zeke. We have a truck to unload. Are you game?"

The truck was crowded, but there was room to spare. Everyone learned a new song and everyone sang of a new beginning. All the way to Augusta, tales of the sea were exchanged for stories of the jungle and a love that started over a bowl of Jell-O.

We dropped Zeke off in Augusta, with the handshake of a brother, the kiss of a girl who would have been true, the hug of a mother who was scared no more and a father who was so proud.

We lost a little time, but we gained so much more. We picked up our load in Charlotte, North Carolina, and blazed our trail north. Zeke was home and so were we. We had money in our pockets and plenty of fuel in our tanks. We were living a dream, and Eddie was along for the ride.

It would take thirteen hours of driving to reach New York City. We took an essential side trip to plant our feet in the Atlantic Ocean. Our love had travelled across one ocean and on to another, and only we would decide where it went from there.

Sandwiches on the road made up the time, alternating naps renewed our ambition, and stubborn determination got our load to New York on time.

We hopped in a cab and handed the driver the address of the YMCA. We were swallowed into the concrete jungle of the city, and gaped at sights that blew the minds of a hayseed from Kansas and a cowgirl from Texas.

Towers of civilization dazzled our eyes and corner hotdog stands charmed our hearts. People thronged in numbers greater than a county fair, but we were in search of only one, Tommy.

We scrambled from the cab and into the YMCA. Our pulses quickened as we looked for Tommy.

"Do you know Tommy Weeks?"

"Who doesn't know Tommy? But I haven't seen him for a while."

"Do you know Tommy Weeks?"

"Yeah, I do. If you see him, tell him he missed our swim yesterday."

Tommy missed the hugs we had in store. He missed the stories we had waited to tell over the last two hundred miles. He wasn't there.

We begged the time of many who knew him and all who missed him, but only the YMCA director knew where to find him.

"Mr. Williams, we've got to find Tommy," I pleaded. "We saw him at our wedding just a few days ago, and this is the address he gave us."

Director Williams put his pen to paper and said, "I need to give you another address for the VA Hospital."

"Oh, my God! What happened?" I erupted.

"Take it easy, sir," Williams insisted. "Tommy's in no danger — but — he had a — a problem. Hey, Marty, would you get these folks a cup of coffee?"

Williams avoided our eyes and looked out the window. "Tommy's only under observation at the hospital. I know about the wedding, and Tommy came back the happiest I had ever seen him."

"But then something changed. Something snapped. I've never seen a guy in that much pain."

Williams rubbed his brow and collected himself. "There was a hell of a ruckus, and screams like I've never heard. Tommy's room was trashed, and he was blubbering like — well – he was just a mess."

I grabbed the hospital address from the desk and demanded, "Let's go, Cassie!"

"Wait, young man," Williams beseeched. "I heard your name. Tommy kept shouting, 'Retreat! Retreat! Run Jake, Run!'"

I chastised the cab driver without mercy. "Get the lead out fella! Step on it, before I put my boot up your ass!"

Without a word, Cassie grabbed my face and pressed our foreheads together. I saw nothing but the calming blue of her eyes, and I panted and gulped for strength.

Cassie gave the cab driver a generous tip and herded me into the hospital. "Let me handle this, Jake. Just hold on to me and keep breathing."

I submitted and put my trust in my partner. Within minutes, Cassie got results.

"I'm Tommy's Doctor, Bartholomew. What are your questions?"

"Where's Tommy!" was my only question.

Cassie put her arm around my shoulders, to keep me in my seat.

"Are you Jake?" Doctor Bartholomew presumed.

I nodded in acknowledgement and hoped for understanding.

"I'm sorry, Jake, but Tommy's not ready to see you yet."

Cassie couldn't hold me in the chair any longer. "THE HELL YOU SAY! There's no power on earth that's going to keep me from seeing Tommy!"

I was wrong. The power of Cassie's touch still commanded my attention. "Please, Jake."

"Cassie, you don't understand. Tommy is…"

Doctor Bartholomew interrupted, "You're Cassie?"

We both nodded, and the Doctor advised, "You need to talk to Tommy. Just you, Cassie."

Cassie wheeled around and again locked those blue eyes into mine. "Do you love me, Jake?"

My head involuntarily nodded.

"Do you trust me, Jake?"

My nod was slow but sure, and I collapsed in the chair as Cassie walked away.

I don't know if it was minutes or hours, but it was an eternity that I held on to that chair. I feared the worst and I prayed until Cassie returned to my side.

"Let's go get a cup of coffee, Jake."

"NO! I've gotta see Tommy!"

"Buy me a cup of coffee, Cowboy."

Cassie led me away and got the cup in my hand. But the coffee sloshed out as I shook. "I'm not leaving here without seeing Tommy."

Cassie stirred her coffee and instructed, "Tommy asked me to relay an order to you."

My posture became obediently erect as I listened for my orders.

Cassie reported, "Tommy said to head due west and don't look back. Take charge and complete the mission. Then get the squad home. He'll rendezvous with you on the bank of the pond at dawn."

My orders were clear, but my heart was confused. "Why won't he see me, Cassie?"

"Your friend wants to see you, my love. But your leader can't. The buddies you lost, the buddies you mourn, were in Tommy's care."

"But Tommy did all he could!" I swore.

Cassie held Tommy's ring on the chain around my neck, and pressed it against my lips.

"He knows that, Jake. He just needs to cry, but your leader can't let you see his tears."

I held my head in my hands and rocked. "Even the rock must weep," I moaned. "But it will not break. I will carry out my orders, and I will be there at dawn."

Chapter 11

Cassie and I headed due West, and North and South, and back East again. We saw beauty and wonder, prosperity and despair.

You sometimes have to be looking for despair. It is so easily masked and so easily ignored. There were Eddies and Tommys everywhere, and we could spot them all. They were in diners or hitchhiking down the road. They were wandering aimlessly through the rich land they had fought for, or hiding under a blanket from a country that had forgotten their name.

Some needed a ride home, others just needed to talk. The one thing they all needed was someone who understood.

We collected names, addresses, phone numbers and birthdays. We wrote postcards every night. We wrote about beauty and wonder and we wrote about hope. Every postcard was signed: "Remember Your Way Home, Cassie and Jake."

We worked through flat tires, breakdowns and bad weather. We became the unbeatable team that Tommy said we would be. We fought over big things, and made love over little things. There always seemed to be more little things than big.

We tasted lobster in Maine, gumbo in Louisiana, and the finest steaks in Omaha. We stored up memories for a lifetime and never looked back.

We cruised the streets of Baton Rouge, until we found the home in the old Broadmoor neighborhood. We knocked on the door and hesitantly said, "We're friends of Eddie."

Eddie's dad was barely verbal as he sucked oxygen from the tank. But I saw the desperate longing in each breath the old man took. Eddie's mom could not get the doily to lie straight on the arm of the chair. She turned it around and turned it over. She just couldn't let it rest.

"Eddie saved my life," I claimed. "He was a hero."

The old man's breathing soothed and weights of sorrow fell away.

Cassie bit her lip as she listened to my lie, and she offered a life-line to Eddie's mom.

"Here's our address in Kansas. Write me when you can and tell me how you raised a guy like Eddie. I want to have a son someday; whose last thought is about his mom."

Eddie's mom smoothed out the wrinkles in the doily and let it rest.

I don't think we saved them any tears, but I think the tears were easier to bear.

Fort Worth was not on our route to North Dakota, but close enough. We were on our way to family. I pushed the speed limit a little and made it to Tyler, Texas before Cassie began, "You can't lie like that, Jake."

"Lie like what — oh, you mean about Eddie saving my life?"

"Yes," Cassie scolded. "You can't sugar-coat the truth."

"Ah, come on, Cassie. Didn't you see how the old man's face lit up?"

"Yes, I saw. And I've seen it before!" Cassie raved. "It doesn't work!"

I pulled off the road and turned on the flashers. This had all the markings and all the feel of an emergency. Cassie's hand was poised on the door handle, as her shivering quickened.

"Look, Cassie, I'm sorry — but I thought a little white lie did a lot of good."

"So did I," Cassie wept. "You know Eddie wasn't the first guy I ever lost!"

With a yank of the door handle and a leap from the truck, Cassie was running away, and I was only seconds behind. Cassie crawled under the fence and I leapt over. I snagged my pants on the barbed wire again and saw Cassie disappearing in the tall grass.

It took every ounce of strength I had to catch up with Cassie's lead. She set the pace of one escaping the past, and I churned my legs forward to catch up with my future. Cassie went down with a wail, as I lunged to capture my fleeing heart.

Cassie pounded my chest. She pounded her head, and then she pounded the earth. All that was within my power was to hold on tight until the demons had been pounded back.

We lay in the tall grass and breathed together. Words would have to wait until love caught its breath. I carried Cassie back to the truck and she buried her face in my sweaty neck. "I'm sorry, Cowboy."

All I possessed to console was a tighter hug and, "I love you too."

The flashers on the truck blinked for hours as Cassie's nightmares were unveiled.

"So many broken bodies and so many broken hearts. I could never do enough, and sometimes I couldn't do anything."

My fingers never left Cassie's hair as I listened to memories of sorrow, of pain, and of horror. Cassie had never faced a bullet and she had never fired a shot. But she had fought many battles and bore many scars.

"Tell me about the white lie, Cassie."

Cassie shuddered and her voice broke, but she went on. "His name was Ben. He was from Wisconsin."

Cassie filled the last handkerchief and braced herself.

"I sat with him for hours, waiting for the times he would be conscious for just a few moments. One time he asked where he was. Another time he asked me if he was going to die. The next time he asked me to call his mom. Each time, I told him what he wanted to hear. And each time he relaxed back to sleep."

Cassie grabbed my shirt and yanked and pushed and yanked.

"I told his mom what she wanted to hear too. They were all lies! LIES! Ben never had a chance!"

I had no words to offer, only my ears and my arms. Cassie sat up and rubbed her temples.

"I talked to Ben's mom one more time, after Ben died. She screamed and she screamed."

Cassie rolled down the window and screamed across the prairie. "WHY DIDN'T YOU TELL ME MY SON WAS GOING TO DIE? WHY DIDN'T YOU LET ME SAY GOODBYE?"

I held Cassie and we rocked and we cried. We rocked until the red and blue lights flashed in the mirror. I laid Cassie's head down in the seat and said, "I'll be right back. Don't you move."

I climbed down out of the truck and assured the Texas State Trooper that all was fine. Except, as I explained, for the heartache of a woman named Cassie.

"Cassie Johnson?" the trooper asked.

Cassie heard her name and climbed down out of the truck. "I'm Cassie Marshall now."

The trooper asked, "Do you remember a young fella named Billy Thornton?"

"YES!" Cassie gasped. "The boy who would never walk again."

"That's what the doctors said," agreed the trooper. "But that's not what you told Billy. You said he would run."

Cassie clasped her hand over her mouth and feared to hear more.

"My little brother, Billy, walked to the bus stop last week and went downtown to buy a box of chocolate-covered cherries."

Cassie threw her arms around the trooper's neck, and Trooper Thornton hugged back for Billy.

The trooper escorted us down the road, with red and blue lights flashing and an occasional "whoop" of the siren. We turned off toward a small diner just outside of Fort Worth, and the trooper departed with a "whoop, whoop, whoop."

We buttered our bread after a prayer for the boy who died in peace, and we hoisted a toast to the man who walked to the bus stop.

The honeymoon was over and the love affair had just begun. We had learned things about each other that no one else would discover. We had learned things about the world that others either failed to notice or failed to care.

We had seen and tasted heaven on earth. And we had seen and felt the pain of hell on earth. Love needs a purpose to endure, and our purpose would be to ease some of that pain.

We didn't eat steak or lobster anymore. We saved every dollar we could. We never passed by family if we were within two hundred miles and we never passed by Eddie on the side of the road.

We kept those eighteen wheels turning for eighteen months, and then Winter took the reins when we entered North Dakota. We braved the snow and the ice, until a blizzard left us on the side of the road.

We hunkered down and shared our warmth under the blanket. We shared our cans of pork n' beans and yellow cling peaches. We shared the peace and solitude God had granted us, as long as He would grant it.

The storm subsided the next day and we reluctantly left the warmth of the blanket to switch on the radio. On a crisp, bright day in January 1973, we heard that a peace agreement had been signed, and the P.O.W.s would be coming home soon.

Cassie and I marked the spot with "snow angels," and showered each other in icy splendor. We danced with God, and we danced with Eddie. Every soldier, sailor and airman danced with us, to the end of the worst chapter in our lives.

We broke free from the snow bank and we plotted our course. Every mile was a new mile and every laugh was a new laugh. The biting cold before dawn held a new promise, and the sun would never set on our bitter-sweet memories.

A new chapter had begun, but the old chapters would never be forgotten.

Seattle was our next stop, and we were ready for all the city had to offer. A two-day layover found us strolling down the wharves, riding the ferries to wherever and back again, and ascending to the top of the Space Needle to overlook the world.

We walked through quaint little shops, dropped coins in the cups of street musicians, and road the trolley wherever it wished to take us.

I stopped in front of a small Vietnamese restaurant and asked, "Cassie, have you ever had Vietnamese Pho?"

Cassie shook her head and I grabbed her hand. "Noodles! Meat! Herbs! You're going to love it!"

We found a quiet table and I beamed with excitement. But I twitched at the sound of the waiter's Vietnamese accent.

"Two orders of – of Pho, please. I'll have the uh – beef."

I was shielding my eyes as I rubbed my brow. "Do you want beef or chicken, Cassie?"

"Chicken sounds good," Cassie answered.

The waiter left and Cassie reached for my hand. "Are you ok, Cowboy?"

"Yeah, sure. I should have ordered a couple of beers with that."

I didn't understand much of Vietnamese, but I recognized the sound. I felt the fear that comes with not understanding. I felt the need to…

"I have to go to the bathroom. I'll be right back."

I needed water in my face to douse the emerging tremors. I needed to feel the water that carried me downstream away from the fear. I needed it now, but a small man stood in my path.

He bowed slightly, and then looked up. He slowly reached for Tommy's dangling ring and smiled. "I am happy for you."

I knew those tender eyes, and I knew those fingers that had held that ring before. They were the eyes of that boy soldier who had given me my freedom, and I owed everything to the man holding Tommy's ring.

"Please, what is your name?" I whimpered.

"I am called Hi-Hi."

I turned to call out, "CASSIE! COME QUICK!" I couldn't turn back around fast enough. Hi-Hi was gone.

Cassie found me sitting on the floor with my back against the wall and my head in my hands. She sat next to me, pulled me to her bosom and said, "I think it's time for us to take the squad home."

Chapter 12

Spring was back when we unloaded in Wichita. We had supper at that same café and danced to that same song on the juke box. We were a little older and a lot wiser, and ready to rest our weary souls.

"It will be pretty late by the time we get to Hays," I observed. "Should we get a room?"

Cassie grabbed me by the ear and led me to the truck. "It's going to take more than a shiny ring and a flashy truck, Cowboy. Take me home."

The farm house was dark, except for that light in the kitchen. We crept past the house, parked in front of the barn, and rolled down the windows to let in all the smells of the farm. The plowed fields, the last remnants of hay, and even the manure combined into a fresh breath of home. We cuddled under a blanket, gazed at the moon, and drifted off to sleep.

The rooster never got a chance to wake us. We were startled awake by a girl in overalls and a straw hat, banging on the truck door with both fists. Cassie dove out of the truck, taking Josie to the ground. They rolled around in the dirt like puppies at play. Momma and Daddy came running as fast as two old folks could, for a hug that brought this farm boy the rest of the way home.

There was no question who would be doing the morning chores. That domain of sisterhood belonged to Cassie and Josie. Momma started breakfast, and Daddy sat me down.

"How long are you staying, Son?"

"I don't rightly know, Daddy. Can you handle us here for a couple weeks, maybe a month?"

Daddy smiled and Momma hummed louder.

"Cassie and I need a little down time to catch up on some things. We agreed to each get a check-up at the doctor's. I have some banking to do, and then I'll work on finding our next load."

"How's the truck running," Daddy asked, hoping there was work to do.

"I think I could use your help with some maintenance, Daddy."

Daddy smiled even broader.

The girls walked in, soaking wet from the pump head, and joined at the hip. Miles and miles, and months and months had not dimmed the love of sisters, and they were ready to eat.

Momma piled my breakfast on the plate that she had kept since I was four years old. Painted around the rim of that plate, Jack and Jill went up the hill, and the cow jumped over the moon. A life so sweet, and a life so sad lay in that plate, and I dove in.

"What's up with Mike?" I asked.

Josie stabbed at her food and replied, "He enlisted in the Marines. He ought to be about done with basic training now."

That was all that needed to be said. That was the Mike I knew, and I hoped that I would someday wrestle again with the Mike I loved.

A moment of fond recollection was broken when Josie asked, "So how many states have you two made love in now?"

Milk spewed from mouths, utensils clattered on plates, and voices choked, "JOSIE!"

Work filled our days, and our nights were consumed with stories. Laughter was dampened with tears, and tears were wiped away with love. Life's trials and triumphs are so much easier and so much sweeter when shared within the warm confines of home.

Sunday rolled around and I laid out my best clothes. The shirt was pure white, and the pants had never been worn. The shoes were gleaming, and I clipped on the old bowtie that I knew Momma would like. I mussed up my hair, so it would be ready for the comb from Momma's purse. I pranced down the stairs with my same old jig, and Daddy was waiting at the bottom.

"We need to talk, Son."

Daddy's voice was stern and his face was set. Though bewildered and a little scared, I followed Daddy without question. The sun was teasing the horizon, as Daddy led me outside and down the path to the pond. I counted the stones Daddy picked up, and weighed the size of the lesson Daddy had in mind.

Daddy stopped to tie his shoe and instructed, "You go ahead, Jake. I'll catch up."

I marched on, in total obedience to the man who had taught me everything from here to the pond. I followed his path that had never steered me wrong, and trusted the guidance that I couldn't wait to hear.

The pond was reflecting the first rays of sunshine, and shadows began to appear. The quiet solitude of nature's sanctuary was being guarded by a lone figure that called out to me. It was a call that is impossible to describe. It was unlike any sound I'd heard from another man or animal. It was the signal call that belonged only to Tommy!

You can imagine, but you cannot know how hard I ran. You can imagine, and I hope you one day find the salvation I found in those arms. It was our rendezvous at dawn, and the squad was back home. Daddy did not join in our rollicking reunion. He just rested on his knees, and watched, and prayed.

"I knew you'd make it, Tommy! But how did you know we were here?"

Tommy squeezed tighter on the back of my neck and said, "I told you to marry that girl."

Tommy made it back to the house for breakfast under his own steam, with only a cane at his side. He wielded that cane like a weapon against the foes of life, and he brandished it like the spearhead of a leader. I had no choice but to follow.

Tommy remained through more Sundays, more church services, and more of Momma's breakfasts. We caught many a catfish together, and many a sunset found us living life as brothers should live it. Tommy spoke his worst memories to me, and he listened to mine. He described the peace and strength he had found, and he offered it to me.

It was one late evening, sitting by Daddy's garden. We remembered Borgelt's boyish grin as he lifted me from the bottom of the swamp. We recalled how Sanchez would howl softly at the moon, letting the jungle know that El Lobo had the watch. We could smell Cooper's raunchy feet when he finally changed his socks, and we totally lost it at the thought of Kowalski scratching his ass and picking his nose at the same time. Every member of the squad was accounted for in the quiet of that evening.

Hi-Hi was accounted for as well. I told Tommy about meeting those eyes again, and about the fingers that held his ring. Tommy took his ring in his hand and said, "You don't have to wear this for the rest of your life. It's served its purpose."

"I've been thinking, Jake. There's got to be a reason you and I made it off that battlefield."

Tommy paused at the sound of a seedling breaking the surface of the garden.

"I think that's it right there. The sound of new life. I don't know if all the other boys heard that, but you and I did. What do we do with it, Jake?"

I picked up the water hose and sprayed a fine mist over that new little seedling. The mist wafted back over Tommy and me, and we knew that the answer would come, if we just kept listening.

When all had been said and all had been shared, Tommy packed his bag, as all soldiers must. He never said good-bye. He said farewell, as all soldiers do.

"Where do I look for you next, Tommy?"

Tommy answered in his factual manner, "Department of Defense, Washington, D.C." A smirk of humor followed, "They're putting me in charge of a desk."

After Tommy had received all the hugs he could handle, he got one more from me. Soldiers hug in strength. There is love in that strength, and that love is softly spoken.

"Travel well, my friend."

"Until we meet again, brother."

I spent many more evenings by the garden, spraying a fine mist into the wind, and Tommy's voice lingered. For more than a month, we were replenished with everything we needed to hit the road again. Our burdens were lightened and our hearts were topped off to the brim with family and farm.

The doctor visits were over, and the truck was ready to go. Cassie and I mapped out our travels and I presented our plans at supper.

"I found a load in Kansas City," I gloated. "By this time tomorrow, we should be half way to Detroit."

Daddy's reaction could only be seen in the long, slow stroke of the knife, as he carved the roast. Momma forced a smile as she clutched the dish towel close to her face. Josie held nothing back.

"I want to go with you! I can help! I won't be any trouble, honest."

Only Cassie's hand could stem the tears, and only Cassie's voice could calm.

"I need you to stay here with me, Sis. We have chickens to feed, hogs to slop, and cows to milk."

It could not have been more silent around the table if the earth had stopped turning and had stood still in its orbit.

"We?" Josie gasped.

"We?" Momma echoed.

"Yes, we," Cassie confirmed.

Cassie turned toward me and winked. "You're going to be making this trip on your own, Cowboy."

Daddy dropped the knife and I dropped my jaw.

There was a sparkle in Cassie's eyes that only Momma could interpret. There was an expectation in her voice that Josie could feel. Cassie announced to all she loved, "I have an appointment with the doctor next week for pre-natal care."

Momma twirled the dish towel over her head, and Josie leapt from her chair. Only Daddy and I sat in catatonic confusion, exchanging dumfounded looks.

"Pre-natal — what?" I stammered.

Momma screamed to the rafters, "I'm going to be a Grandma!"

Josie demanded to be heard, "Call me Auntie Jo!"

Daddy's more experienced eyes were the first to bulge, and my incredulous thoughts finally caught up. "I'm going to be a Daddy?"

Our nearest neighbor was half a mile away, but surely, they heard. The foundation of the old farm house quaked and every window pane shook, as the Marshalls danced and roared.

"WHEN!" I bellowed over the deafening din.

"Just make sure you're back home by March, Cowboy!"

I strangled Cassie. I suffocated her, and I swirled her off her feet. Cassie grabbed me by both ears and ordered, "Eat your supper, Daddy Jake, and get your butt to bed. You have a big haul in the morning, and I don't want you missing any exits."

Plates were swimming in gravy, and the roast was consumed down to the last piece of gristle. Stomachs were gorged and hearts were ready to explode. I trotted off to bed and Cassie soon followed. She snuggled next to my racing heart and quieted my delirious mind.

"Do you mind that I didn't tell you until the family was all together, Cowboy?"

"Oh, no," I was convinced. "That was — it was just - perfect."

I'd had some tough goodbyes in my time, and I'd had more than my share of joyous hellos. The next morning was somewhere in-between. They were all happy tears, but they were tears just the same. The family was worried, but they would be fine. They would worry together.

I was not fine. I was scared stiff. But a good point man does not show fear. He blazes the trail into the unknown. He keeps his eyes on the objective. He fears not for himself, but for those who follow, and he must make the path safe. I was now being followed by a child to be born from the greatest love the world could conceive, and I was scared stiff.

Cassie chased the truck down the road. She never stopped running, and she never stopped waving, until I drove out of sight.

I will never tell a soul how much I cried on the way to Interstate 70. No one would believe how much I laughed as I headed east. I had to gather my wits. I had to follow all the rules that had served Cassie and me so well. So, I began to count.

I counted telephone poles all the way to Kansas City. I counted flagpoles all the way to Jefferson City. By the time I reached Terre Haute, I had counted 38 places Cassie and I had made love, but I would never tell Josie. When I entered Detroit, I had lost count of all my blessings.

Beyond Detroit, I counted 132,248 miles, 122 dawns, and 61 calls home. The truck faithfully climbed to the crest of the hill, and the countless colors of a Missouri autumn reminded that harvest was near. The load of machine parts pushed me down the other side of the hill, and the St. Louis Arch graced the skyline of early morning. I was 512 miles from Hays, Kansas, and eight hours from home.

A blinding glare of sun splashed across the windshield and pierced my eyes. Only sound remained to record the unfolding horror. Tires screeched with a cry of helplessness. Bending metal groaned in agony, and glass shattered lives.

"CASSIE!"

The cab tilted and I reached up to pull myself into the sleeper. But my leg was caught in the twisted dashboard. I pulled and strained until my skin tore.

"MOMMA! DADDY!"

I hung upside down and the blood streamed from my leg to my eye. I let go and cried.

"Josie."

I could faintly make out that boyish grin as Borgelt walked through the smoky haze. His broad shoulders bore a small child that held on tight to his hair. Borgelt knelt by my side and greeted, "Hey, Jake, this is Gretchen."

I reached up with a hand that could not touch and a voice that could not speak, "Gretchen?"

I woke in a St. Louis hospital, with an angel standing over me. "It's about time you woke up, Cowboy."

I reached with a hand that could now touch a tear on Cassie's cheek, but a voice that could barely speak. "Cassie — I…"

"Take it easy, Cowboy. You're pretty banged up, but the doctor says you're going to be fine."

"I saw her, Cassie — I saw her."

"It wasn't your fault, Cowboy. Just rest."

"But I saw her, Cassie."

"Who did you see, Cowboy?"

"Gret – Gret…"

"Gretchen?" Cassie whimpered.

"The picture, Cassie — the picture. It was her."

Cassie buried her face in the pillow next to mine. She trembled with me and she believed with me. With one quick gasp, she swore, "I'm never letting you out of my sight again."

Chapter 13

I dreamed of Gretchen many times over the coming weeks. Each time, those searching brown eyes spoke to my soul. And each time, I woke to those gently parted lips curved across Cassie's face.

"Good morning, Cowboy. We're walking half a mile and back today."

I asked Cassie the same questions again, to help separate my dreams from reality.

"The people?"

"Nobody died, Cowboy, and it wasn't your fault."

"The truck?"

"Gone, Cowboy, but we had good insurance."

"Home?"

"Yes, My Love, we're home."

I held Cassie until the only reality was her hair entwined in my fingers.

I groaned as I pulled my clothes over the mending joints and complaining muscles.

Cassie knelt to tie my shoes, but I kissed those gently parted lips and said, "It's high time that I tied my own shoes."

We drew in the cool morning air as we rounded the mailbox, and we set a pace down the road that was perfect for me, perfect for Cassie, and perfect for the baby who was along for the ride. We sang as we marched.

"And those caissons go rolling along."

We laughed as we sang.

"Ain't no use in lookin' down. Ain't no discharge on the ground."

At the half mile mark, Mr. Taylor was leaning against his mailbox, leafing through the early morning delivery.

"Great Day in The Mornin', Mr. and Mrs. Marshall!"

That genuine greeting came from the man who had once called me "Little Sprout." It was his arms that had handed me my new puppy, Blondie. It was his back that carried me home when I had lost my way. This was an unsung hero of my boyhood who now called me "Mister."

"When is that new little sprout due?"

Cassie blushed with her answer, "March. We're half-way there."

"Mr. Taylor," I excused. "I'm sorry I haven't come by to see you for quite a while."

Mr. Taylor stopped leafing through the mail and crumpled an envelope in his fist with a vengeance.

"I understand, Sprout. You've been busy fighting wars and wrecking trucks."

I lowered my head in the shyness of a boy who gave credence to anything his elders said. I bent down to pick up the crumpled envelope and cast a hesitant gaze at Mr. Taylor.

"That's another letter from that damned corporation that wants to buy my farm," Mr. Taylor confided. "Now that Millie's passed on, I figure I'll sell someday soon. But I'll be damned if I'll let my home go to that pack of heathens that's grabbing up all the small farms!"

I nodded in respect of a farmer who called his place home.

"Maybe I'll buy your place someday soon," I mused with a sheepish grin. "Uh — when did — Sir — when did Mrs. Taylor pass away?"

"When you were over there in Vietnam. April 19, 1969."

My face paled and my knees buckled. Mr. Taylor brought me back to my feet.

"Are you okay, Sprout?"

Cassie claimed my arm and assured, "He'll be alright, Mr. Taylor. I just need to get him home to rest."

Mr. Taylor supported me with a strong arm, and walked me home with the same care as when he carried that boy who had lost his way. Cassie clutched my hand and swiped her tears. She knew the date, April 19, 1969. It was the day that the earth rumbled beneath me and a torrent of death thundered above. It was the day that eight young men died before they were old enough to vote. And now I knew that the neighbor lady who always had the warmest cookies and the coldest milk had also died on my nineteenth birthday.

I stayed in bed the rest of the day and all of the next. Momma came with food and Josie came with laughter. Cassie came with whatever I needed, but even I didn't know what I really needed.

Daddy stayed away, as I knew he would. He was one to provide, to protect, and to love, but he was not one to coddle. He would have no part of the pit of pity in which I wallowed.

The third morning of my useless retreat, Daddy woke me with a hardy tug of my big toe.

"Don't let the sun catch you sleepin', Jake."

Winter was hinting at an early arrival, and the cold hardwood floor startled me awake. I ambled down the stairs, following Daddy's call, and found him sitting with a ruddy-faced young man who appeared to have a fire under his butt. He stood up on his one leg and leaned on his crutch. He offered his hand with earnest intent, and Daddy handed me the young man's note.

It was nothing more than a twice-folded paper that simply read,

"This is Sam. Give him a chance.
Tommy

Daddy rose and left the room, while Sam and I talked. We talked about before and we talked about after, but we did not talk about the war. Veterans understand all they need to about war, and no amount of talking will change it. The only thing that can be changed is the after.

"I've studied agriculture," Sam offered. "I've worked the farm and I've lived the farm. Ask me anything and I'll have an opinion. But I'll do things your way and Eddie's way."

I reeled in shock. "Eddie's way?"

"Yeah, your father said you had some project planned with a guy named Eddie."

Daddy had done it again. He had defied and rejected despair and pointed the way to a new dawn.

"That's right," I confirmed. "Eddie and I are partners. I'll tell you all about him, as soon as we get you squared away."

"All I need is a spot in the barn to bed down and some chow," Sam declared.

"No, no," I objected. "You're not sleeping in the barn. Winter's on top of us."

"Listen, Mr. Marshall…"

"Jake," I corrected.

"Listen, Jake, I need a place in the barn. I'll work as hard as any man with two legs. But I need a place of my own to rest."

"Alright, Sam. Go pick your spot in the barn, and we'll bring you some blankets, a lantern and such. We'll talk about your pay over supper."

"I'm not worried too much about pay," Sam declined. "I've got a little disability check coming from the government."

"We'll talk about it over supper," I repeated.

Sam hoisted his bag over one shoulder and wedged his crutch under the other.

"Well, I could use a couple bucks to flash in front of the ladies on Saturday night."

I called to Sam when he was half way to the barn. "Do you think you'll ever tell me how you lost that leg?"

Sam didn't stop. He just waved and shouted, "I slipped while I was shaving."

Daddy made himself easy to find. I could hear the rhythmic creaking of the porch swing. I eased into the swing, and Daddy rubbed his chin to blot out his grin. I gave a slight push to smooth out the sway of the swing.

"I don't know what to say, Daddy, except thank you."

"Thank you for what, Son?"

"For dragging me out of my hole."

"You dragged yourself out, Son. We've all had to climb out of a few holes. All we can do is cover them up and try not to fall in the same hole again."

Daddy allowed time for his poetic wisdom to sink in before he went on.

"You knew that Mrs. Taylor had passed away, but I didn't plan on ever telling you she died on your birthday."

Comfort was exchanged to and fro, as the swing swayed from back to forward.

"I understand, Daddy. You've always looked out for my best interest."

Daddy slapped a hand on my knee and asked, "What do you remember about April 19, 1956?"

"My first two-wheeler," I blurted.

Daddy chuckled. "And a few scrapes and bruises."

"Oh yeah," I vouched. I got so good at falling down, that it became my favorite game. I would pedal that bike as fast as I could, and then fall off like a cowboy being shot off his horse."

Of course, in my play, I would always fight through my imaginary pain and shoot all the bad guys before I died. If only that could have been the case in 1969. I didn't shoot the bad guys that day. Eight good guys fell and the bad guys got away.

"What about April 19, 1959?" Daddy asked.

The day I could have lived in forever flooded my mind. "Fried chicken — potato salad — ice cream — fishing."

"What flavor of ice cream?" Daddy pushed.

"Banana," I was sure. "I remember everything, Daddy, everything you gave me and everything you taught me."

I leaned forward to rest my elbows on my knees and stared at my feet. "I know for certain, that's why I'm still around."

I felt Daddy's hand briskly stroke my back. "How about April 19, 1966?"

I reared back into the swing. "My driver's license! I headed straight from the DMV to pick up Julie McHenry and took her to the malt shop."

"And you got caught, didn't you?" Daddy reminded.

"Oh yeah," I confessed. "The car wouldn't start and I had to call you."

Daddy dismissed his valiant rescue. "I just banged on the battery terminals, but we got it started, didn't we?"

That's the story that I wanted Daddy to remember. I would never disclose my long-held secret. While Daddy banged under the hood of the car, I noticed my idiotic mistake. That old Plymouth would only start with the automatic transmission in park. I had left the gear shift in drive. While Daddy banged, I slowly and unperceptively moved the gear shift into park.

"Try it now," Daddy suggested.

The engine fired and hummed. I yelled out the window, "Daddy, you're a genius!"

Only Julie and I know the truth, but Daddy knows the better story.

"Oh!" I excitedly recalled. "Julie had set her milkshake on the dash, and when I stepped on the gas to take off, the cup slid right into her lap."

Daddy roared and I cackled. Daddy slapped my knee again and concluded, "April 19 isn't such a bad day to remember."

"DADDY!"

The frenzied call pierced the air and drowned out our laughter.

"JAKE!"

Josie was furiously waving her straw hat from the barn door. Daddy took the steps and I sailed over the porch railing. I flew like that bull was on my tail. Fear pounded in my ears louder than when the bullets were whizzing by them. Pain could not slow my legs. Not a stride was wasted. Not a breath was spared.

I lunged into the barn and saw a horror beyond imagination. It was a hideous scene of the cruelest torture, and the most humiliating humor.

Sam was laid out on his back. The tines of a pitchfork were held an inch from his neck. Holding the other end of the pitchfork, Cassie yelled, "DROP THE KNIFE!"

I couldn't catch enough breath to laugh at poor Sam. I coughed and lumbered my way to Sam and reached out a saving hand.

"Look out, Jake! He's got a knife!"

I grasped Sam's crutch with one hand, and lifted him with the other. Cassie stood braced with her weapon at the ready.

"I was just gonna cut a hunk of rope, Jake," Sam pleaded.

I curled my arm around his shoulders and said, "Sam, meet my body guard, Cassie. And this is her back-up, Josie."

Pale faces drooped in disbelief, then relaxed in relief, and slowly creased and flushed into laughter. Daddy caught up in time to witness the gaiety and joy of poor Sam's initiation.

The triangle dinner bell rang out, as Momma clanged the three-quarter time waltz music calling us to breakfast. Sam was now welcomed with smooth country gravy, steaming biscuits, and warm hospitality. Momma buzzed around, doting on her new mouth to feed.

"I made plenty of food," Momma emphasized. "I'm expecting you to have seconds, Eddie."

A shocked moment of silence and darting eyes brought Momma's hand to her mouth. "I'm sorry — I meant Sam."

"It's okay, Momma," I excused.

"Is that the Eddie you're partnered with?" Sam assumed.

"Yes," I confirmed. "I'll take you on a tour of the farm and tell you all about Eddie. Dig into those biscuits now, Sam."

Sam was not much of a conversationalist, but he listened intently. He nodded when he understood and nodded faster when he agreed. He cocked his head quizzically when he didn't concur, but spoke only after he had carefully weighed and measured his thoughts. He smiled every time he heard his name, and we made sure he smiled a lot.

It was nip and tuck as to who was keeping up with whom, as we walked the farm. Sam charged through furrows and stubble, around stones and stumps, and nothing escaped his surveillance.

"We have more hogs than ever before," I bragged.

"I counted fourteen," Sam responded. "You might be pushing that for this size of farm. Tell me about Eddie."

Sam continued his visual sweep as I recounted the story of the boy with no arms or legs, but a heart full of boundless love. I described the contagious smile of the boy who wanted only to go home.

"I've seen six milk cows and twelve head of beef cattle," Sam interjected. "I think I might have run across this Eddie in the hospital. Did the little fella have big dimples and ears that kind of stuck out?"

"And a front tooth missing," I added.

Sam nodded faster. "Looks like soybeans were here, corn over there, and timothy hay on the south forty. So now you and Eddie are partners?"

Sam's pace slowed as I told about Eddie's letter home. He fell to his knee when I quoted from memory the return letter stained with the colors of chocolate and cherry.

"Eddie has been with Cassie and me every day. I wish I could have been his arms and legs, and Momma wishes she could have just fed him breakfast."

Sam dug in the ground with his crutch and smelled the composition of a handful of topsoil.

"You might think about adding more nitrogen in the spring. And let your Momma know she can call me Eddie anytime."

Daddy was waiting for us when we circled around to the pond. He was nursing the fledgling flames that danced among the kindling, and beckoned us to join him around his small council fire.

"What do you think?" Daddy asked, as Sam warmed his hands over the growing flames.

"I think I'd like to make a fire pit, not too far, but not too close to the barn," Sam requested.

"Sounds good to me," Daddy agreed. "I do some of my best thinking around a fire. Now, what about our little farm?"

"It's well laid out," Sam began. "Uh — the animals look healthy — uh…"

"Look, Sam," Daddy leveled. "There's always room for improvement. If you know about any new farming techniques we could use, I'd appreciate a straight answer."

Sam looked Daddy straight in the eye. "With the right fertilizer, we could increase your crop yield by at least ten percent. You need to decide whether you want to do dairy or beef. Unless you have a good market for milk, you have too many dairy cows. And you don't need the milk for slopping the hogs. With a good brand of feed, we could fatten and sell those hogs faster than a merry-go-round. You can buy young hogs down in Arkansas for a third of the price here and more than triple your money."

"And," Sam added. "Mrs. Marshall makes the best gravy I've ever tasted."

Daddy sat with his knees pulled to his chest, and his body gently shook with a laugh that comes from inside. He grinned in excitement, and fire sparkled in his eyes.

"Oh," Sam remembered. "You have enough equipment to farm twice the acreage you have."

Daddy and I looked at each other and shared a revelation.

"Maybe we should pay Ed Taylor another visit," I urged. "How about we invite him to supper."

I left Daddy and Sam basking in the warmth of the fire and dashed to the house.

"Momma, we need one more place setting for supper, and Daddy says that Mr. Taylor is partial to your chili and corn bread."

I kissed Momma hard and loud, and grabbed Cassie by the hand. "Let's walk a half mile and back."

Cassie noted a purpose in my gait that had too long been absent. It wasn't a stroll or even a walk. It was a drive toward something I had in my sights.

"You want to let me in on it?" Cassie probed.

I could have joked. I could have pretended innocence and ignorance, but this felt too real.

"Would you mind being married to a farmer?"

"I thought I was married to a farm boy."

"Not a farm boy. A farmer. You — me — the baby…"

"And Mr. Taylor's farm?" Cassie finished for me.

Now Cassie was the playful innocent. "What do you like about farming, getting up with the chickens or slopping the hogs?"

I switched gears in my step and began to stroll. "I like having to get up before dawn, so I don't miss the sunrise. I like having to work the land so I feel part of it. I like every sight, sound and smell that tells me I'm home. That's what I want for our kids. I don't want them to have it better than I had. I want them to have it as good as I had."

"Cowboy," Cassie beamed. "I think you just made my life."

Mr. Taylor had a porch swing also, and he was making good use of it. His eyes were serenely closed and his lips moved as he talked silently with the other half of himself. Mrs. Taylor was in that swing with him, as sure as she had lived, and as sure as she had died.

Mr. Taylor's eyes fluttered at the song of a meadowlark, and he sighed at the sight of Cassie and me. "Hello, Sprout. Hello, Mrs. Sprout."

"Mr. Taylor," I honorably addressed. "You remember that I said I might buy your place someday? I want to make — uh — I want to make an offer — uh — of chili and cornbread."

"What time?" was all that Mr. Taylor wanted to know.

Mr. Taylor attacked the big bowl of chili as if his life depended on it. He savored each buttery mouthful of cornbread and asked for more. He no longer took breathing for granted, as most folks do. Nor did he let a smell escape his nostrils or let a taste evade his tongue. He missed the smell and taste of Millie Taylor, and he was starved for another reason to live.

"It looked like you had a pretty fair crop this year, Ed." That was Daddy's way of asking, "How ya doin'?"

"It was a decent yield, "Mr. Taylor allowed.

Daddy extended his neighborly chatter. "They say we're in for a hard winter."

"I've got my firewood stacked," Mr. Taylor proclaimed. "We could use a good cold snap to kill off the bugs."

The harshest of winters would be taken in stride by two old friends of the earth who knew its hardships and its bounty. Sam listened and learned what no textbook can teach. Tried and true wisdom was heard over that chili and cornbread.

The crow's feet in the corners of Mr. Taylor's eyes wrinkled in the early stage of a smile, as he watched me perched on the edge of my chair. I shifted indecisively, leaning on one elbow and then the other. The twitching of my knees could be detected in the tell-tale vibration of the table.

"Speak your piece, Sprout, before you burst at the seams."

The vibrations stilled and my posture straightened.

"When you're ready to sell your farm, Sir, I'd like to put in my bid."

Mr. Taylor pushed his bowl away, making room for the steaming cup of coffee Momma offered.

"Thank you, Rose. That has to be the best chili in five states, and your corn bread is out of this world."

Momma beamed with satisfaction, then blushed as Mr. Taylor announced, "Roy Marshall, you don't deserve this woman."

Everyone chuckled except Daddy. He put his arm around Momma's waist and agreed, "You're absolutely right, Ed, but I'm working on it."

My proposal had not been forgotten. Mr. Taylor was waiting until he felt the vibrations in the table resume.

"I'm sure you know that farming is a hard life, Sprout, but I guess you just can't take the farm out of the boy."

The vibrations ceased for good, and I boldly asked, "Any thoughts on when you might sell?"

Mr. Taylor rested his eyes behind tired eyelids.

"I was talking to Millie earlier, and I came to realize that time won't make it any easier to move on. I think Millie would like it if I went down to stay with our daughter in Corpus Christi. I have a grandson I haven't seen yet."

Mr. Taylor opened his eyes and looked at the future reflected in mine. "Make me an offer, Sprout."

Cassie put her hand in mine and held her breath. Momma and Daddy smiled at each other. Josie bounced in her chair, and Sam nodded faster.

"I want to get a bank appraisal for a fair price," I insisted. "Cassie and I have some money stashed away for a down payment on a bank loan, and we could share the crops with you as long as need be to make it right between us."

The deal was set in stone with one simple, binding handshake.

Chapter 14

Night after night, the family gathered around the glow of Sam's fire pit. The snowflakes stacked around us, while the fire blazed within us. Stories were exchanged and dreams were shared. Plans were made and commitments were sworn. The cocoa simmered on the embers until the last drop was sipped, and Sam retired to his layers of blankets on a bed of straw.

One bitingly crisp morning, Sam was out and about when Josie entered the barn. She measured the chicken feed and shook off a chill. Her wandering eyes fell on the stall that Sam called home, and her curiosity drew her close. Just a peek was all she wanted, but that peek would plunge her into a world beyond her innocent grasp.

Around the railings and wall of Sam's inner sanctum, drawings were impaled on rusty nails. Charcoal sketches graphically portrayed faces of agony, and twisted bodies recorded the gruesome reality of war. Josie could not comprehend or escape the indescribable horrors that lived in Sam's mind.

Josie shrieked at the touch of Sam's hand. She retreated to a corner and covered her ashen-white face. "This can't be real!"

"You weren't supposed to see these," Sam quaked.

Josie sobbed and Sam groaned. He ripped a drawing off its nail and sighed, "This was Curt. He was real."

Sam snatched another sketch. "This is Gene, and that's me he's dragging through the brush. That was real."

Josie peered through her quivering fingers at the scenes of fear and heroism depicted as one. She sank to the ground and tried to shake the carnage from her eyes.

Sam frantically ripped all the memories of hell from their nails and buried them under the straw. He reached a cautious hand to lift Josie's chin and coaxed, "Hold still little darlin'."

Sam settled on an upturned bucket and put charcoal to paper. He formed the likeness of a spirited young girl in overalls and a straw hat. Pigtails were in mid-twirl, and her face was to the sky. Fanciful leaves and dainty butterflies swirled in a bird's-eye view of the world that was meant to be.

Sam entrusted his vision of a brighter day into Josie's hands. "And this is real," Sam implored.

The tears trailing over Josie's lips turned from bitter to sweet. The pain of unwanted knowledge was swept away by the beauty of truth.

Never again did Sam sketch by lantern in the shadows of a dismal past. He sketched by sunlight and by firelight. He sketched life as it came, not as it had gone. From the first snowfall to the first hint of spring, Sam captured a new world with charcoal and paper.

The snow yielded to green, and the winds blustered us into March. Preparations had been made to greet the next cycle of life, but I was ill-prepared for the greatest of all life's events.

"It's time, Cowboy."

I blinked my eyes until the alarm clock emerged through the blur. "But dawn is still five hours away," I argued.

I grumbled into the folds of the pillow, "It's time." The mental light bulb switched on and I shot straight up. I saw a bead of sweat meander down Cassie's forehead.

"It's time? IT'S TIME!"

The clatter in the house and the slamming of doors woke Sam in the barn. In precious minutes, Cassie was secure in the car, and I fumbled the key into the ignition. As we drove away, Sam leaped up and down on that strong, triumphant leg and shouted, "And this is real!"

Cassie was panting and Josie was swiping a cool cloth over Cassie's embattled brow. Daddy and Sam were pacing outside, and Momma was rocking and humming. I scrambled from Cassie, to Momma, to nurse, and back to Cassie. I was a helpless witness of this fight for new life. I could not lead and I didn't know how to follow. I was a helpless, witless mess, but I held on to Cassie's hand for dear life.

The doctor and nurse considered the hard facts. The contractions were now one after another.

"Why isn't she in the delivery room yet?" The doctor demanded.

"She isn't fully dilated," The nurse informed.

"Grab a gurney, we've got to fly!" the doctor ordered.

The nurse raced ahead, clearing the hall. The doctor and I pushed the gurney forward in high-speed pursuit.

The head was crowning when we got to the delivery room, and Cassie was pushing with all her mortal might.

"She's not dilated enough for that size of head," the nurse worried.

"You're going to have to push harder, Mrs. Marshall. This is a big baby," the doctor advised. "Get a nursery nurse standing by to check for clavicle fractures! MOVE!"

I had never been more frightened in my life. The rapid-fire action and the intense shouting of orders spun in my head like the chaos of the battlefield. The will and determination in Cassie's beet-red face equaled that of the fiercest warrior.

The baby's shoulders appeared and Cassie screamed. She collapsed on her back and her eyes glazed over.

"I'M LOSING HER! CASSIE!"

The doctor calmly and authoritatively instructed, "You better push, lady, or you're going to lose this child."

Cassie sprang up with fury in her eyes. She found the breath and she found the strength from somewhere beyond this mortal world. With one last relentless push, and one last unyielding battle cry, Gretchen Marshall was presented to the world.

The baby was whisked away before I caught a glimpse. I couldn't take my eyes off Cassie. Her eyes opened and closed with each deep, recuperative breath.

"Stay with our baby, Jake. Go."

I tore myself away from Cassie, to follow the miracle of Gretchen.

My explicit instructions were to sit in a rocker and wait. To wait for the nurse to check each finger and toe, each bone and lung, and that new little heart pounding in the next room. I hadn't heard Gretchen cry, and I hadn't heard any news. I remembered hearing only, "Big baby." "Check for clavicle fractures." "You're going to lose this child!"

I stood in a flash at the sound of the opening door.

"Sit, Papa," said the nurse holding my tightly wrapped child.

I obeyed and stared and gulped.

The nurse placed that child in my arms as gently as if it was a bundle of stardust.

"She's a fighter," the nurse declared. "And she's perfectly healthy. All ten pounds and two ounces of her."

You cannot feel a heart so pure and not melt in awe. You cannot hold a miracle so profound and not feel the presence of God. I made so many promises to my little girl that day. Promises she would not recall, but promises I would keep with my last breath.

An even greater joy followed, as I relinquished that precious gift into her mother's arms. I was now a witness to an instant bond, stronger than any force within the grasp of a living soul.

"Ten pounds and two ounces!" Momma swooned.

"Isn't she gorgeous?" Josie squealed.

"She's a keeper," Sam asserted.

"Amen," Daddy prayed.

Cassie had fought the good fight. She had finished the race to which no man could aspire. No battle was more glorious and no victory sweeter. Cassie was my hero, and Gretchen was ours.

Spring had new meaning that year, 1974. Each task had an added purpose with Gretchen in our midst. Gretchen would grow along with this year's crop and many more to come. Backs strained twice as much with a labor of love for two farms. Mr. Taylor lent a hand for his final planting. Two old men and two young ones plowed and planted and dreamed.

The papers were signed in May and Mr. Taylor's farm was ours. Mr. Taylor headed south; with Millie Taylor making sure he found his way to Corpus Christi.

He left behind the porch swing that Millie loved. He left behind the sofa where Millie spilled her popcorn every Saturday night. He left everything that he could not bear seeing moved from its sacred spot.

Cassie and I moved in with Gretchen and little else. We pictured the home we would create; we treasured the memories before they happened. We painted walls and we hung pictures, but we did not budge the sofa. We placed a TV in front of it and made a batch of popcorn.

The crops were standing tall, when Sam and I doused our heads under the pump and flung the invigorating water from our hair. The droplets evaporated in the afternoon swelter and Sam reclined in exhaustion.

"I think we've bit off more that we can chew, Jake."

I hung the bucket on the pump head to catch the last flow of water. "Yeah," I confessed. "But I'm still hungry."

"Well chew on this," Sam challenged. "The easy part is over. I don't think we can handle the harvest."

"It is going to be a big harvest," I conceded. "And that's your fault, brother.

You and your soil-sniffling nose."

I emptied the bucket of water over Sam's depleted body, and he gasped and sputtered and laughed.

"I'm going to do you a favor," Sam countered. With a sweep of his crutch, Sam separated my feet from the ground, and I was flat on my back, looking at the same sky as Sam.

"Okay," I surrendered. "You've got my attention. What's the favor?"

Sam cocked his head at the clouds shifting and shaping into familiar forms and asked, "You ever know a guy you would march into hell with?"

The clouds rolled and transformed into faces I remembered. "I could name a couple," I recalled.

"Gene," Sam called out. "He was the best of us. He was too dumb to be afraid of anything and too stubborn to let me die."

Sam and I watched the clouds furl and collide. I knew Gene, without seeing his face. I had seen his valor in many other faces. Those faces were all afraid. Bravery is driven by an all-consuming fear that blinds one to logic and numbs one to pain. Extraordinary acts of heroism come from terribly frightened men who value the lives of their buddies more than their own.

"So, what's this favor you're going to do for me?" I pushed.

"It's already done," Sam surprised. "Gene will be here tomorrow. We'll get your harvest in, down to the last kernel. I'll split any increase in yield with you, and I'll split my share with Gene."

Sam's favor was more of an instruction than a proposal. We needed help, and Sam needed Gene.

"I guess I'm asking you for a favor, boss. Gene is strong as a bull and he could use some good hard work. All that shit in the war kind of messed with his mind, if you know what I mean."

"I think I know what you mean," I hinted.

"But you won't have an ounce of trouble from Gene," Sam swore. I'll stake my life…"

"Hold on there," I interrupted. "Keep your life; I just want your promise."

"Name it, Jake."

"If Gene is still here after the harvest, we're building a bunkhouse for you two."

Sam reached for that binding handshake and agreed, "I can live with that."

Tomorrow came and Gene came. He was a quiet young man, who tended to look down a lot. There was gentleness and sorrow in his demeanor, but a conviction in his stance. When he said, "Yes, Sir," he meant, "You have my word."

He had the strong and able body that Sam had described. No disability was apparent to the common eye, but I saw it. This was a warrior who was wounded in the depths of his heart.

"You know anything about farming, Gene?" I queried.

Gene looked up and ventured, "I know it's a lot of work. And that don't scare me none."

Josie appeared in Gene's sights, as she skipped across the barnyard. Gene froze, as if he had been overrun by a dominant force over which he had no power. I imagined that look on his face was the same look I had at my first sight of Cassie.

"Gene? Gene!" I warned. "That's my little sister, Josie."

"I wasn't — I didn't mean to — I was just…" Gene flustered.

I eased Gene's embarrassment with an accepting smile and called, "Josie, come on over here."

Josie's skip faltered as she neared, and her feet abruptly halted as her eyes gaped wide. Her lips parted and her jaw dropped.

"You're Gene," Josie knew.

Gene nodded in dumb-struck wonderment.

Josie's eyes watered and her lips quivered. She had no choice but to run and embrace that face that had leapt into her life in charcoal and paper.

Josie softly wept on the shoulder of the man that had drug Sam through the brush, and pressed her cheek against the face in which she had seen the meaning of love, of valor, of everything that mattered.

"Josie — do you know — how do you know…" I stammered.

"Let's go for a walk, boss," Sam insisted. "I'll tell you all about it."

I looked over my shoulder as Sam led me away. Gene looked as bewildered as I, but his was the look of a man who had just found heaven.

That look continued, as the harvest began. Gene kept a vigilant eye on Sam's back as they put their shoulders to the task. But Gene's other eye watched as Josie matured into her eighteenth year. Her skipping became a glide, and her smile became allure. Gene was hopelessly bound and hopefully found in that flowing red hair, and his broad sweaty shoulders did not escape Josie's eye.

Sam's promised harvest was fulfilled, and it was time to build. Sam and Gene would have a real home this winter, warm enough for two and big enough for more. Hammers were flying and saws were buzzing, and Daddy took charge.

"Make sure the foundation is square. It won't turn out right if you don't start right. We need more pitch on those rafters to hold up under the snow. Get a good seal around those windows."

Each of Daddy's instructions made Sam and Gene work a little harder and smile a little broader.

Christmas was only days away when the last nail was driven. Sam crouched over the fire pit, breathing life into the flames. Gene was turning a harmonica over and over in his fingers and watching the glow of the first embers.

"You've got magic in your hands, Gene," I informed.

Gene looked at his hands, then looked up for more.

"My sister loves Christmas carols."

Gene's eyes smiled and his nose crinkled as he put music to his lips.

"The first Noel, the angels did sing…"

Josie appeared before the second verse, and melted next to the warm strains of Christmas. Momma brought the cocoa, Daddy brought the fiddles, and Cassie brought Gretchen. Carol after carol filled that night. Christmas was never so perfect and never so right.

Josie rose after the last carol ended. She spread her arms wide and sang, "Make me dance, Gene."

Gene led the way and Daddy and I followed. The harmonica blared and the strings were on fire. The tune didn't matter to the flame that night. Gretchen clapped in glee, and Josie twirled and twirled.

The snow piled deeper than I had ever remembered and it was a winter without equal. Holidays shined brighter and nights passed warmer with Gretchen in our arms. Daddy felt the sweet hugs he had known once before and Momma held the child she had swaddled before she was too big to be held.

Josie held a new wonder she had never known. All the confusing yearnings of womanhood could never be understood until she held the magic of her own childhood. Gretchen learned to laugh with uncontrollable joy and Josie learned to give with uncontrollable love.

Josie taught Gretchen a little game of her own invention. Josie flung her arms up in the exuberant sign of a touchdown and cheered, "Happy Baby!"

Over and over, Josie performed to the giggling delight of Gretchen. Gretchen finally mimicked Josie's inescapable joy, and reached her tiny arms above her head.

"Happy Baby!"

It was more than Momma could bear. With each explosion of joy, Momma laughed harder. The more Momma laughed, the higher Gretchen reached.

"Make her STOP!" Momma begged.

Cassie came to Momma's rescue, scooping up the baby and declaring, "Time for your bath." Cassie paused in her waltz from the room, "How's your speech coming, Josie?"

Josie hung her head as Momma asked, "What speech?"

Cassie looked at Josie and regretted, "Sorry," and vanished from the room.

"I was named Valedictorian of my high school class and I have to speak at graduation," Josie moaned.

Momma screamed in that faint, shrill voice that could barely contain her elation.

"Ah, Momma, it's no big deal."

"No big deal?" Momma blustered. "It's the biggest — the most wonderful…"

Momma couldn't always find the words, but she could always find the hug.

"I don't mind writing the speech," Josie whimpered in Momma's arms. "I just wish someone else would give it."

"You'll do fine, Sweetheart," Momma had no doubt.

Josie dutifully wrote that speech and rehearsed and rehearsed. The chickens heard the strains of hope and the challenge of a new generation. The cows listened to the memories of youth and the dawn of wisdom. Josie knew her thoughts and she knew her heart. But she didn't have the answers, and she was scared to death.

The entire family was sitting in the front row at graduation, as Josie approached the podium to speak. She avoided any eye contact as she thanked all the appropriate people. She cleared her throat and excused herself as she stuttered and grasped for words.

She backed away from the podium and stumbled toward the steps. Momma was on the edge of her seat, ready to rescue her baby, but Daddy held her tight and trusted and prayed.

The audience gasped as Josie teetered on the brink of collapse. Her breathing was shallow and her vision was blurred. All the faces of expectation were obscured in the blinding lights. I saw that face of fear that I knew so well. It was the fear that infects us all at the moment of truth. It was the moment in which one has to decide to run, to fight, or to hide.

Josie couldn't run and she couldn't hide. Not after she saw that tiny glimpse of movement from the front row. Gretchen was clapping and bouncing and bursting, and that's all Josie needed to see.

Josie took three deep breaths and returned to the podium.

"We are not the future,
Class of 1975.
We are the now.
The past has shaped us and the future is among us, but the now is in our hands.
I know the past, and I have seen the future.
The past has taught us what needs to be done and what cannot be repeated.
Justice must be done.
Peace must be won.
I have seen war in the faces of those who endured it, and it must not be repeated.
I have seen hope in the faces of the future and it must be nourished.
It will not happen without us.
It must happen because of us.
I have known you all my life, Class of 1975.
I won't forget you. Please don't forget me.
And don't wait for the future. The future begins now."

Josie quelled the burst of applause with a sweep of her hand. "Hold on a second, please."

She walked down to the first row and gathered Gretchen in her arms. The audience watched in anticipation and silence as Josie carried the baby onto the stage. She sat Gretchen on the podium, gave her a tender kiss, and turned her to face the audience.

Josie leaned toward the microphone and said, "Ladies and gentlemen, this is the future."

Then she put her lips to Gretchen's ear and said,
"HAPPY BABY!"

Chapter 15

It was three o'clock in the morning, and Josie had given up on sleep. She sat on her bed, with her legs crossed and Raggedy Ann tucked in her arms.

"You're going with me, Raggedy, so you've got to help me choose."

Josie and Raggedy surveyed the myriad of choices spread out on the quilt. Letters of acceptance from universities far away demanded their attention. Scholarship offers from half of them required their consideration.

"Of course, you're right, Raggedy. Why even look at the ones that don't offer any help?"

Josie and Raggedy joined hands and tossed half of the papers through the air.

"Purdue is much too far away, Raggedy, and Stanford is even farther."

More papers floated to the floor. One by one, the choices were narrowed, and only Raggedy's choice remained.

"The University of Kansas, huh? I knew that was your choice all along, Raggedy."

Josie hugged and Raggedy whispered, "What about Gene?"

"Don't talk about things you don't understand, Raggedy!" Josie scolded. "You just — just sit here."

Josie set Raggedy on the pillow and kissed her farewell. She slid her hand down the stair railing that was worn smooth, and listened to the creak each step had acquired. She squinted her eyes through the kitchen light and stepped out into the mist. Her steps were slow, but measured and sure. Moonlight could not disguise the feel of the damp grass or the sound of the gritty bare earth. She groped her way through the dark barnyard with her eyes half open, and pressed her face on the bunkhouse door.

The door flung open, and Gene caught her fall. Neither sound nor smell alerted Gene, he just knew Josie was there.

"What wrong?" Sam muttered from his broken sleep.

"Go back to sleep, Sam. I've got this watch," Gene reassured.

Josie and Gene walked aimlessly as one. Each step was matched and each heartbeat was echoed. "I've got to go, Gene," Josie braved.

"I know," Gene courageously relented.

Gene's pace slowed and Josie held her breath. "You go," Gene insisted. "Go be the best, wherever that takes you."

Gene didn't flinch or show any doubt, but a rogue tear escaped down his cheek.

"I'll be home for Thanksgiving," Josie promised.

A coyote howled and challenged the moon. Josie hid in Gene's arms and shivered. "I never liked coyotes."

"I'll be here," Gene committed.

Shapes were becoming sharper and forms were taking on color, as the sun previewed its coming.

"You get the chicken feed and I'll gather the eggs," Josie decided.

Josie raced to the chicken house and Gene sprinted to the barn. They each ran their separate ways, knowing they would soon meet again.

The door on the chicken house stood ajar and Josie stood still. Feathers floated out the door and the hens sounded the alarm. Squawking and growling filled the air, but Josie screamed louder. A coyote appeared with a mouthful of prey, and then dropped it to bare his teeth. A coyote's first instinct is to flee from deafening human screams, but this coyote was seconds too late.

Gene's hands were around the coyote's throat, and the two combatants began a deathly spiral. Gene spun and the coyote sailed around and around. The coyote snarled and snapped in fear for its life. Gene roared and bled in fear of much more. Death was an old acquaintance of Gene's and could not defeat him. Life was what scared Gene and life screamed in his ears.

"GENE! NOooo!"

The coyote's body slammed onto a fencepost and fell limp at Gene's feet. The coyote was done but Gene was not. The enemy was defeated but still breathed.

So many lives had been lost in battles that should not have been fought, and more deaths had to be accounted for. Gene pounded his fists in unrelenting fury. Each blow mourned a life that had ended too soon and each blood curdling wail begged for forgiveness.

"GENE! STOP! GENE!"

Sam wrapped an arm around Josie from behind, and shielded her eyes with the other. "Let him be," Sam prayed. "Let him wear himself out."

The aftermath of war is always the same. Victor and vanquished lay side by side, and loved ones are left behind in shattered pieces. Then come the gatherers to carry away the wounded and bury the dead.

"Give her to me, Sam," Cassie requested.

Josie jolted at the sound of Cassie's voice. She lunged and grasped like a drowning victim and cried the desperate sobs of "WHY?"

Momma and Cassie led Josie away, but Josie looked back and called once more, "GENE!"

Sam and I huddled over Gene and understood his pain. We saw it, we felt it, and we remembered it.

"Josie?" Gene panted.

"Josie's okay, brother," I guaranteed. "Let's get you in for some stitches."

We sat Gene erect, and Sam grabbed him like a sack of potatoes. "You big, dumb son of a bitch!"

Sam and I carried away the wounded, and it was Daddy who stayed behind to bury the dead. With wheelbarrow and shovel, Daddy dug the hole and buried the only possible outcome of war.

Cassie stroked and Momma petted, while Josie cuddled Raggedy under her chin.

"Why, Momma?"

"We're not likely to ever understand the why and how of love, sweetheart," Momma answered.

"Love?" Josie denied.

"Even Raggedy knows you're in love, little sister," Cassie teased.

Josie hid behind Raggedy and mumbled, "Maybe I do love him, but…"

"There are no buts in love young lady," Momma reminded.

"But Gene's crazy," Josie cried. "He scares me to death!"

"Yeah, he's crazy alright," Cassie agreed. "He's crazy about you. Let me tell you about another boy who went crazy."

Cassie centered herself in front of Josie on the bed and smoothed Raggedy's hair. Momma fluffed the pillows and propped Josie up. Josie's eyes were as wide as Raggedy's as Cassie began her story.

"A boy was stolen away in the middle of the night. Far from home, he was stripped of his clothes and dressed in olive drab. Other boys were stolen as well, and dressed to look the same."

Josie pulled Raggedy closer, in case she was scared.

"They were given guns and taught how to kill. Their faces were shoved in the mud, while orders were shouted in their ears."

"DON'T BE THINKING ABOUT YOUR MOMMA, THAT'LL GET YOU KILLED!"

Momma gasped with her hand to her mouth.

"Their bodies were pushed beyond limits they had never imagined and their minds were tested and prepared."

"DON'T BE THINKING ABOUT YOUR GIRLFRIEND, SHE'S PROBABLY WITH ANOTHER GUY!"

Tears were rolling down Josie's face, but Raggedy caught them all.

"Comfort and compassion were ripped out of their lives, and the only thing left to love was the buddy next to them in the mud."

"YOUR MISSION IS TO KILL AND YOUR DESTINY — IS DEATH WITH HONOR!"

Raggedy was trembling, but Josie held her tight.

"Well, death was foretold and death was delivered. But those who died were the lucky ones. Flags were draped over their coffins and guns were fired over their graves."

"Bugles were played to mourn their senseless loss, and honor was theirs as promised. Others were not so lucky."

Josie waved her hand frantically toward the dresser and Momma passed her the Kleenex.

"Others were sent back home with only half of their bodies and even less of their hearts. They were put in wheelchairs and pushed out the door; your check will be in the mail."

Josie covered Raggedy's ears. She could hear no more.

"Then there was the boy who went crazy," Cassie recalled.

"He did everything he was told and gave everything he had. He fought as hard as he could against an enemy that kept coming and coming. He fought against memories of life and love and home. He fought to forget those who died in his arms."

Momma tried to shelter Josie from the horror. "Cassie, PLEASE!"

Cassie looked away from the fear she had kindled and stuck to her purpose.

"This boy finally came back, with all his fingers and toes. He was told to go home; we're done with you. They gave him a medal and a plane ticket, and said, 'Have a nice life.'"

"All the way home he heard the greeting, "Baby Killer!" "Dope Head!"

"Scum!" All the way home, he wished he had died with honor."

Cassie cried with Momma. She cried with Josie. She cried with Raggedy, because the story was true.

"This boy felt his Momma's arms again. He heard his Daddy's voice again. But he hadn't made it home. He was still in the mud, in the blood, and in his own personal hell."

The bed was shaking with Josie's and Momma's sobs, and even Cassie's. Josie asked, with a gasp between each word, "Was – Gene – that – boy?"

"Yes, little sister, I was talking about Gene. And I was talking about your brother. I was talking about all the boys who went crazy because they loved so much and lost so much."

The Kleenex box was empty when the boys returned. Sam and I forced Gene up the stairs and left him standing in Josie's doorway. His bandages matched the paleness of his skin, and he couldn't look even Raggedy in the eye.

"I'm sorry. I'm sorry if I — I didn't mean to…"

Josie bounced off the bed and Raggedy fell to floor with a smile on her face. Josie wrapped her arms around Gene's wounds.

"You big, dumb, wonderful boy!"

Chapter 16

It was quieter on the farm with Josie gone. But quiet does not equal peace. Peace requires laughter and love. For so long, Josie had been the reason for laughter and love. For so long, she had been the reason to come home. Now we all waited for her to come home for Thanksgiving.

It was Friday evening, and Thanksgiving was only thirteen days away. The jack-o-lanterns were shriveling into figures more grotesque than when they were carved.

There were seven of us seated at the table, and we started passing the meat and vegetables around. There wasn't enough room for the big bowl of mashed potatoes, so Momma walked the bowl around the table. She had that pout in her lips and that staggered breath I knew so well.

"What's wrong, Momma?" I had to ask.

"Nothing," was all I received.

Momma set the bowl aside, took her seat, and forced a faint smile across her face.

"You never let me get away with fibbing, Momma."

All forks were laid to rest and all eyes were on Momma. She wasn't going to get off that easy.

"It's really nothing," Momma fumbled. "It's just that — Thanksgiving is almost here. Josie will be home. Tommy will be here. Cassie's folks are coming."

Momma was working herself into a full-fledged tizzy. "I'm going to be cooking for eleven people, plus Aunt Colleen and maybe Uncle Ralph."

"We'll help, Momma," Cassie pledged.

"I know, dear," Momma sobbed. "But I don't even have room on the table for a bowl of mashed potatoes."

Momma was beyond blotting tears; she was in shambles.

"Momma Rose," Sam spoke up.

Momma lifted her eyes from her apron at the sound of her new name.

"We'll take care of it, Momma Rose," Sam swore.

Momma breathed easier and nodded in belief, and Sam nodded faster.

Friday night was noisy and all of Saturday was worse. Hammers and saws were the chorus, while wood and varnish carried the melody. The sun set on that Saturday serenade of metal and wood. The varnish needed to dry, so Sam and Gene headed to town.

The girls would be partying, and Sam had a few bucks to flash. Gene wouldn't be looking for any girls. There was only one girl that had claim to his heart. Gene went along to watch Sam's back.

Sam and Gene were out late, and brought a new friend home. Far from beautiful and far from sober, Timmy shared the bunkhouse in the wee hours of Sunday morning.

We came home from church, and Momma handed Daddy the ax. "I've got potatoes to peel," Momma droned. "Bring me two chickens."

Momma climbed in weary steps and opened the kitchen door wide. Her mouth flew open and her arms flew out. The aroma of wood and varnish filled the room, and sixteen place settings of Momma's assorted china dazzled her eyes. Seven places were set on one side, and seven on the other, while two places of honor adorned the ends of Momma's new table.

There was little room between the chairs and the walls, but there was plenty of room for a big bowl of mashed potatoes.

Sam and Gene stood waiting for their reward, and they would have it. Momma lavished her kisses and spared no hugs. For the first time in their selfless, valiant lives, Sam and Gene felt like heroes.

"Let's go wake up Timmy." Gene proposed.

"Who's Timmy," Momma queried.

"We'll take care of it, Momma Rose," Sam disguised.

The chickens were dressed and cooked and the potatoes were boiled. Timmy sat at Momma's table with a hangover banging in his head.

He was a slight young man, rather small in stature. He didn't converse and tried not to impose. He accepted each platter and bowl with a humble nod and said his prayers over his modest portion.

"Where are you from, Timmy," Daddy welcomed.

"I'm not really from anywhere," Timmy denied. "I was just passing through, but my last foster home was in St. Joseph."

"We found Timmy at the American Legion last night," Sam explained.

"His last station was in Da Nang," Gene interjected.

"You were one of the last troops on the ground in Nam, weren't you?" I recognized.

"I guess," was all that Timmy wanted to acknowledge.

Timmy kept his head low as he peeked at Gretchen. Her innocent curiosity and her probing eyes were irresistible. Timmy lifted his head and smiled like he had not done in a long while.

Gretchen gasped and toddled her way over to Timmy's side. She reached up with her tiny fingers and almost touched Timmy's face. She retracted her hand as if she had touched a hot stove. She was scared to touch the scars burned into Timmy's face, but she was drawn to the soul beneath.

The scars were deep and covered his face, but they did not cover his soul.

"It's okay punkin'," Timmy murmured. "It doesn't hurt anymore."

Gretchen touched and Gretchen hugged and Timmy showed his crooked smile.

Timmy offered the first bite to Gretchen and savored the next himself.

"This is fantastic, Mrs. Marshall!" Timmy wowed.

"Call me Momma Rose."

Timmy hurried another bite to Gretchen's lips and devoured an even bigger bite for himself.

"You threw a bay leaf in the pot, didn't you, Momma Rose?" Timmy detected. "And I can taste the garlic."

Momma's face was filled with shock and wonder and expectation.

"Did I mention that Timmy can cook?" Sam bragged.

Momma shot straight up and implored the heavens, "Praise the Lord and pass the potatoes to that boy!"

Momma was beside herself with joy. "How many potatoes do we need for up to fifteen people?" Momma tested.

"I'd go with twenty-five just to be sure. I once peeled three hundred potatoes for our company mess hall," Timmy remembered.

Momma slapped her hands together in front of her gaping mouth and wondered, "Do you think we need two turkeys?"

"One good size turkey will do it, if I carve it right, Momma Rose."

Momma Rose became very accustom to her new name in those next few November days. She taught Timmy how to cook for a king, and Timmy taught her how to cook for an army. Timmy scrubbed pots and pans in rhythm to Momma's hymns and Momma fell in love with yet another child.

"You're not like my foster moms, Mrs. — I mean, Momma Rose. And you're a darn sight nicer than my drill sergeant," Timmy laughed.

Momma took it like the compliment it was and swiped the dish towel across Timmy's nose.

There was barely enough room in the cupboard for that last pot Momma wiped dry. Perplexed, yet determined, she shoved and prodded to make it fit. Pots and pans jostled and shifted until all collapsed. Cast iron hit the floor with a resounding thud, and aluminum clanged against it in a ricochet ping. It was a barrage of thundering sounds that could almost be felt. Momma turned with her hands covering her ears and Timmy was gone from sight.

There was only one foot exposed from under the table. Timmy was cringed in a fetal ball, with his arms and hands shielding his head from the barrage. A shrill whimper could be heard and a delirious spasm could be seen in that foot.

Momma knelt in slow, cautious movements and crawled under the table. She cooed and soothed and held her child. She hummed a lullaby until the spasms subsided. She patted and stroked until the sounds of mortar fire were gone from Timmy's ears.

For months to come, my Momma was on loan. Wherever Momma Rose was, Timmy was not far away.

There were fifteen place settings for Thanksgiving. It was everyone Momma expected, plus one new face.

"This is Denny," Uncle Ralph introduced. "He's the nephew of my first wife's sister. That makes him your — uh — well, I guess you're not really related, but he's family."

"Good to have you here, Denny," I extended.

Denny sat erect and nodded in respect. "Thank you for having me, Sir."

There was no question that Denny was a vet. Manners can be seen everywhere and polite indulgences are easily feigned. But true respect is learned in only a few places.

"Army, Navy, Marines?" I explored.

"National Guard, Sir, but I was attached to an army unit," Denny reported.

I knew that Denny had not spent his week-ends in Denver or San Francisco or Hoboken.

"Where was your last duty, brother," I inquired.

"Somewhere in Cambodia," Denny thought.

Daddy was amazed. "I heard that some National Guard units were sent to Viet Nam, but Cambodia?"

Denny remained silent, but I intervened. "It's a fact, Daddy. The government doesn't want to admit it, but we stepped over the border."

I passed the cranberry sauce to Denny, but held on to it until he looked me in the eye. That was a combat vet. I just knew.

The women took over the conversation, while the men filled their faces. The turkey was devoured and every bowl was scraped clean. Sam rose and limped away, stopping to give Momma Rose a kiss on the cheek.

"I'm going to get the fire pit lit."

All the men followed when I announced, "I have cigars for everyone."

The women talked, and the men joked. The women shared and the men smoked. The fire pit came to life, and Cassie's folks watched the flames dance in their darling Gretchen's eyes. Josie and Gene cuddled in the warmth and peace that had returned to the farm.

Inevitable sleep took over Gretchen's eyes, and Cassie carried her off to bed. One-by-one, family bid goodnight to the everlasting embers of Thanksgiving.

"Say, Jake," Uncle Ralph suddenly spoke up. "Could you use another hand around this place?"

I looked at Daddy, and he looked at the stars. He wasn't going to give me an answer. He was going to wait to hear what I had learned.

I looked at Tommy, and he looked at the ground. He drew a battle plan in the dirt and pointed his stick at the objective.

This was my mission, and Daddy and Tommy understood that. This was my call, and I was just learning that.

"We're doing fine for now, Uncle Ralph, but what's on your mind?"

"The thing is," Uncle Ralph advanced. "Denny here — he's a good boy — but he…"

"I had a drug problem," Denny opened up.

I looked at Sam, and he was not pleased. I looked at Gene, and he was not surprised.

"But that's all behind him now," Uncle Ralph assured. "He just needs some good, clean, hard…"

"I didn't catch your last name, Denny," I interrupted.

"Borgelt, Sir. Daniel Borgelt."

I grabbed Tommy's sleeve and made him drop his cigar. Tommy didn't move. He sat solid as a rock.

"Borgelt?" I asked to confirm. "I served with a Lester Borgelt."

"Yes, Sir," Denny acknowledged. "That was my cousin, Les. We enlisted together, but he didn't make it back."

"I know," I answered, and looked back at Tommy. Tommy clenched his jaw tight and crushed the cigar under his heel.

"Were you there when Les — when he…?" Denny hoped.

"We were there, Denny," I grumbled.

"What happened?" Denny begged. "Was he — did he…?"

"He died quick and he died a hero," I granted Denny. "I wouldn't be here right now if it wasn't for Les Borgelt."

I reached to touch the shoulder of a Borgelt. Denny looked in my eyes and knew it was true.

"Sam," I ordered. "Get Denny set up in the bunkhouse. And let Cassie know that I'll be down at the pond. Do you want to come along, Tommy?"

"Nah," Tommy refused. "I'm going to head back to the motel. I'll swing by before I leave tomorrow." As always, Tommy would hold his tears until he was alone.

Borgelt's was not the only face I saw as I sat by the pond. I saw Sanchez handing me that meal of ham and lima beans. I heard Cooper and Kowalski swapping stories about what they were going to do as soon as they got home. I heard all the voices that had been silenced by that hailstorm of death.

I laid back and looked at the same moon I had seen over Viet Nam. It loomed over me like a blood-red ball. I pressed my hands over my eyes and chanted, "Remember your way home. Remember who created you. Remember…"

Dreams can be real. When you are locked in the inescapable torment of their visible horrors, they are very real. I felt the chill of the water as I floated back upstream. Distorted faces of "Charlie" taunted me from the dense jungle. I felt the rifle butt against my back and the sting of the lashes to my face.

Cassie looked out the window at the darkness. "I'd better go check on Jake."

Gene heard the quiver in Cassie's voice and bounded from his chair. "Josie and I will come with you."

Before they reached me, Cassie could hear the frightful moaning she had heard in countless other dreams. Josie heard the moans she had heard after I had gotten a good whuppin', and raced ahead to be with me.

As Josie reached to stroke my hair, Cassie yelled, "JOSIE, NO!"

At the touch of Josie's hand, I rolled over on top of "Charlie" and raised my hand to drive his nose into his brain.

Cassie jumped on my back and put a choke-hold on my throat that took us flat on the ground. I couldn't breathe and started clawing at the plastic bag I felt over my face.

We rolled over and over on the ground. Cassie held on as if I was dangling over a cliff, and life depended on her never letting go.

Gene grabbed my shirt and instructed Cassie, "Let him go. I've got him."

Gene pulled me to my feet and stood face to face. I swung my fist in reflex and broke the skin next to Gene's left eye. Gene recoiled and stood his ground.

"JAKE, IT'S ME, GENE!"

I did not hear my name and I didn't hear Gene's. I heard screams of agony and cries for help. I swung with the other fist and landed on Gene's nose. Blood poured down Gene's face, but he held on tight.

"IT'S ME, BROTHER!"

I heard the call of a brother, but it was a call for help.

"HELP ME, BROTHER!" Sanchez screamed through the exploding air.

"WHERE ARE YOU, BROTHER?" Borgelt searched through the smoky haze.

I raised my hand for one more strike at the enemy that would not let me go.

"COWBOY!"

There was only one voice in the world that called me Cowboy. It was the only voice that could pull me back from the grips of hell.

The guns silenced, the screams subsided, and the haze drifted from my eyes. I saw the blood trailing down Gene's face and the anguish in his eyes.

I saw Josie tightly curled in Cassie's arms. I saw the devastation wrought by my own hand, and I ran.

I ran from everyone I loved. I ran as fast as I could because I loved them. I ran to protect them from me.

"JAKE, STOP!"

"JAKE, COME BACK!"

Gene was right on my tail, so I took the car. I made the tires spin and the gravel sprayed behind me. I got the speedometer to forty before I even shifted. I got it to fifty and my family was safer.

Sixty miles per hour would keep them safe, and eighty might end my pain. Telephone poles whizzed by and speed limit signs were a blur. The speedometer said ninety when the neon light flashed in my eye.

"Hayseed Motel."

My foot left the accelerator and my hands locked tight on the steering wheel. The car slowed to sixty and I thought of Tommy's face. The car slowed to thirty and I heard Tommy's voice. The car coasted to a stop and I cranked the wheel hard. The U-turn was tight, but I came up out of the ditch and headed back to the "Hayseed Motel."

"I'm looking for Tommy Weeks," I requested of the manager.

"I saw him headed across the road an hour ago," the manager responded.

There was only one destination across the road, "Casey's Tavern."

Tommy was slurping his fifth beer, give or take. I slid onto the stool beside him and ordered the same.

"Tommy?"

"Yeah?" Tommy just stared into his glass.

"I got scared and ran, Tommy."

"We were all scared. And, of course you ran. I told you to run, you dumb-ass farm boy."

"No, Tommy, I ran again. I'm still running."

Tommy turned his head and looked me in the eye. "Running from what?"

"From Cassie and Josie and Gretchen."

Tommy slammed his glass on the bar. "WHAT THE HELL?"

The bartender stepped over and cautioned, "Hey, keep it down over here."

Tommy shoved his dollar bill and change across the bar. "How about you keep that and go wash some glasses over there."

The bartender had to have felt the glare of Tommy's eyes as he walked away.

I swung Tommy around on the bar stool. "I had that dream, Tommy."

Tommy shuddered, "Yeah. We always will, because it wasn't a dream, was it? But it can't hurt us anymore, Jake."

"But it can!" I burst back. "I almost killed Josie!"

Tommy trembled until beer splashed out of his glass. His face contorted into creases that tears ran down. He threw the glass against the wall and it shattered into sparkling pieces of shrapnel.

The bartender brought his ball bat and slammed it on the bar. A loyal patron from the other end of the bar walked up behind me and asked, "Got a little trouble here, Casey?"

"Nah," Casey bragged and tapped the bat on the bar. "I'm going to give these two Vietnam misfits a chance to hit the door running."

Tommy rubbed the ever-present pain in his leg, and kept his eye on the tapping bat.

"I don't know about that running, Jake. What do you think? Should we keep running?"

Tommy waited for me to give the signal. He waited like a runner waits for the starter pistol to fire, and like a warrior waits for the call to battle.

We both watched and listened to the bat tapping on the bar. One – two – "NO!"

I threw my beer in Casey's face and Tommy grabbed the bat. Tommy jabbed with the bat and landed a solid hit to Casey's forehead.

The guy behind me grabbed me by the hair, but I spun and caught him in the eye with my elbow. I swept his foot out from under him and dropped on one knee in the middle of his chest. That had to have broken a rib.

Four more loyal bar patrons kicked their chairs back and headed to join the action. It was the same story we had lived in a different life. We were in a place we should never have been. We were out-numbered by an enemy with which we should never have had a quarrel.

Tommy and I were not fighters. We were trained and seasoned killers that could have left a pile of dead bodies around us. But we had enough of war and death. It was time to go.

Tommy threw himself over my shoulder and yelled, "Fall back to higher ground!"

I lifted Tommy and barreled out the door. We were out in the open and I was steaming across the parking lot. Tommy was grunting and groaning in pain, but still swinging the bat.

We made it across the road and into the drive of the Hayseed Motel. The dogs of war were close and gaining. But I would not stumble and I would not drop. Tommy and I made it off that battlefield together, and we would regroup on higher ground.

The bellies full of beer that were chasing us came to a sudden stop when the hammer on the shotgun clicked and cocked. The motel manager sighted down the barrel and said, "These boys are guests of mine. You – are not."

The beer bellies retreated to their side of the road and I laid Tommy down. Tommy was groaning and laughing.

"That was like riding over thirty miles of bad tank trail!"

"I would have done thirty more, Tommy!"

The motel manager knelt beside us and asked, "You boys got any holes in you?"

"Not me," I answered. "How about you, Tommy?"

Tommy was still laughing. "I feel like hell, and it feels great!"

"You boys got a place to call home?" the manager asked.

"Yes, Sir, we do," I thanked.

Tommy could recognize a veteran by the sound of his words and he wanted to know, "What unit were you with, brother?"

The manager rose and spoke his final words. "It doesn't matter what unit I was with. What matters is that I fought my way back across the "pond." You boys fought your way back across that road. That's what matters. Now get your asses home."

We gathered Tommy's belongings out of the motel room and piled in the car. The motel manager watched our backs as we headed home. We waved farewell to one more man that had our undying gratitude. If he ever needed us, we would be the first ones there, but we hoped he never did.

The headlights lit up the front porch and everyone was gathered. They breathed a collective sigh and waited for Tommy and me to lumber up the steps.

Daddy was the first to grab me. He hugged and said, "I guess I should call the Sheriff and tell him to call off the hounds. Am I going to have any more trouble out of you?"

"No, Daddy. I got a little lost, but I found my way home."

Momma hugged and pounded. She had no words, just hugs and pounds.

Gene had a hug for me too, with a well-deserved jab. "My grandmother punches harder than you."

Cassie and Josie were sharing the porch swing and waiting their turn to give me my due. Josie leapt out of the swing and attacked.

"What you need is a good whuppin'!"

Tommy spewed out a laugh, "He damn near got one!

Josie pounded and pounded and I hugged and hugged.

Cassie did not budge from the porch swing. "We have a sofa with your name on it, Tommy."

Tommy limped to the door and appealed, "Take it easy on him, Darlin'. He doesn't deserve you, but you could do worse."

Only Cassie and I remained. I eased into the swing and tried to explain. "Cassie, I…"

Cassie shut me up with her hand over my mouth. "I ran away from you once, but you tackled in the tall grass. I would have tackled you, but you run too fast."

I held Cassie as if she were dangling over a cliff, and life depended on me never letting go.

Chapter 17

Tommy was sore all over the next morning and grinned in between sips of coffee. I hid my eyes from Cassie and stifled a laugh.

"What's so funny?" Cassie interrogated.

I was still choking back a laugh. "You should have seen Tommy swinging that bat."

"And Jake was running like a bat out of hell."

"And Tommy yelled, 'Look both ways before you cross that road.'"

Cassie was infected by our victorious joy and laughed harder than both of us. "What am I going to do with you two?"

"Well," Tommy surmised. "I think you're stuck with us Darlin'. We're done running – aren't we, Jake?"

"Yeah, we are, Brother. We fought our way back across that road and that's all that matters."

Tommy pulled a couple of file folders out of his satchel and laid them on the table. The folders bore the emblem of that proud American eagle, with the arrows in one talon and an olive branch in the other.

"I see you brought your work with you," I observed. "How's that Defense job going?"

"You know what I've been doing for a living lately?" Tommy asked, without waiting for an answer.

"I sit at a desk all day, analyzing reports and I make estimates," Tommy disclosed.

"I estimate troop casualties for military operations big and small," Tommy went on. "My bosses ask how many American lives we'll lose if they execute their plans, and they don't really want to hear my answer."

Tommy sighed in weary discontent. "It's a hell-of-a thing to be doing for a guy who's trying to forget."

Cassie reached for Tommy's hand, but Tommy withdrew. He wasn't looking for sympathy, he had a plan. He opened a folder and tossed a report across the table. Names and ranks were listed from Private to Colonel, and there were many pages.

"I'm not supposed to have that, but I do," Tommy admitted. "That's more than 58,000 names, and all of them died in Viet Nam. They say they might build a memorial for them one day. I guess that's all they can do."

I flipped through the pages, and they seemed to go on forever. Borgelt was listed, and so were all the others.

"I've put in for a transfer," Tommy resolved and downed the last of his coffee. "I'm going to find a job with the Veteran's Administration, and see if I can find some boys we can still help," Tommy vowed.

Tommy opened the next folder and shared a different list. "These are all the names I've found of disabled vets. That's where I'm going to start."

There were more pages than I would have dared to imagine. They were pages of names that had not died in honor, but struggled to live in peace. Eddie's name was on that list.

Cassie and I trembled at the magnitude of grief. "I wish I knew how to help," Cassie wept.

Tommy reached for Cassie's hand, and Cassie did not withdraw. "You've got a pretty good thing going here," Tommy judged. "Sam, Gene, Timmy, Denny, they're all where they need to be. They all have a piece of that Eddie you lost. Put all those pieces together, and I think you're helping more than you realize."

Tommy packed away his folders and his plans. "Well, I've got a cab on the way. Thanks for that fine cup of coffee, Cassie. You let me know if this Farm Boy doesn't treat you right."

Tommy rose into Cassie's waiting arms and hugged until the cab honked outside.

Tommy paused at the door and hinted, "I just might send another vet your way. Be ready to put him to work."

"I don't know, Tommy," I hesitated. "The bunkhouse is pretty full already and we only have so many acres to work."

"Think big, Jake," Tommy prompted. "You're the best trail blazer I know."

Cassie and I watched Tommy amble off the porch and wave farewell from the back of the cab. "Think big" is what I would remember.

Cassie and I thought big all through the coming winter. The more I dreamed about those who had fought their way back across the "pond," the less

I dreamed of those who did not. With my compass around my neck and the map stuffed in my shirt, I would someday find a way to bring more Eddies home.

Denny had never seen snow in Tucson or in Viet Nam and he was excited. "What's next, boss?"

Daddy was poking the fire pit and raised his stick to point to Sam for an answer.

"There's a lot to do before winter sets in," Sam advised. "The first thing is to disc that cornfield before it freezes."

"I want to drive the tractor," Denny volunteered. "Show me how."

Daddy passed his poking stick to me and offered, "I'll show you how to hitch up the harrow."

Daddy rested his arm on Denny's shoulders as they sauntered away. If Denny had a tail, it would have been wagging.

I stirred the fire and Gene tossed on another chunk of wood. "I need to ask you guys a question," I began.

Eyes darted around the fire, wondering what trouble was afoot.

"Relax, guys," I diffused. "Sam, you know how much we've come to depend on you. I need to know how much longer we'll have you around."

Sam studied the question in his usual manner, and spoke only when he was sure. "I've got no other plans. I figure on sticking around until you tell me to go."

"I don't see that ever happening, Sam," I predicted. "And I don't think a Sherman Tank could move Gene off this property until Josie tells him to go."

"You got that right, brother," Gene committed.

Timmy was trying to conceal his fear of being alone and dreaded his turn to speak.

"What about you, Timmy?" I pressed.

Timmy was Momma's favorite, but Timmy did not presume. "I've got no place else to go."

"You're not going anywhere," Sam voted.

"Not in this lifetime," Gene seconded.

"There's a word for that, Timmy," I mused. "When you've got no place else to go, that's called home."

Timmy beamed and his scars yielded to that crooked smile. "What about you, Jake?"

The end of Daddy's stick caught fire and I was too lost in thought to notice, but Sam noticed.

"You've got something stuck in your craw, Jake. Spit it out."

I tossed the stick and let it be consumed in the fire. "I've got bad dreams — and I've got good dreams. If I could make the good dreams come true — maybe the bad dreams would stop."

"Tell us about the good dreams, Jake," Timmy entreated.

"Yeah, the good ones," Gene hoped.

So, I talked about Eddie and the vows I had made. I talked about Tommy's list of names that numbered more than the stars in the sky. I told the story of the one who spit on my shoes, and of the red-headed little girl who said, "God Bless America, and you too."

I recounted the story of the man with one leg who smelled a handful of earth and found a home.

I thanked the man who had offered his blood in my darkest hour and loved my sister more than life.

I hailed the man who had borne his scars and bared his soul, and touched my Momma's heart.

"The good dreams have already started," I realized. "And I don't want them to end."

"I don't know where you're headed with this dream," Sam spoke up. "But I'm in."

"I want to build a place where vets who…" I didn't get a chance to describe my lofty dreams. Seemingly out of nowhere, a man approached our council fire.

"Top of the mornin', brothers."

His presence was genuine and undeniable. His voice was clear and carried across the barnyard to Denny's ears. Denny knew that voice, and Denny came running.

"CHAPPY!"

Chappy braced himself, Denny collided, and we all looked on. Denny was weeping and Sam tried not to. Chappy was laughing and Gene couldn't hold back. Timmy raised his arms high in jubilation, and I did all the above.

"Is this part of your dream, Jake?" Sam guessed.

"I reckon so," I marveled. "Hey, Denny, are you going to introduce us?"

"Oh!" Denny exclaimed. "This is Captain Edwards, my battalion chaplain."

The Captain made the rounds, shaking every hand. "Call me Chappy," he insisted.

There was something different in that handshake, something special. None of us could define it, but we all felt it.

"It's an honor to meet you, Chappy. How on earth did you get here?" I asked.

"I hitched a ride from town," Chappy explained. "All Daniel told me in his letter was Hays, Kansas and the Marshall farm. Who painted the "R" backwards on your mailbox?"

"She's in college now," I laughed.

Denny was just shy of bursting. "Come on, Chappy! We've got a field to disc!" And Denny was off.

"Catch you guys later," Chappy shrugged.

"I'll look forward to it," I returned.

Denny pounced on the tractor seat and Chappy took a commanding stance behind him. Chappy thrust his fist forward and shouted, "Onward, young Daniel! We shall turn our swords into plowshares!"

Chappy could be heard well into the field. "And the lion shall lie down with the lamb!"

The sun was setting when Denny shut the tractor down and Chappy joined us for supper.

"Would you do us the honor of saying grace?" Daddy enjoined Chappy.

Denny grabbed Chappy's hand to the right and Timmy's hand to the left. An unbroken chain of hands and hearts awaited Chappy's blessing.

"Dear Lord, bless this food and us to thy service. We thank you for friends, for family, and for your good earth that sustains us. We lay our burdens at your feet and ask that you give us the strength to take up your cross. We hope to walk in your ways the remainder of our days, and we shall study war no more."

Chappy's prayer was sanctified with an instant and unanimous "Amen."

"We could use a pastor like you," Momma remarked in awe. "What denomination are you, Chappy?"

Chappy chewed and chuckled and swallowed. "I've studied many a religion and many a denomination in my day. But all I've ever claimed to be is a Christian."

"That's my kind of chaplain," I decreed. "How much leave time do you have?"

"Oh no," Chappy disclosed. "The Army is done with me. They discharged me and I disavowed them."

There was a disturbing solemnness in Chappy's reply, and Denny hurried to defend. "It's the Army's loss and our gain. I wouldn't be here if it wasn't for

Chappy, and I for sure wouldn't have had a shot at heaven."

Chappy bowed his head and glanced sideways toward Denny. "You knocked and the door was opened. It wasn't me who saved you."

I sensed a deeper truth in Chappy and I wanted that truth to stick around. "Snows are coming soon, Chappy. You may as well stay till the spring thaw."

"We can squeeze one more in the bunkhouse," Sam vouched.

"I'm keeping my top bunk," Gene clarified.

"I'd like to learn how to pray like you," Timmy welcomed.

And so, Chappy stayed. He worked, he listened and he loved. Faces glowed warmer around the fire pit that winter. Hearts asked the questions, and souls sought the answers. Chappy didn't have all the answers, but he knew where to look for them.

Chappy told Gretchen story after story about Jesus, and the boys listened. Chappy and Gretchen sang, "Jesus loves me, this I know..." and the boys clapped along.

I watched, listened and dreamed. I always looked forward to the first sign of spring, but I must admit that I mourned that winter's last skiff of snow.

Denny was awfully quiet that April morning. He savored each bite of his breakfast as if it was his last. He swiped a tear and choked a whimper.

"Denny?" So much was communicated when Momma Rose spoke your name. You knew that someone was on your side and that someone needed to know what was in your heart.

Denny could not find the words, so Chappy came to his rescue. "Daniel's moving on, but he's finding it a little difficult."

Chappy gripped the back of Denny's neck. Denny drew agonizing breaths and smiled as if he was ready to cry.

"Where are you headed, Denny?" I coaxed.

"First, I'm going to visit my family all over Arizona and New Mexico," Denny struggled to answer.

"That's a good idea!" Daddy tried to comfort.

"Then what?" I prodded.

"Then I'm going to start school in the fall. I'm going to be a veterinarian."

Sighs and smiles surrounded the table. "Yes, you will," I affirmed. "Yes, you will."

Cheers and well wishes were not what Denny needed. He needed to learn how to say farewell.

"I haven't been here very long," Denny braved. "But you've all been so, uh

— I'm going to miss, uh…"

"We're going to miss you too, Denny." Cassie persuaded.

"You'll always have a place to lay your head here," Daddy promised.

"You better write to us, young man," Momma instructed.

"Go," I demanded. "Give 'em hell, Daniel Borgelt," I challenged. "And don't say good-bye, brother. Say farewell, and travel well, my friend."

Denny waited until Josie returned home from school, or it wouldn't be a proper farewell. Everyone got their hug and Momma got two. Chappy drove and Denny waved. We watched, as we always did, for that last dwindling glimpse.

Gretchen was still waving as we headed into the house. Timmy had the table arranged with an offering of comfort for our happy and sad crew. It was Gretchen's favorite, milk and gingerbread. In the middle of the table was an envelope with a note.

"I'll be back for this," was all it said.

Wrapped inside the note was a snapshot of two fresh-faced boys standing in front of the welcome sign at Fort Benning, Georgia. Their uniforms were neatly pressed and their hats were slightly cocked. You could almost hear them laugh through their goofy grins as they posed for the camera. They were arm in arm, as if forever, and that's what they would be as long as I held that picture of Denny and Les Borgelt.

Chapter 18

I quietly approached to watch Chappy tend his flower garden in the front yard. It was July 1, 1976 and red petunias, white alyssum and blue lobelia bloomed in tribute to 200 years of American independence.

Chappy had packed his bags more than once, only to unpack them again. Sometimes he stayed because he had another gospel story to tell Gretchen. Sometimes he stayed because I begged him. Sometimes, I think, he stayed because he didn't know where to go.

I had yet to learn what misfortune had befallen this man of God. It was Chappy's words that had cast the shroud of mystery. "The Army discharged me, and I disavowed them."

I wondered how many soldiers had come to believe before they died in the grace of God, because Chappy was there? How many soldiers had carried on in faith, because Chappy had shown them the way? What kind of Army could turn its back on a man who nurtured the flowers of red, white and blue?

"That's the most beautiful thing I've ever seen," I startled.

Chappy flinched and then smiled. "It's the perfect union of God and country."

"You have a gift for growing things," I observed. "Things that matter."

Chappy did not respond. He went back to plucking a stray weed here and smoothing the warm, rich soil there.

"How would you like to grow a congregation?" I proposed.

Chappy's hand froze, and then clinched, and the good earth was in his grasp. He sat back on his heels and squinted his eyes at the brilliance of the sun. "Watch my flock," he mouthed.

"I want to build a place where a vet can come home," I finished my thought.

Chappy stood, with his head still tilted back and his eyes still squinted.

"I want a place where..." I labored on. "Where someone understands and someone cares. I want a place that war can't touch and loneliness doesn't exist."

I paused. I watched. I waited for an answer from Chappy, perhaps even from God.

Chappy lowered his head and opened those eyes of solace. He twitched his head in the direction we needed to go and began to walk.

I followed him to the mailbox and we turned to the west. We walked a mile and spoke not a word. The meadow lark sang and we stopped to listen. The wind gusted and we breathed it in.

"Where do we start, Chappy?"

Chappy walked on with his only advice, "Feed my sheep."

I grabbed Chappy by the arm and spun him around. "Feed your sheep with what? It takes land to feed sheep. It takes money. It takes…"

Chappy spun back around and resumed the march. *"God doesn't require us to succeed; he only requires that we try,"* Chappy quoted. "Mother Teresa of Calcutta," he acknowledged.

We were two miles from home and I was no closer to an answer. The big red letters read "FOR SALE," and Chappy stopped in his tracks.

"Oh, no," I admonished. "That's the Chambers farm. It's 1,500 acres and it's way out of my reach."

Chappy proceeded down the dirt road to meet Mr. Chambers, and I pleaded. "Mr. Chambers and I are not on really good terms, Chappy. CHAPPY!"

Chappy just kept walking and I followed.

Mr. Chambers was rocking on his front porch as we neared. He rocked peacefully, but his eyes were vigilant. His hands were resting on the shotgun that ensured his tranquil pose. The breech was open and both barrels were plainly loaded.

"Top of the mornin'," Chappy greeted.

Mr. Chambers rose and the chair rocked on its own. It rocked in time, slower and slower, until time finally stopped.

"Did you enjoy that watermelon from my patch?" Mr. Chambers gruffed.

"Gee, Mr. Chambers," I relented. "That was more than fifteen years ago."

That was not a good response and the breech of the shotgun was closed.

"Look, Mr. Chambers," I faltered. "I was just a dumb kid, and I'm sorry."

The shotgun was laid into the fold of Mr. Chambers arm, and Chappy poked me in the ribs to spur me on.

"This is Chaplain Edwards," I introduced.

Chappy bounded onto the porch and offered his hand. "Just Chappy."

Mr. Chambers eyed Chappy from head to toe, and then reached to accept that hand as all farmers do. He must have felt that something special in Chappy's grip, but revealed no particular interest.

"Chappy and I served in Vietnam," I tried to relate. "My Daddy says you're a veteran of World War II, Mr. Chambers."

"U.S. Marine Corps," Mr. Chambers boldly proclaimed.

"We have a few more vets working with us on our farm," I added.

"I've seen them around," Mr. Chambers acknowledged. "Most of them need a haircut."

"I'm sure you're right, Mr. Chambers. But they're all good men, and we take care of each other."

Mr. Chambers leaned the shotgun against the porch railing and declared, "I take care of myself."

"Well," I tried to explain. "These guys saw a lot in that ugly war, and it's good to have a friend that understands."

"You boys don't understand squat!" Mr. Chambers defied. "How many Americans died in battle in Viet Nam?"

"Over 58,000," I knew.

Mr. Chambers reflected a moment on that staggering number, and then remembered, "Over 300,000 were killed on the battlefields of World War II."

"Yes sir," I dutifully recognized. "But I learned two things in war. There are worse things to lose than your life. And losing one friend hurts as much as losing 300,000."

"You ever hear of a place called Pleiku, Mr. Chambers?" I groped.

"Is that someplace in Viet Nam?" Mr. Chambers guessed.

"Yes sir," I confirmed. "That's the last place my buddies and I had a beer together."

Mr. Chambers lowered his gaze and lowered his guard. "You ever hear of a place called Normandy Beach?"

"Oh, my God!" I gasped. "Were you there?"

Mr. Chambers opened the front door and invited, "Let's have a beer."

My head was on a swivel as we walked through the living room. On the right was a picture of Mr. Chambers in his brown boots and muddy helmet. On the left hung his purple heart and all that it meant. On the shelf was a picture of Doris Chambers and her new-born child. The picture was framed, but it was wrinkled and worn from having traveled in a pocket many thousands of miles.

Chappy and I sipped our beer and Chappy reached for the vase of flowers. A wilted petal fell into his hand and he offered, "I have some fresh flowers I could bring you."

Mr. Chambers opened the door and spoke into the cupboard. "Anyone want salt in your beer?"

"No, thanks," Chappy and I declined.

Mr. Chambers sat at the table and added just a shake or two of salt to his beer. "Doris picked those flowers."

Chappy slipped the wilted petal into his pocket.

"Maybe I could take your fresh flowers to the nursing home for her," Mr. Chambers accepted.

Chappy grabbed his pen and opened his hand as a tablet. "Where can we visit her?"

Mr. Chambers gulped the salt down and his beer was half gone. "She won't know you're there," he belched. "But she knows I'm there. I know she does."

"Mr. Chambers," I spoke up. "Could I talk you into coming to our place for the 4th of July? I'd like to pay you back that watermelon."

Mr. Chambers added another shake of salt and chugged his glass empty. "Could I talk you into another beer?"

We had no fireworks on the 4th of July, only fire. The fire made the hot dogs sweat and the marshmallows flame. Hearts burned and Mr. Chambers' face radiated. That is, of course, when his face was not buried in a slice of watermelon.

Mr. Chambers had a few hotdogs and too many marshmallows. He washed them down with copious amounts of beer and floated them with all the watermelon he could hold. Sam and Timmy lifted Mr. Chambers and guided his steps to the bunkhouse.

"Were you really in the Normandy Invasion?" Sam tried to imagine.

"Ah — you don't want to hear about that shit," Mr. Chambers resisted.

"I probably don't," Sam agreed. "But tell us anyway."

"OK," Mr. Chambers slurred. His voice trailed off as the boys led him away. "There I was, ass-deep in the water. German bullets were ripping past my ears. I ran — I ran — and I ran…"

The bunkhouse lights dimmed, but the fire lingered. Josie and Gene were snuggling and Momma's eyes were drooping. Daddy was poking the fire and Chappy was waving the smoke from his eyes. I was keeping watch over Gretchen as she roasted her last marshmallow.

"One more," I allowed. "And then off to bed."

Cassie stood, and all the attention was hers. Then she sat back down and smiled in blissful delight. "I'm pregnant again."

Momma's eyes flashed open and Daddy reached for the stars. I grabbed Gretchen about the middle and she held on to the stick with the flaming marshmallow on the end.

"When?" Josie exploded.

Cassie blew out the flame on Gretchen's marshmallow and spoke only to her. "You're going to have a new baby brother or sister in March."

"On my birthday?" Gretchen fancied.

"Maybe," Cassie proposed.

"Can I keep him?" Gretchen asked.

"Forever," Cassie endeared.

Gretchen filled her mouth with marshmallow and gave her muffled permission, "OK."

Minds raced against sleep that night. Sleep finally won, as it usually does, but dawn came just as early.

Cassie cracked the eggs, I started the toast, and we met in the middle.

"What do you think about the name, Mark Antony?" I teased.

"What do you think of the name, Cleopatra, Queen of the Nile?" Cassie teased back.

A small voice entered the room. "Joshua."

Gretchen climbed onto the chair and planted her elbows on the table. She cradled those fleshy white cheeks in those chubby little hands. "Joshua fought the battle of Jericho."

Cassie leaned over the table and touched her nose to Gretchen's. "And the walls came tumblin' down."

"What if it's a baby sister?" I asked of Gretchen's innocent wisdom.

"Then Cleopatra, Queen of the Nile," was her judgment.

"I guess I better hope for Joshua," I snickered.

Gretchen rode on my shoulders as I walked that half mile. Grandma stole her from me and I headed to the bunkhouse. I heard the raucous laughter coming from inside.

"You boys ever kiss a French girl?" That was Mr. Chambers' booming voice.

"No, but I French-kissed a girl," Timmy howled.

I sat on the step and listened to the voices of World War II, of the Viet Nam War, and every other war meld into one.

Mr. Chambers opened the door and caught me in nostalgic content. He sat on the step and nudged my shoulder with his.

"You want my farm, don't you?" he deduced.

"Well, yes sir," I confessed.

Mr. Chambers swayed and bumped my shoulder again. "You get these boys a haircut, and you've got a deal."

"It may not be as sweet of a deal as you hoped," I warned.

We'll work it out," Mr. Chambers warranted. "I'll even pay for the haircuts."

Heads were cropped like new recruits that summer. Brotherhood was forged between generations. Peace was imagined across continents. Wounds were shared and hope felt real. Loneliness didn't exist that summer, and war couldn't touch us.

Chapter 19

Dear Tommy,

I have the compass around my neck and the map stuffed in my shirt. I know where the objective is, but I'm not sure about that next hill, that next ravine.

I wish you could look at the map with me and tell me if I'm on the right path. Should I climb that hill? Should I cross that ravine, or should I go around?

I'm on point, Tommy, and I'll lead the way. Just tell me you'll be right behind me.

Jake

Dear Jake,

Climb that hill, or you won't see what's on the other side.
Cross that ravine, but keep your eyes peeled.
The squad is right behind you, so don't worry about your back.
Keep following that compass. You're on the right track.

Tommy

Dear Tommy,

Daddy and I just got back from the bank.
A fair price for the 1,500 acres is $570,000.
The bank will loan $427,500 against it, plus another $91,440 against

Daddy's farm.

Mr. Chambers has agreed to carry $40,000 on a personal note, which leaves me $11,060 short.

I don't know if I should cross that ravine, Tommy. I'm taking fire from all sides and I'm running low on ammo.

Jake

Dear Jake,

Maintain your heading, Jake. We're right behind you.
Now you're only $10,000 short.

Tommy

Enclosed in Tommy's letter was his check for $1,060.

I started the engine on the old 54 Ford and Chappy flung the passenger door open. "You headed to town?"

"Yeah, Chappy. I have another letter to Tommy, but I need some more stamps."

Chappy threw his suitcase in the back seat and claimed his ride. "Just drop me off at the school district office."

"Where in the hell — I mean — where in the heck are you going?"

"I'll be back in time for the harvest, little brother," was all that Chappy disclosed. "I'll make you fishers of men," were his last words on the subject.

We rolled into town and Chappy's knees started bouncing at the first stop light. "Come on! Come on! It's green now, Jake, GO!"

"I don't know where you're going, Chappy," I chuckled. "But you sure are in a hurry."

"I wait only on the Lord," Chappy persisted. "There it is, 12th street, turn right!"

I slowed in front of the school district office, and the wheels stopped after Chappy was out the door.

"What do I tell everyone at home?" I asked, as Chappy reached for his suitcase.

"Tell them to pray for me," Chappy paused to request. "And be sure to read to Gretchen every night, the Gospel of John. And God so loved the world…"

I stopped by to see Mr. Chambers on the way home, and there was no shotgun in sight.

"We're still working on coming up with the money," I reported. "But I think Chappy is off looking for a miracle."

"If anybody can find a miracle, it's Chappy," Mr. Chambers divined. "And if anybody can find a beer, it's me."

Mr. Chambers' door was open and I walked through. I decided that this time I would have salt in my beer.

It was three weeks that we labored and fretted and missed Chappy. A place was always set for him at the table. Timmy said grace, and Gretchen waited.

The harvest moon was rising when we saw that yellow bus pull up, with the horn blaring and the lights flashing. In the dim light, I read, "Hays Public School District 489."

Chappy stepped down from the bus, fell to his knees, and flung his arms to the sky. He was surrounded in a heartbeat with his small flock, talking all at once and reaching for a touch.

The crowd parted, as Gretchen plowed her way through. "The Prodigal Son," Gretchen shrilled.

"Out of the mouths of babes," Chappy rejoiced.

Gretchen choked Chappy's neck, and he announced, "I want you to meet some folks."

He rapped his knuckles against the windshield of the bus, and twelve young souls filed out of the bus into a loose formation. Before us, stood ten men and two women. Some stood at attention and some stood at parade rest, while others shuffled their feet and gazed in trepidation. Each face hinted at a different story. And each face spelled VET.

Chappy knew his young pilgrims and did not hesitate to introduce. "This is Gabriel, from Fayetteville. But I like to call him Samson. This boy is strong."

"An honor to meet you folks," Gabriel shied.

"And this is Annette, from San Antonio," Chappy went down the line.

"Do you have any horses?" Annette hoped.

"I'll introduce you to them," Sam offered and gawked.

There were smiles and there were frowns as Chappy continued. There were two legs, and there was one. There were two arms, and there were none. Twelve faces looked at that harvest moon and twelve hearts beat together.

"It'll be dark in an hour," Chappy warned. "Unload brothers and sisters!"

Chappy's throng scrambled to the rear of the bus.

I grabbed a moment with Chappy's ear. "What's going on, Chappy? What are we going to do with all these people?"

"We're going to have faith," Chappy consoled. "Faith the size of a mustard seed."

Out of the bus poured tents and lanterns, blankets, dishes and utensils. There was enough canned food to feed for a while, and enough faith to last a while longer.

Cow chips were cleared and tents were pitched. Blankets were spread within and lanterns were hung without.

"Timmy," Momma determined. "We're going to need to get up an hour earlier to start breakfast."

The old oak tree sheltered that motley crew from a light sprinkle of rain. Hungry stomachs were fed, hungry souls were nourished, and hungry eyes desired.

Ears turned toward the sound of crunching gravel under the wheels of a Channel 4 News van.

Tommy stepped out of the van and a silver-haired gentleman stood beside him. The silver hair matched the two stars on the shoulders of his uniform. A chest full of ribbons accounted for the stars, and the voice of command boomed. "Get those cameras rolling."

I was the first to make it to Tommy, and the nation saw me pour myself into a hug. Tommy let my hug linger as long as he could, but he had a mission to accomplish.

"This is General George Weeks."

My instinct was to salute, but I took the handshake that was offered. "As in George and Thomas Weeks?" I presumed. "You never told me your father was a general, Tommy."

"I never told anyone," said the soldier I knew. "I told him about Chappy and he opened a few doors and we did a little digging. We came to let everyone know what we found."

The general and the news cameras surveyed the terrain. Twelve tents in neat rows were displayed on televisions across the country.

"Are you preparing for war?" the general joked.

"Preparing for war and praying for peace," Chappy exclaimed.

"That's him, Sir," Tommy informed.

"Captain Rollen Edwards?" the general asked.

"Yes, Sir," Chappy responded.

"FALL IN!" the general commanded.

Eighteen troops fell in at attention, and the general ordered, "Captain Edwards, front and center!"

Chappy stood motionless until anxious hands grabbed and pushed him into the glaring camera lights.

The general read in solemn declaration, "Captain Rollen Edwards. Your military service has been reviewed at the highest levels. For your unwavering service to your country, I present you with an Honorable Discharge from the United States Army. And for gallantry under enemy fire, with total disregard for your own life, while rendering spiritual strength to hundreds of comrades-in-arms, you are hereby awarded the Bronze Star."

The general pinned the Bronze Star on Chappy's flannel shirt, and Chappy quaked with tears. The formation exploded with shouts and cheers that must have vibrated in all those television sets.

"Now tell me," the general implored. "What's going on here."

Chappy hid his eyes from the cameras and sobbed, "Feed my sheep."

"Permission to speak, Sir," I shouted.

"Permission granted," the general allowed.

"Home is what's going on here, Sir," I told a nation of listeners.

The cameras zoomed in and I spoke our cause. "Faith is what you see here. Faith the size of a mustard seed. Every man and woman in this formation is a veteran who defended that faith. They each gave full measure to their country and lost a little of themselves along the way. But that faith will bring them home, because a man named Chappy will show them the way."

The camera man wiped his tears on his sleeve and tried to focus the camera on Chappy.

"Do you have any comment for us, Chappy?" the reporter asked.

Chappy shook his head in his humble way, but then spoke. "All will work and all will be fed. All will console and all will be consoled. Love will be given and love will be received."

The cameras were packed away and the general shook every hand. He climbed into the news van, but Tommy remained for the party.

It was a party like no other. It wasn't planned. It wasn't even expected. There were no invitations, but everyone was welcome.

Chappy was hailed and Chappy wept. Wayward souls became friends and

Chappy wept. Daddy's fiddle and Timmy's vittles carried the party all through the evening, then Chappy disappeared.

"Where's Chappy?" I asked Cassie, when only the light of the moon remained.

"The last time I saw him, he was dancing with Josie," Cassie recalled.

Cassie and I joined hands and walked. It was a nice night for a stroll, but we swung our arms with a stride of purpose.

"I didn't like the look on Chappy's face," Cassie revealed.

"We'll find him," I assured. "Let's check the bunkhouse."

"I thought Chappy was already discharged from the Army," Cassie questioned.

"I guess the last discharge wasn't "Honorable," I explained. "But now it is. Let's head to the pond."

Chappy was not in any of the usual places, but a faint sliver of light exposed his silhouette kneeling in the field.

"Have mercy on me, Lord!" Chappy wailed.

Cassie and I approached quietly and knelt by Chappy's side. We touched and waited, but didn't say a word.

"They don't give purple hearts for the loss I suffered," Chappy finally spoke.

Chappy let a handful of soil sift through his fingers and divulged, "I had a daughter, but I lost her."

I heard Cassie's gasp, and I tightened my grip on Chappy's shoulder.

"Rachel is a couple years younger than Josie," Chappy described. "Each time I came home from Viet Nam, she was another year older and it was another year missed."

Chappy held his head in shame. "But I begged and pleaded to be sent back across the "pond."

Chappy rubbed his face with the gritty soil. "I was going to make it up to Rachel, but my boys needed me. I had to be there at Christmas, when so many boys wanted to end it all. I had to be there for those who couldn't find the hope in Easter or the thanks in Thanksgiving."

Chappy went from his knees to his butt and sank into the dirt. "I spent four consecutive tours in Vietnam."

Chappy was slumped as if he didn't have a bone left in his body. "When I came home the last time, my wife and child were gone. All I found was my wife's wedding ring on the dresser and empty closets."

Chappy wiped his face with his flannel sleeve and smeared the dirt with his tears. "I tried to find them. I looked everywhere. I searched until the Army declared me a deserter. They arrested me in the daylight and dishonorably discharged me in the dark of night."

"How can I lead a flock, when I am the sheep who is most lost?"

Cassie held Chappy like no one else could and I made a solemn oath, "We'll find Rachel. You have my word. You have my faith."

Chapter 20

It took Momma Rose no time at all to turn our new encampment into a home. Each morning she made her rounds tent by tent.

"Wake up and smell the bacon, Gabriel. That's right; let me see those baby blues."

"Annette — Annette — I'm sorry to wake you, Dear. You look like an angel in your sleep."

"Stan — oh — you're awake. Show me how you put this arm on. How do these straps work?"

Momma Rose opened the flap on every tent, and every tent was warmer.

Michael's tent was always empty when Momma Rose made her rounds. Michael had not slept at night for a very long time. Evil threatened in the dark recesses of Michael's mind, and only daylight would allow him to sleep. Each new member of our family would find their daily chore, but Michael's was to stand guard while others slept.

"I brought you a couple of bacon and egg sandwiches, Michael. Then it's off to bed for you, young man," Momma Rose directed.

"Yes, Ma'am," Michael nodded. And the weary guardian stood down. "There's a young lady on your front porch," Michael reported. "I've been watching her all night. She's just sleeping like Goldilocks."

Momma tip-toed up the porch steps and found Goldilocks curled up in the swing. A golden lock of hair was stuck to her face, and another tickled her nose. Goldie swished the hair back and the swing swayed. Goldie woke with a start and leapt to her feet.

"And who's been sleeping in my bed?" Momma bear asked.

"I'm sorry — I just — I didn't want to wake anyone."

"Come inside, dear. You must be frozen."

Momma sat her new wayward child on the couch and summoned her troops. "Timmy, get this girl a cup of cocoa. Gretchen, bring Grandma a blanket."

Momma wrapped the blanket around those shivering shoulders and all the way down to those trembling knees. All that could be seen was a bright pink nose and sapphire eyes.

"I saw you folks on the news," came from under the blanket.

"Ah," Momma coddled. "And you found your way here. What is your name?"

"Rachel Edwards," echoed off the walls.

Momma choked, "Gretchen, go ring the dinner bell."

Gretchen hopped on Timmy's back and rode out the door. Gretchen rang that dinner bell like a five-alarm fire and Timmy howled.

One-by-one, our hearty band barged in and grabbed a breakfast plate from the stack.

"That's Stan," Momma softly said to Rachel.

"I could eat a horse," Stan quipped.

Annette gave Stan a sharp slap on the back of the head.

"And that's Annette," Momma whispered.

Rachel watched all the faces parade in and out. The faces were familiar from the TV news, but the one face she sought was always the last to take a plate.

"DADDY!"

Chappy's plate clattered on the floor. Rachel flew out from under the blanket and nested in Chappy's arms.

Momma shooed all her little ducklings out the door, and looked back once more at Chappy and Rachel, slowly turning, slowly swaying, and sobbing more and more.

"Mom said you were missing in action," Rachel cried.

"I was missing," Chappy lamented. "I was lost, but now I am found."

Chappy and Rachel walked for miles and talked endlessly. They talked about days when Rachel's hair had pink ribbons and Chappy's hair had no gray. They talked about things that Chappy had missed and about things Rachel wanted to know.

"You graduated from high school this year," Chappy calculated.

"Yeah," Rachel giggled. "I was voted Most Likely to Become a Green Bay Packers Cheerleader."

"So, you live in Wisconsin," Chappy surmised.

"Three years now," Rachel protested. "Three years of tears and hopes and fears! How could Mom do that to me?"

"Don't," Chappy pleaded. "Please — don't blame your mother. I was the one who left."

"But you left to save souls, Daddy," Rachel rebelled. "I saw them give you a medal."

"NO!" Chappy shouted. "They gave me a medal because I put you last. Blame me — please, blame me."

Chappy knelt on the side of the road, hanging between condemnation and redemption. Rachel dried her Daddy's tears with her hair and conceded.

"Ok, Daddy. I'll blame you for caring. I'll blame you for loving. Just hold me, Daddy."

The next time Chappy saw those golden locks was on national TV. Rachel was leaping and cheering for the Green Bay Packers. The camera zoomed in and captured those sapphire eyes, and Chappy knew they were looking at him.

Chapter 21

The Packers won that game, but I was losing mine. The nights were getting colder and the ground was getting harder. My team was out on the frozen field, while Cassie and I lay in our warm bed.

Cassie was searching for that heartbeat in her belly. She often fell asleep with her stethoscope in her ears.

I was opening mail and catching up on the bills. The mortgage payment was due and the feed store bill was overdue. Dollars and cents didn't add up to getting my team off the frozen field.

I laid my spectacles on the night stand. Only Cassie knew I had them. I rubbed my eyes, and the stack of mail cascaded to the floor.

"Listen, Jake!"

Cassie had found the beat. I listened to the steady rhythm of life that could not be measured in dollars and cents, and I fell asleep with the stethoscope in my ears.

I swung my feet to the floor at the sound of the alarm. I switched on the lamp and stared at the floor. The mail was strewn about my feet, and one unusual piece caught my eye. "Channel 4 News."

The bed shook as I ripped open the envelope. "What's wrong?" Cassie called out of her slumber.

"It's a letter," I babbled, and reached for my spectacles.

"Who's it from?" Cassie pulled herself upright and peered over my shoulder.

"Blah, blah, etc., etc." I mumbled. Then the words became clear.

"In response to the Channel 4 news reel at the Marshall Farm, we are in receipt of an overwhelming number of donations to your cause. Please find enclosed a check for $14,071. Also, please accept our congratulations and best wishes."

The springs of the bed squalled in concert with my victory yell,

"TOUCHDOWN!"

Cassie laughed and cried, watching me dance on one leg, then the other, trying to get my jeans on. I laced one boot and Cassie laced the other.

"Go, Cowboy, GO!"

With one kiss, I could fly. The first mile, the ground disappeared under my feet and I scarcely took a breath. The second mile challenged my resolve and my heart pounded in my chest. I stumbled and grappled through the last half mile and used my last breath.

"MR. CHAMBERS!"

I was still heaving, half sprawled over his table. Mr. Chambers brought a glass of water and laid his hand on my back.

"What the hell, boy? Are the Russians coming?"

I held up the letter, clutched in my hand. Mr. Chambers read and slapped the table with his hand. He dashed around the house, switching on every light that had too long been dark. He cranked up the furnace and the air warmed the walls. Home emerged out of its dormant shell, and Mr. Chambers directed, "Let's get those kids out of the cold."

The chores were done and breakfast was packed away in the stomachs of my team, when Mr. Chambers drove me back to those twelve tents.

"Strike those tents!" Mr. Chambers bellowed. "Prepare to move out!"

The encampment was stripped bare in less than an hour. Two columns were formed with forty or fifty pounds on each back. Everything they owned and everything they needed was packed and ready to go. Six wind-blushed faces stood in each column, and waited for the command of the United States Marine who had stormed the beach at Normandy.

"FORWARD, MARCH!"

No one knew how much they carried. They carried Eddie and all that would follow. They carried the beginnings of something bigger than they ever dreamed.

I raced back home that last half mile. The lights were unusually dim, and Gretchen punched the door open and sailed into my arms. "Daddy! Help! It's Momma!"

Gretchen and I stormed through the door and up the stairs. Cassie was lying still on the bed, afraid to move a muscle. The stethoscope was pressed deeply in her belly and she held her breath to listen.

She passed the stethoscope to my ears, and I listened to what I could barely hear. It wasn't the strong, steady rhythm that had lulled me to sleep. It was the heartbeat I had heard only once before, in a wounded soldier clinging to life.

A phone call to Momma had her standing at the mailbox. Gretchen was left in her arms, and the 54 Ford left dust in its trail.

The clinic had just opened when the brakes squealed on the Ford. We had no appointment, but no was not an answer we heard. Other patients waited while Cassie lay on the table.

Her stethoscope searched and searched, and then came to a rest. That strong heartbeat was back in her ears, and she spoke a sigh of relief. "False alarm, Doctor. Everything's ok."

The doctor listened with his own stethoscope and agreed, "Sounds good. You just keep listening to that."

The doctor's stethoscope moved and probed every inch of our baby's domain. He listened to every gurgle and burp, and nodded in reassurance. Then his stethoscope stopped.

"Mrs. Marshall, tap out your baby's heartbeat."

Cassie tapped on the right side of her belly and the doctor tapped on the left. The doctor hung his stethoscope around his neck and looked at the floor.

"I think we have two heartbeats."

"Twins?" Cassie erupted.

"Maybe," the doctor qualified. "I can't be sure. It could be an echo, but we need to confirm."

"Tell us what to do, Doctor," I pleaded.

"I want to send you to the University of Kansas Medical School," the doctor advised. "They have the latest in ultrasound equipment."

"What's that?" I had no idea.

"He wants them to shoot sound waves at our babies, Jake," Cassie shuddered.

"Nobody's shooting anything at my babies!" I raved.

The doctor backed up a step and raised his hands. "Your babies will be perfectly safe," he ensured. "It's a new technology that will allow them to do a more specific amniocentesis."

"What's that, Cassie?" I asked with my eyes locked on the doctor.

"It's ok, Jake," Cassie calmed. "Stand down, Cowboy."

The doctor leveled with us the best he could. "It could be nothing, but it can't be ignored. That second heart beat doesn't sound good, and it could be a warning sign for other developmental issues. We need to do this."

"Take me to Lawrence, Jake," Cassie decided.

Dawn doesn't wait on anyone, and sunset cannot be delayed. Cassie and I were on Interstate 70 while the sun was still rising in the East.

"Stick to the speed limit, Jake," Cassie cautioned.

"Did you call Momma?" I finally remembered. "What about Gretchen?"

"I called, Jake. Everything's fine. Just watch the road, watch that speedometer, and think of another name."

"Not Cleopatra, Queen of the Nile," I begged and relaxed. "How about Benjamin? How about Cassie?"

"I think I'll hope for Benjamin," Cassie smiled.

Three and a half hours of pavement lay in our wake and the University of Kansas was just ahead. We stopped to pick up Josie and she plugged the stethoscope in her ears.

"I'm sure it's ok," Josie tried to encourage, and a tear stole down her face.

Josie waited with me as Cassie put on the gown. Cassie entered the battlefield alone as Josie stroked my hair.

"How's school," I tried to ease the waiting.

"It's fine," Josie responded, but there was more.

"I'm ready to come home, Jake," was what she really meant.

"Any time, Sis. Any time."

"How's Gretchen?" Josie couldn't wait to hear.

"She's the spitting image of you, Sis, except for the red hair."

Josie and I watched the hands on the clock go around and around, until the nurse invited us in. Josie beat me to Cassie's arms and Cassie let me know, "It'll be days before we get the results. Take me home, Cowboy."

Josie didn't budge when we stopped to drop her off. She was going home with us, but Cassie would not allow.

"Look, Little Sister, I've got enough on my hands with your brother. I don't need you worrying over me. Stay here and do me a favor."

"Anything," Josie swore.

"Come home after you finish the semester, and bring me two Jayhawk shirts, the smallest you can find."

It was the bravest thing Josie had ever done when she stepped out of the car. She blew a kiss and watched us pull away. She ran to keep the car in sight, if only for another moment. I couldn't see her in the mirror anymore, but for all I knew, she was waving still.

Chapter 22

"You're staying right here with me," Momma insisted.

"No, Momma," Cassie declined. "I want to go home."

"Alright," Momma persisted. "I'll come stay at your house."

"No, Momma," Cassie refused. "I'll be fine."

Gretchen settled the matter. "You're supposed to do what Grandma says." And that was that.

I drove down to the Chamber's place to check on the progress. I was looking for something I could wrap my troubled mind around, something I could see and touch and help.

There had been enough money for two truckloads of lumber. It was all neatly stacked because Daddy was in charge. New toilets and sinks were included and a couple of refrigerators. Everything was going to be built to Daddy's specifications, and that old farm house would soon house a platoon. Daddy would answer to no one but Momma, who ordered, "You're building a home, not a barracks."

Everything was buzzing, saws and drills and voices. The saws and drills wound down to a stop and the voices surrounded my Ford.

"How's Cassie?"

"How are the babies?"

I reached out to each of those voices and said, "I don't know."

The voices faded. Eyes searched and faces cringed. Then Daddy handed me a hammer.

I pounded out the rhythm of one strong heart and missed the nail when another heartbeat faltered. I hit my thumb but didn't stop to notice. It swelled and blackened and I pounded on. Then Daddy took the hammer away.

"Sam, you're in charge! Let's go fishing, Son."

I caught a few fish that day, but I released them all. They swam for their lives, and those hearts kept beating.

"There's something I never told you, Jake," Daddy hesitated.

Anytime I got to thinking that Daddy had taught me everything I needed to know, there was always something more.

"Your Mother had twins."

"What — When — Daddy?"

Daddy released a fish, letting it slowly slip through his fingers. "You were born first, Jake, but your brother didn't make it."

This was something that had never been revealed to a boy who was too young, but now I needed to know. I had never seen so much pain in the face of man or woman. I planted my face next to Daddy's ear, and shared that pain.

"What was his name, Daddy?"

"There was no name," Daddy trembled. "There was no headstone. They just took him away, and I didn't — I should have…"

Daddy cupped my face in his hands and gave me the most important lesson he ever had.

"Make sure all your babies have names."

Daddy and I reeled in our lines and threw the rest of the bait in the water. "I will, Daddy. Even if it's Cleopatra."

A few days are never a few when you are waiting to hear. But they finally passed and we sat in front of the doctor's desk. Crenshaw was his name. Best in his field, so they said. Trust what he says.

Crenshaw laid out the fuzzy ultrasound images that we could barely make out. I could see a head, and maybe a foot. And one of them, I think, was sucking his thumb.

"They're both boys," Crenshaw unceremoniously droned. "Fraternal twins, each in its own placenta."

That was the last time Cassie and I smiled in that office. We had heard all we needed to hear, but there was so much more.

Crenshaw looked over his glasses like a judge about to impose a sentence. He held up the images one at a time. "This one is perfectly normal."

The next image was shown in a much dimmer light. "This one isn't quite — uh…"

Cassie lunged forward and pointed at the boys. "This is Joshua, and this is Benjamin."

"Yes, well," Crenshaw retracted. "It doesn't look good for Benjamin. The amniocentesis revealed an extra chromosome that indicates Down syndrome."

"What's that?" I had to ask again.

Cassie knew, but she listened to Crenshaw's version. Crenshaw proceeded to crush my world, with the bedside manner of a lab rat.

"Well, it explains the heart problem, which he will likely always have. And he will probably have severe complications in his digestive system."

Cassie nodded in understanding and acceptance of each challenge, and then Crenshaw spoke even colder.

"It's doubtful that he will ever exceed the mental age of an eight or nine-year-old. And the odds are against him outliving you."

Cassie was still nodding and I was bracing myself against the odds.

"I've been outnumbered before," I scoffed. "Benjamin can beat those odds."

"Look, Mr. and Mrs. Marshall, I've been giving you the best-case scenario. The fact is that three quarters of all Down syndrome babies die in the womb, and fifteen percent of those born will die within a year. After two years, leukemia takes some more of them."

Crenshaw took off his glasses and leaned back, as if the world was only a matter of simple facts.

"Now we need to be more concerned about Joshua."

Cassie stopped nodding and her eyes burned into Crenshaw's face. Crenshaw pushed harder.

"In the best of cases, sixty percent of twins are born prematurely. If they're born too soon, there's the risk of cerebral palsy. The average twin is a pound or two smaller than normal at birth. Either or both of these babies will likely spend their first days or weeks in intensive care."

Cassie's nails were digging into the upholstery of the chair like a lioness ready to pounce.

"There are also dangers to the mother," Crenshaw further condemned. "There's a greater chance of preeclampsia, gestational diabetes, placental abruption…"

"Look, Doc," I cut him off. "You don't know the price of soybeans and I don't know Latin. What are you saying?"

"Well," Crenshaw academically huffed. "Medically speaking, it would be best for Joshua and his mother if the other fetus — uh — Benjamin was…"

"ABORTED?"

The shock waves of Cassie's scream were felt as much as heard, and Cassie pounced. She crouched and tensed over Crenshaw's desk and growled, "Medically speaking…"

Crenshaw didn't have a chance to dodge Cassie's fist. Blood gushed from his nose and his lab coat was no longer pure white.

Cassie stormed out of his office and took her babies with her. Crenshaw grabbed tissues that could not hold back the tide. He reached for the phone and I slammed his hand hard against the receiver.

I handed him my big bandana handkerchief out of politeness and promised, "If you try to press charges against my wife, I will put you in the ground. And if I can't do it, there are fifteen guys back home that will do it for me."

People stood aside as Cassie barged out of the building. I trailed behind and waited till she tired and stopped.

"I'm not giving up either of them, Jake! Don't you even…"

"Of course not," I assured. "Our boy, Josh, will never leave his brother behind."

"We'll teach them how to love, Jake."

"And I'll teach them how to fish."

"I don't know if I'm strong enough, Jake."

I almost laughed. "From Jell-O to tapioca to oatmeal. We're strong enough. Let's go tell Gretchen."

Gretchen almost burst at the news of twin brothers and could hardly wait. Momma was doubly happy and she knew how to wait. And Daddy said, "Joshua and Benjamin are their names."

We told everyone about our joy and our fears. The vets were relieved and had no doubts. Sam summed it up.

"You're saying those twins may come out with some battle scars. They'll fit right in."

The saws continued to buzz and the hammers continued to pound. Cassie fell asleep each night with her stethoscope in her ears.

Mr. Chambers bid his little brothers and sisters farewell and moved into town. He found a room to rent just down the street from the nursing home, and I firmly believe that Doris knew he was there.

A small package came in the mail, not long after. It was addressed to Joshua and Benjamin Marshall. A letter was enclosed, written on faded yellow paper. It was brief and the handwriting was lousy, but each word was pure gold.

Boys,

You listen to your Mom and Dad. They won't steer you wrong.
Respect the earth. It's the only thing under your feet.

Respect the Lord. He's the only thing above you.

Remember that the only good reason to fight with your brother is to learn how to fight for him.

Learn all you can.

Work all you can.

Love all you can.

And if temptation ever gets the better of you, pay the man back two watermelons.

Ned Chambers

I recognized the box the letter came with. I opened the smooth soft lid and let the light shine on the Purple Heart that was earned on Normandy Beach.

Chapter 23

The harvest was in and so were the sinks and toilets. The vets worked hard and happy that fall and winter. Walls came down and walls were raised. Beds were built to last a hundred years. First there were four and then there were ten. But the beds stood empty, waiting for more. No one wanted to sleep in a nice warm bed while their buddies were still on the floor.

Momma stayed close to Cassie for a while, and Cassie let her dote. Cassie didn't need her fussing about, but she knew that Momma needed to fuss.

Momma kept the cocoa simmering in between stitches. She embroidered and rocked and listened while Cassie read to Gretchen.

"It says here that it will take Benjamin longer than Joshua to learn how to crawl and walk."

"That's ok," Gretchen decided. "That means I get to hold him longer."

"It also says here that Benjamin is going to need a lot of help learning to talk."

"I'll teach him how to sing," Gretchen vowed.

"And there's one more thing, Sweetie," Cassie taught. "His heart might not beat as strong as yours, but there's something special inside. Way down deep in the heart of a Down syndrome child, there is more love than you can possibly hold."

Gretchen grasped the stethoscope and begged, "Let me hear, Momma."

Cassie shared the stethoscope and found that strong, steady heartbeat. Gretchen giggled and her eyes bulged wide.

"That's Joshua," Cassie introduced.

"Hi, Joshua. I'm your big sister, Gretchen. If you're nice, I'll share my turtles with you. I've got bunches of them."

Gretchen waited until Cassie found the heartbeat with more love than she could hold.

"Hi, Benjamin. I'm Gretchen. Don't tell Joshua, but you're my favorite.

"Jesus loves me, this I know, for the Bible tells me so..."

Momma swiped her eyes and put her embroidery away. "Cassie, dear, I have to be going. I have some other kids who need me more than you do."

"Thank you, Momma. See you tomorrow."

A few vets went home for Thanksgiving that year, but they all came back. They were part of something they had to see through, and it was part of them. No one left for Christmas. Some had nowhere else to go, and others had no place they would rather be.

Gene drove to Lawrence and brought Josie home for Christmas. The back seat of the car was piled high with everything Josie owned. I knew that look and I knew that hug. Josie would never leave again.

"Momma, Daddy, I'm transferring to Fort Hays State University next semester," Josie announced.

"Oh?" was Momma's usual response.

"You think so, huh?" was more Daddy's style. "You think we should talk about this, Rose?"

"No," Momma answered, with that smile that always started in the corners of her eyes. "Go to your room, young lady."

Josie shrieked and hugged and bounded up the stairs.

We hadn't been allowed near the Chambers' property for days. It was all very top secret and even Daddy was turned away. We received our invitation to Christmas dinner and the grand opening tour.

At 1 pm, December 25, 1976, we piled in the car. The sun was bright and there wasn't a hint of snow. But the air had that unmistakable Christmas crisp. Gretchen was singing, *"Away in the Manger..."* The words were not all right, but her melody was nothing short of divine.

"Oh, look, they built an arch over the entrance." I could see it a quarter mile away.

"And there's a sign hanging from it," Cassie noted.

The gravel pinged lighter on the bottom of the car as I slowed to make the turn. I threw in the clutch, slammed on the brakes and looked up.

Gretchen sounded out the words on the sign above our heads. "Edd — ie's — Pl — Pla — Place. Eddie's Place. Who's Eddie?"

"A very good friend, Sweetie," Cassie answered. "A very beautiful boy."

I wiped my eyes on my sleeve and slowly let out the clutch. I glanced at Cassie and then the road, at Cassie and then the road, and then at the sky.

A Hays School District bus was parked near the house and I felt a shiver of impending dread. "You don't suppose Chappy brought home another bus load of vets, do you?"

Chappy came out to greet us. "Merry Christmas! Come see the house."

Gretchen hopped into Chappy's arms and Cassie and I trotted behind.

"What's up with the bus, Chappy?"

"Oh, that," Chappy dismissed. "School's out and that's mine for a week."

The eggnog was flowing inside and Momma, Daddy and Josie were surrounded by Santa hats and garland dancing about. The kitchen was huge and the table was set.

"That table must be twenty feet long," I guessed.

"Twenty-four," Chappy exacted. "Let's go upstairs."

First came the men's room, all shiny and bright. Toilets and sinks glistened and mirrors lined the south wall. Light flooded in and sparkled on the new floor. Mops and brooms hung on the east wall to keep it that way.

The women's room had a few extra accouterments. Floral designs on the walls and vases of flowers distinguished them from the heathens across the hall. Every accessory was there to ensure that a woman could return from the fields covered in dirt and sweat and close the bathroom door, feeling like a lady.

Each bedroom had a wall full of racks for coats and hats and fishing poles. Each dresser was graced with a copy of the Holy Bible. And each bunk bed was wrapped in a blanket that bore the occupant's name, all stitched by Momma Rose's hand.

The house was warm and secure and spoke of home. Cassie oohed and Gretchen aahed, and I hoped that Eddie could see.

Timmy out-did himself with Christmas dinner. Two turkeys were in the oven this year, and all the trimmings were peeled and chopped and blended. Everything was perfected and timed, and dinner would be served at 4 pm.

"It's two o'clock," Chappy announced.

Dozens of feet thundered out the door.

"Come on, Jake, try to keep up," Chappy beckoned.

I looked at Cassie and Cassie grabbed Gretchen, and we dashed to the Ford.

The yellow school bus was loaded with a whoop and a holler, and we followed that bus all the way to town. Arms were waving out the windows, with Santa hats flapping in the wind. The bus turned and we turned, and found a place to park in front of the Prairie View Nursing Home.

Chappy hoisted Gretchen to his shoulders and escorted us to Room 24. "I think you should go in first, Cassie," Chappy advised.

Cassie walked in on the union of Ned and Doris Chambers and listened to his voice. *"I want a girl, just like the girl that married..."*

Ned looked up from his serenade. "Oh, look, Doris, it's..."

"Cynthia!" Doris called out. "The brightest student I ever had."

Cassie looked at Ned and Ned bowed his head.

"Yes, Mrs. Chambers," Cassie answered. "It's Cynthia. I'm married now, and I have a beautiful little girl."

"That's wonderful!" Doris exclaimed.

Cynthia listened and thanked and loved. Doris lived the life she remembered and loved every minute.

"I have to be going now, Mrs. Chambers. My husband and daughter are waiting for me. Merry Christmas."

"Oh, yes. You run along, dear. Merry Christmas."

Cassie walked out and fell in my arms. "Be whoever she says you are, Jake."

I walked in and shook Ned's hand.

"ROBERT! Doris screamed. "I knew you would come back! They said you were captured, but I knew."

"That's right," I stammered. "I was captured, but I escaped. I just got back yesterday."

Doris would not let me go. She clung to me and all her past, and her present was Christmas peace.

Ned stood and turned toward the window. Against the backdrop of the rolling prairie, stood a single file of wind chill-flushed faces. Their clothes were mismatched, but their hair was cropped short. Fifteen brothers and sisters raised their fingertips to their brows and saluted Ned and Doris Chambers, of the United States Marines.

Chapter 24

I once heard how to tell the difference between a fairy tale and a war story. A fairy tale begins, "Once Upon a Time." A war story begins, "Hey, man, you ain't gonna believe this shit."

Once you hear that introduction, you know that the storyteller has not seen the horrors of war that cannot be told.

Our vets did not tell war stories. They talked about friends that could never be replaced and about regrets that they did not die instead. Their pain could be understood only by someone who had felt it and seen it and lived it. Someone who said, "I'm your friend now."

Gabriel was not surprised when his friend Brad was not in his bunk. Brad didn't sleep much, and was often the first to arise. He was probably in the barn, talking some nonsense to the cows.

Brad had lots to talk about and the cows always listened. They didn't judge and they didn't care whether Brad made any sense. They listened to the darkest secrets that a man can carry. They listened to the deepest despair that a man can bear. They listened, but they didn't have any answers.

Gabriel donned his two pair of socks and bundled himself for the January freeze. He stopped in the men's room to lighten his load, but Brad was not there.

He walked through the kitchen and the coffee was ready. Timmy offered, but Brad was not there.

He checked out the barn but the cows had no answers.

Gabriel ran and searched. There was nowhere he didn't look and his hope dwindled. There were so many places Brad could be lost and fear took over. Gabriel called out to the only shepherd he knew.

"CHAPPY!"

Chappy was pounding on my door before the morning light. "Lost sheep!" was all he had to say.

Cassie grabbed the phone and I grabbed the car keys.

"Do you have an admission for a Bradley Cunningham?" Cassie asked the hospital.

"Do you have a record of a Bradley Cunningham?" she asked the morgue.

"Do you have a report about a Bradley Cunningham?" She asked the police.

"Yes, Ma'am, we do."

Chappy, Gabriel and I headed to the police station.

"Do we have money for bail?" Chappy worried.

"All I have is this Ford," was all I could offer.

"Brad's in trouble!" Gabriel shouted. "Step on it, Jake."

Officer Monroe was on duty that morning. "Hello, Clyde," I greeted.

"Hey there, Jake," Clyde recognized. "Did you hear? We beat the Wildcats last night."

"We always beat the Wildcats, didn't we Clyde?" I recalled.

Clyde verified, "That we did."

Clyde Monroe was not the sharpest tool in the shed, but there were a few touchdowns I wouldn't have made, without Clyde keeping the Wildcats off my back. He wore his police uniform with the same pride he had worn a football jersey and pads. He puffed out his chest as he stood, but he was still just Clyde.

"We're looking for Brad Cunningham," I got back to business.

"Oh, yeah," Clyde confided. "We've got that loony locked up in cell number two. What a nut job that kid is."

Clyde jangled the keys from his belt. "He was fixin' to jump off the highway overpass when we nabbed him. We're holding him for a psych evaluation."

Clyde's key rattled in the lock and the cell block door hinges squeaked that eerie sound of doom. Cell number one was empty and cell number two was quiet. Brad lay twitching on the bunk, halfway between conscious memories and unconscious nightmares.

Gabriel pushed his way through and blocked our way. "Let me talk to him, Jake, Chappy, please."

Chappy joined foreheads with Gabriel and blessed, "Whatever you do for the least of my brethren, you do for me."

"You got any coffee, Clyde?" I took a chance.

"The worst you've ever had," Clyde warned. "But we've got doughnuts."

Gabriel was left alone with Brad at cell number two. He gripped the bars and began to shake. He shook the bars in a slow, rhythmic sway that quickened with each exasperated breath. He shook faster and harder until the bars resonated with rage.

"DAMN YOU, BRAD!"

Brad came off the bunk, as if he had heard the most fearsome word a soldier can hear. "AMBUSH!"

Gabriel was trying to break down those walls of iron. "I'm going to kick your ass all the way back to Kentucky!"

"I'm sorry, Gabe, I just…" Brad tried to grovel.

"You just tried to leave without me, you dumb-ass hillbilly!" Gabriel rampaged.

Brad was drowning in tears. "I didn't want you going where I was going!"

Gabriel had only a few thrusts at the bars left in him and very little breath. "How did you get to town, Brad?"

Brad didn't know. "All I remember is walking — and being very cold. I saw an International pick-up. I think I got in. I saw red, Gabe. I SAW RED!"

Brad fell to his knees at the base of the bars. "It was her blood, Gabe — that little girl — that beautiful, bloody little girl!"

Gabriel reached through the bars with his hand that could crush, and laid it like a downy comforter on Brad's head. "You can't run from it, Brother, and you can't die. I won't let you. Not without me."

No more could be said that had not been said before. But there was always more to be felt in the silence of a touch. After fifteen minutes, the hinges creaked and Clyde spoke his duty.

"Time's up, Bud. You've got to go."

"I'm staying," Gabriel snarled.

Did I mention that Clyde was not the sharpest tool in the shed? He grabbed Gabriel's bicep that was larger than some men's thighs.

"Let's go, NOW!"

Gabriel spun and landed a left hook. Clyde careened off the wall and stumbled back to his feet. Gabriel lay face-down on the floor and put his hands behind his back.

"Can I stay now?"

Gabriel now owned cell number one and Brad was not alone.

I saw it all unfold and watched Clyde rifle the files for the right form to fill out. His pride was hurt, but justice would be done, if only he could find the right form.

"You know, Clyde," I calmly intervened. "That boy could have separated your head from your shoulders, but he didn't. All he was doing was keeping the Wildcats off his buddy's back."

Clyde lost his place in the files and closed the drawer. He didn't turn around; he just talked to the wall.

"Come back to get him tomorrow, Jake."

"I'll be here, Clyde," I thanked. "Give my best to Helen."

Chapter 25

There were two other brothers in custody that winter. Joshua and Benjamin were scheduled to be released in March, but they plotted for an early escape. They were two and a half weeks early, just as Dr. Crenshaw had predicted. Joshua was the first to storm the gates.

He came quickly, as if he was on a mission, and he cried at his first taste of the world without Benjamin. Joshua wailed for half an hour, until Benjamin followed his call.

Joshua tipped the scales at almost six pounds, while Benjamin was barely over five. Both boys were whisked away to intensive care, and there Joshua felt they were safe.

Joshua was released into our care in just two days, and remained in his mother's arms next to Benjamin. Benjamin fought for two weeks. Each day he improved, and each day Joshua grew stronger.

We brought Gretchen's birthday presents home just a few days early and she cuddled one arm around each. "Thank you, Josh, for watching over Ben," Gretchen endeared. "You just sleep now, and I'll take care of him."

A parade of visitors lined up for a reminder of the wonder of new life. The vets each saw their own version of the future in the boys. They saw the frailty in Benjamin, the strength in Joshua, and the beauty in both. A rebirth of brotherhood was felt in those two boys, and the vets at Eddie's Place had only begun to learn.

They learned victory when Josh took his first steps, and they cheered Ben on as he struggled to crawl. The vets had been denied victory in the face of war, but they learned how to begin again with a simple crawl.

They learned patience as Josh waited for his brother to catch up. And they learned hope when Ben never gave up. These lessons were not easy and they would be tested time and again.

President Carter had issued a pardon of all those who had evaded the draft.

It didn't matter why they fled from their duty to their country. Some of them truly objected to the unrighteous purpose of the war in Viet Nam. Some of them were just afraid. And some of them just didn't care. It didn't matter. They were all now free to come home.

A dozen or so vets were gathered around the huge kitchen table and the bottle was passed around. Low grumblings grew louder with each swig of booze, and the language got ugly.

"We've got to do something about these damn draft dodgers," one voice demanded.

"What are you going to do?" another voice tried to reason.

"All I'm saying is they don't deserve to live in a free country."

"You're damn right. And I heard that one of those bastards is living at the YMCA right here in Hays."

"Maybe we should pay that son-of-a-bitch a visit."

Brad had declined his share of the bottle, and he had heard all he could stand to hear. He slammed the bottle on the table and sent his chair crashing into the wall.

"I know one of those bastards that fled to Canada!" Brad roared.

Faces paled and the room fell silent.

Brad picked up his chair and sat staring into his past.

"He was my best friend, Terry."

Brad shook his head and closed his eyes in torment. "There was nothing I wouldn't do for him and there was nothing he wouldn't do for me, except show up for the bus."

Brad opened his eyes and reached for the bottle. Gabriel stopped his hand and urged him on. "Tell it all, brother."

"We were drafted together," Brad went on. "We took the physical together. I got on the bus to go to basic training, and Terry took off to Canada."

Brad was living in the moment and let out his rage. "I cursed that traitor for months! I defiled his name! I saw his face on every target on the rifle range, and I became a damn good shot."

Brad took a moment to calm himself and everyone waited to hear what came next.

"I carried my anger all the way to Viet Nam, and it followed me into the bush on every patrol. I killed men that I thought were better than Terry. At least they had the balls to fight. I lost friends in the field and wished that it was Terry instead. I hated as much as a man can hate."

Brad looked at Gabriel and reached slowly for the bottle. "Just one swig, Brother."

Gabriel allowed and Brad gulped down enough liquid courage to get him through. "Then came the day when they said, "Search and Destroy.""

Brad set the bottle down and pushed it away. "We had just entered the village, and all was quiet. It didn't feel right and rifles were poised. A chicken squawked here and a dog barked there, but no enemy was in sight."

Brad hid his shame behind the palms of his hands and told the story that only the cows had heard before. "A little girl burst out of a hooch and ran for her life. She came straight toward us, yelling, "Tro giup! Tro giup!""

More than a few vets around the table recognized the little girl's call for help.

"A shit-load of explosives were bound around that tiny body, and her arms were reaching out to me."

Brad collapsed on the table and pounded with his fists. Everyone leaned forward, dreading what came next.

"The patrol leader shouted, "Two o'clock! FIRE!""

Brad could only utter a few words between heaving sobs. "I don't even — remember — pulling the trigger. But my rifle fired — and the little girl — dropped."

Everyone reached to lay a hand on a piece of Brad, and Brad raised his head to look them all in the eye.

"In the smoke and fire, I saw Terry's face. Half a dozen rifles had fired, and maybe some of them missed, but I was a damn good shot."

Brad rose from his chair and stated his conviction. "The only thing I knew for sure was that it wasn't Terry's bullet that killed that little girl."

This was not a war story. This was a nightmare of truth. Brad started to walk away, but paused to make one more declaration.

"I wish that I had never gotten on that bus and I'm glad that Terry didn't. I hope that Terry can come home now. I'd give anything to see him again."

One-by-one, the vets slipped quietly off to bed. Gabriel followed Brad and murmured in his ear. "You did it, Brother. You're free now. You're going to be ok."

Timmy took the bottle and poured the last liquid courage down the drain.

Gabriel and Brad lay on their bunks, staring into the darkness. Gabriel hoped that his friend would sleep peacefully tonight and Brad wasn't sure he wanted to.

"Goodnight, Brad."

"Goodnight, Gabe."

It was so quiet, they could hear the minutes tick by on the alarm clock.

"Gabe?" Brad called out softly.

"Yeah, Brad?"

"How long do you figure on staying here at the farm, Gabe?"

"Oh, I don't know. I don't have any plans. And it's not a bad place to be. Good chow, good honest work. How about you?"

"I was just thinking," Brad mused. "You swore you were going to kick my ass all the way back to Kentucky."

Gabriel's smile was concealed under the darkness. "Yeah, I did. And I'm a man of my word."

Brad chuckled for the first time he could remember. "How soon could we go?"

"Well," Gabriel considered. "We probably ought to stick around until the planting's done."

Brad's smile was so big; it should have beamed through the darkness.

"It'll be an honor to meet your folks, Brad."

"There's someone else I'd like you to meet, Gabe."

Gabriel didn't have to guess. "We'll see if we can find your friend, Terry. But not until I've met that pretty sister of yours."

"You just get that thought out of your head right now, Gabe. There's a reason that guys like you don't have a girlfriend. It's because you're butt ugly."

"Goodnight, Brad."

"Goodnight, Gabe."

Chapter 26

I lost count of how many friends we said, "so long" to, over the next six years, but we never said goodbye. New friends came and took the bunks of those who had found their way home. New names were stitched on blankets by Momma Rose's hand.

The new friends came less frequently as time pushed the war further into history. But I remembered the haunting prediction, *"There will always be wars and rumors of wars."* As long as I drew breath, Eddie's Place would always be here.

We received a letter in the Summer of 1983.

Dear Jake and Cassie,

Remember those 58,000 plus names I showed you?

Remember the memorial I said they were going to build for the Vietnam Vets?

You've got to see it.

Enclosed are two plane tickets. Happy 12th anniversary. Who would have thought we would live to see the day?

Now get your asses on that plane.

Tommy

We kissed our boys and left them in the care of Grandma and Grandpa. We kissed our Gretchen and left her in charge.

It had been a long time since we had seen Kansas from the air, and it had been a long time since I had Cassie to myself. I ordered a beer for me and a bourbon and coke for Cassie.

"I'm not one of those easy Kansas girls, Cowboy. You're not going to ply me with drinks and have your way. You're going to have to at least buy me dinner."

"Good Lord, you're a hard woman."

Cassie had the chicken and I had the beef. It was like a second honeymoon, and it wasn't in an eighteen-wheel truck. We talked and we laughed and we soared.

Tommy was waiting at the airport, and I thought Cassie would never let him go.

"Hey!" I objected. "You can mess with my mail and mess with my chow. You can even mess with my pay, but don't mess with my girl."

Cassie let go, and Tommy was mine. We didn't shake hands. We went straight for the hug. The difference between a handshake and a salute is respect. The difference between a handshake and a hug is love.

"I've got a car waiting outside," Tommy gushed. "Follow me."

We followed Tommy into the heat of the South and swiped the humidity from our brows. We careened through the streets and Tommy pointed at all the sights. Cassie oohed and I aahed.

"I have dinner reservations," Tommy revealed. "But we have time for one stop."

The car was parked, and Tommy led the way. Our heads tilted further and further back as we stared at the top of the Washington Monument. We followed Tommy into the elevator, and it lifted us 500 feet above everything that Tommy wanted us to see.

There were two large windows on the north side and two more on the east, the south, and the west. Tommy pointed out the memorials to Lincoln and Jefferson and saluted the flag on top of the capitol.

"That's the Smithsonian." Tommy pointed out. "We'll spend all day there."

Tommy looked at his watch. "Dinner reservations!"

We made it in time for the best meal I'd ever had outside of Momma's kitchen. The place was called the "Prime Rib." The silver shined and the glasses sparkled. The waiter shredded fresh horseradish over the top of the thickest cut of steak I had ever seen. Cassie and I devoured and relished and Tommy savored every precious bite.

We didn't stay at the poshest hotel. That was not in the budget. But the Howard Johnson's we rented was just across the street from "Watergate" and we had another story to tell.

Tommy ran us ragged for the next three days. We saw memorials to the glory of those who fought for our independence. The tragedy of a nation divided into North and South was on full display. The sacrifices of men, women and children through two world wars could not be denied.

Tommy showed us the heights of grandeur and the depths of despair. We walked among the monuments to democracy and freedom, and we walked the streets filled with homeless Americans who knew neither.

We could smell them a block away. They lay on grates in the sidewalk and warded off the nightly chill with the heating exhaust of magnificent buildings. They awoke in their own stench, peed on the sidewalk and begged for change.

Cassie gave one a bottle of water and a few bucks. She gave a pack of gum to another and a few bucks. Cassie ran out of money, but her hand touched many.

"I'm ready to go home now, Jake. I've seen enough."

"You promised me one more day, Darlin'," Tommy insisted. "And don't forget your list."

Cassie summoned her courage. "That's right. We've got to do the list."

"I'll pick you up in the morning," Tommy pledged.

Tommy was waiting the next morning in the restaurant of the Howard Johnson's before the crack of dawn. He shared a Danish and coffee with Cassie as I settled our bill. We loaded our bags in the trunk of the car. Cassie buckled in and clutched her list to her breast.

We drove, we parked, and we walked. Cassie and I held hands and measured our steps. We turned northeast from the Lincoln Memorial and our breaths quickened. The 250 foot "Wall" loomed in the distance and grew taller with each step.

The Vietnam Veterans Memorial cut a gash through the landscape like the wound that was inflicted on a nation of peace. It rose to ten feet at its highest and sloped down to less than a foot at its futile end.

The names were engraved in polished black granite, and we could see our reflection in the shadow of those names. 58,307 names outnumbered the stars in the sky, and we touched them all.

Tommy handed me a wax crayon and held a strip of paper over an engraved name. I rubbed the crayon over the paper from left to right and the letters boldly appeared.

L E S T E R M. B O R G E L T

My knees failed me and I collapsed on the walkway. But I was back on my feet in only a moment or two, when I heard Borgelt's voice. "It's your turn to take the watch, Jake. I'm going to catch some sleep."

Cassie divided up her list and we rubbed. I held Tommy on my shoulders to capture the names that were ten feet high, and Cassie knelt to rub the names that were at the bottom of the "Wall." Over 400 names were on Cassie's list. They were friends, comrades and relatives of everyone that knew of Eddie's Place.

We rubbed until our fingers were raw and covered in wax. We etched until the sun set and the names faded.

They say we use only ten percent of our brains. But we had used all of our hearts. Our minds and hearts were exhausted.

"We are now boarding Flight 129 to Kansas City. We will begin with those needing special assistance."

Tommy searched his pockets until he found where he had tucked away a small scrap of paper. "Here are the names of two more vets coming your way. Give them to your Momma so she can start stitching blankets."

"What do I tell everyone when we get home, Tommy?" I implored.

"We are now boarding rows 1 through 20."

"You'll know what to tell them," Tommy was sure. He held up his fingers, still brown with wax. "You'll know."

"Are we doing enough, Tommy?" Cassie cried.

Tommy grinned and softly closed his eyes. "Remember when you got me out of that hospital bed and into a wheelchair and said there was someone you wanted me to see?"

"You said you didn't want to see anybody!" Cassie burst.

"I said I didn't want to see anybody unless his name was Jake."

Cassie's face turned radiant. "And I said, he has the most gorgeous eyes."

"We are now boarding rows 21 through 40."

Tommy opened his eyes and looked into Cassie's heart. "You started all this, Darlin', one man at a time. Now get on that plane, and that will be enough."

Tommy slapped me on the back and pointed toward the boarding door. "You're on the right path, Private. Keep your eyes peeled and we'll be right behind you."

Cassie and I walked toward the door and I shouted back, "Specialist 4!"

"We are now boarding rows 41 through 60."

I handed over our tickets and heard one more call. "You don't deserve that woman, Jake!"

"I'm working on it, Tommy!"

We buckled up in row 48 and I looked out at the moon. "It wasn't much of a honeymoon for you, was it?"

Cassie asked the stewardess for pillows and nestled her head next to mine. "Just take me home, Cowboy. Just take me home." Cassie mumbled, "I'm going to look for fresh horseradish when we get home." And she was out like a light.

Our first morning at home, Cassie put the boys to work, sorting strips of paper with names etched in wax. Cassie consulted her list and held up each strip of paper.

"This goes in Gene's pile. This is for Sam. Timmy, Brenda, Freddy, Bruce…"

The boys darted back and forth, delivering each name to the stack of names that loved them most. Each stack was bundled and tied with ribbon of red, white or blue.

Josh tied the final knot around Gene's bundle of names. "Did Uncle Gene serve with all these people?"

"Yes, Honey, and he loved every one."

Ben fought back all his tears except one lone drop. "Sam has so many names in his bundle. Won't it make him sad?"

"Sam has been sad for a long time, Sweetheart. We're hoping this will make him a little less sad."

We gathered around the fire pit once more that evening. Harvest time was just around the corner. Plans needed to be made and commitments needed to be heard. Everyone listened and most everyone spoke.

But what they really wanted to hear was about Washington, D.C. "What did you see?" "Was it awesome?"

I poked at the fire and Cassie nudged my shoulder. "Tell them, Jake."

I didn't stand to command their attention. I just started talking into the fire and yearning ears drew closer.

"We saw darn near everything, and yes, it was awesome."

"We saw the monument to Washington, who led us through a revolution for our independence, and I was honored to stand in its shadow. But I wondered, where are the names of those he led in battle?"

"We saw the memorial to Lincoln, who guided the nation through a Civil War. I was humbled to stand at the feet of his giant statue and feel like a small part of history. But I wondered, where are the names of those that fought and died to preserve the Union?"

"We saw tributes to veterans of two world wars that threatened to destroy us, but I didn't see the names of those who died with their faces in the mud."

I stood, and my boys took their cue. Josh and Ben started passing out their bundles of names.

"Then we saw the Vietnam Veterans Memorial, and we found the names."

I watched Sam untie the ribbon in dread, as if he was deliberately ripping out his own heart. He read the first name and his face paled. He felt each letter of the second name and his breath left him. The third name brought a hint of a smile, and every name after that was held close to his heart.

I can't say that we healed all wounds that night, but many a heart was a little closer to peace.

"God willing," I prayed. "These names will remain engraved in granite for hundreds of years. Other folks will read them, but you will always hold them."

After that night, each time another vet joined our ranks, Cassie sent a letter to Washington, D.C. And Tommy sent back a bundle of names etched in wax.

Eddie's name was never etched. It wasn't even on the "Wall." His name was engraved only in our hearts. He was a casualty of war, but he was not a casualty of life. He was the reason that hundreds of other vets found their way home at Eddie's Place.

Cassie and I were talking about Eddie one fall morning. We recalled that grin that spread all the way between those big ears, and couldn't help but smile. We recalled his corny jokes, and couldn't help but laugh. We recalled so many things that only Cassie and I knew. The good memories were even sweeter this time around, and the bad memories didn't hurt quite as much.

Chapter 27

Josie and Gene had been married since the day after her college graduation. Josie was expecting her second child and they were sure they would always be here.

As long as Chappy had a flock to tend, he would always be here.

But time was slipping by faster, as it always does with age, and I dreaded the day that my kids would no longer be here.

Gretchen spread grace and peace wherever she went, and she shared it with every soul she met. Josh filled any room with laughter, with his mischievous ways, and showed the promise of a man who knew no limits. Ben filled the room with love, with his infectious smile, and we were blessed.

Ben learned to walk, and Josh taught him how to run. There was nowhere that Ben didn't follow, and Josh went nowhere without Ben by his side.

Ben was not always happy. His joy was unrestrained, but his sorrows hurt to his core. Ben's saving grace was that he remembered the joy longer than the sorrow. Many a vet learned that lesson from Ben, and we all learned from his patience, acceptance and courage.

Ben's education began with Gretchen. It took three weeks for Gretchen to teach Ben, *"This little light of mine, I'm going to let it shine."* But Ben did eventually learn it, and Ben lived it. His first inclination was to love, and his second desire was to learn.

Ben started school a year later than Josh. No one thought he was ready, but Ben had to try.

"Maybe next year," I tried to advise.

"I want to try now, Daddy," Ben resolved.

"We'll talk about it later," I avoided. "We'll just have to see."

"Daddy," Ben pushed on. "I learned how to ride a tricycle because Josh told me to try. I learned how to like spinach because…"

"Because I told you to try it with a little vinegar," I remembered. I held that boy's face in my hands and wished that I had his courage. "Ok, Ben. Let's add a little vinegar and give it a try."

Josh was so proud and Ben was so unsure on the first day of school. "Now remember, Ben, your teacher's name is Mrs. Henderson. But all you have to say is "Yes, Ma'am."

"OK," Ben shivered.

The Miller boys were blocking the way, and smirked their evil intent as the Marshall boys neared. "So, your retard brother is going to go to school?" they taunted.

Ben cowered and Josh stood fast. "He's not a retard! You take that back!"

Josh took the onslaught of those older, bigger Miller boys. He fought and got in a lick or two before he fell down. He stood and took all the punches he could before he fell again.

"RUN, BEN! RUN!"

Ben ran and the air swooshed with the wrath of God. Gretchen was swinging her backpack around her head.

With a THUD, and a THUD, the Miller boys went down. Gretchen raised her backpack high and triumphed, "WITH THE JAWBONE OF AN ASS, SAMPSON SLEW THE PHILISTINES!"

The Miller boys slithered away as all cowards do, and Gretchen knelt beside Josh. She touched his battered face, and Josh winced and cried, "We have to find Ben!"

Ben was not far away. They found him hugging the nearest tree.

That's the account we heard in front of the principal's desk. Chappy was with the kids, while Cassie and I listened to the bravest story we had ever heard.

Ben later asked, "Why, Momma?"

Cassie tried to explain. "Because they don't understand, Honey. But the world will one day understand how special you are."

Josh vowed, "I did my best, Daddy."

I made sure Josh saw my eyes. "You did better than best, Buddy. You're my hero."

Gretchen hid her face as she confessed, "I didn't turn the other cheek, Chappy."

Chappy pulled Gretchen's head into his chest and reminded, *"There is no greater love than this, my child, than to lay down one's life for a friend. And thine enemies shall fall at your feet."*

Ben spent two years in the first grade, and took two more years to finish the second grade. But Ben didn't try to be normal. He tried to be the best of himself.

The alphabet came slowly, even though Gretchen sang the letters to Ben every night. Then came the meaning behind those twenty-six letters. Many like to begin with A — pple, Buh — Boy. I taught Ben an alphabet he could recite to his veteran friends around the fire pit.

"Alpha, Bravo, Charlie — uh…" Ben rehearsed.

"Delta," Bridget helped.

"Oh, yeah. Delta, Echo, Foxtrot…" Ben persisted.

Each night, the fire burned brighter for Ben, and each night the vets had something to write home about.

Josh was Ben's numbers man. Josh stood outside the chicken house with an egg basket in his hand. "Go find me three eggs, Ben."

Without question or delay, Ben tackled the job and came out of the chicken house, gingerly cradling three fresh eggs.

"Put them in the basket, Ben. Now how many eggs do I have?"

"One, two, three," Ben pointed out one-by-one.

"Now go get two more eggs," Josh encouraged.

Ben delicately delivered two more eggs into the basket.

"How many eggs do we have now, Ben?" Josh quizzed.

Ben counted all the way to five. Josh handed him the basket and finished the lesson. "Now, go tell Momma. Three eggs plus two eggs equals…"

Ben's eyes lit up and his heart throbbed. He ran as fast as he could without endangering those precious eggs. "MOMMA! Three eggs plus two eggs equals FIVE EGGS!"

Chapter 28

Peace is not the absence of war. Peace must be sought amidst relentless war. It had been fourteen years since the Viet Nam peace agreement was signed, but the world was not at peace.

The U.S Embassy in Iran was seized and fifty-two American hostages were held for two years. The Soviets invaded Afghanistan. President Reagan was wounded by a crazed gunman. Even the Pope was shot, but he survived.

John Lennon sang, *"Give Peace a Chance,"* and he challenged us to *"Imagine"* nothing to kill or die for. But, Dear God, someone shot him dead.

There was nowhere to escape the battle between good and evil, and it haunted Eddie's Place.

"I think the next war will be in Central or South America," Andrew predicted.

"Nah," Brenda disagreed. "It's going to be somewhere in the Middle East."

"I'm with Andrew," Curt chimed in. "We already invaded Grenada down in the Caribbean. Now I hear talk about going after that General Noriega in Panama."

"But what about that explosion in Beirut that killed 237 marines?" Brenda countered. "It's the terrorists we're going to be fighting next."

"I have to side with Brenda," Sam weighed in. "The terrorists just blew up a commercial flight and killed 270 people. I don't know where the fight is going to be, but they're coming after us."

Chappy was sitting in the corner, scratching notes on a pad. He hadn't gotten very far with his Sunday sermon, and Sunday might be too late to speak up.

"The war is already here," Chappy announced from the corner.

Chappy laid his pad and pen aside and began to stroll around the table of troubled faces. "The casualties are all around us. I'm sure you've seen them."

Chappy took a chair and sat among his flock. "You've seen them standing in line down at the soup kitchen. You've seen them packing what little they have left after they lost their farm and their home. I've seen them in the classrooms where children practice hiding under their desks in case of nuclear attack."

The vets held their breath in a hush. It was the silence you hear at the height of a movie, when no one dares to speak and risk missing a word.

"We sit here, hunkered down, waiting for the enemy to strike. But all the while, he's right on our doorstep."

A chair scooted and screeched and more than a couple of eyes glanced at the door.

"And you have faced this enemy before. His name is Fear, and his weapons are hunger, loneliness and despair."

The vets exchanged nods and glances, and couldn't help but agree.

"I, for one," Chappy concluded, "Would not still be here if I hadn't found someone who cared."

Chappy traced his finger along the wood grain of the table and waited for the first voice of compassion. Timmy rarely spoke his feelings, but he was the first to respond.

"All I know how to do is make gingerbread and cocoa for the kids. I don't know how I can help save the world."

Chappy took an apple from the bowl and twisted the stem off. "What would a good day be for you, Timmy?"

Anyone looking with their heart could see the ray of peace in Timmy's eyes. "Just watching the kids running through the fields without a care in the world."

"That sounds like a good day," Chappy agreed.

Chappy tossed the apple the length of the table, and Timmy caught it inches in front of his misty eyes.

"Pass it along brother," Chappy inspired.

Timmy wiped his eyes clear and picked his target. The apple soared and Andrew intercepted its flight. Andrew turned the apple in his fingers and buffed a shine with his sleeve.

"One of my best days was when the judge sentenced me to do community service. I made a few friends that day."

Andrew passed the apple back and forth between his hands and smirked. "We all picked up the same trash along the highway. It was empty pop bottles, dirty diapers, everything nobody wanted anymore. At the end of the day, we were covered in the same filth and we all smelled the same. I should look those guys up again and see how they're doing."

Andrew launched the apple and Brenda snatched it out of the air.

"I have an idea! Get your guys together, Andrew, and bring them along. We'll all go down to the supermarket and have a food drive. We'll wash cars. We'll help load groceries. We'll collect so much food; they won't be standing in line for just soup at the soup kitchen."

Brenda took a small, but voracious bite out of the apple and sent it on its way. Curt was the next to catch the spirit.

"I monitor the emergency frequencies on my radio. We can be there for every fire, every car crash."

Sam stole the apple from Curt and added a voice of reason. "Whoa there, Bat Man. Let's not start chasing fire trucks and ambulances. We'll talk to the authorities and find out where we can help. Brenda, how about you talk to the supermarket manager first thing Monday morning. Andrew, you get your boys together and round up some hoses and car washing supplies. Timmy, make me a list of all the ingredients you need for gingerbread. We'll rustle up enough for a huge batch, and you and the kids can take it down to the grade school."

Sam had taken the lead and his troops were saddling up for the charge. There would be little time to worry about Panama or Iran. And the terrorists would be held at bay as long as Eddie's Place was on patrol.

Chappy sat back in the corner with his pad and pen. He scratched out all the sermon notes he had struggled with before and wrote, "Feed My Sheep."

Chapter 29

Daddy cast his line with the grace and beauty of a seasoned angler. His bait sailed only inches above the surface of the pond and dipped into the water, leaving one, two, three ripples. Daddy settled into his peaceful repose and watched me bait my hook.

I cast about ten feet out, just to make sure there were no snags, and cranked the line carefully back onto the reel. I wetted my finger and held it in the breeze, waiting for the perfect moment. I drew the rod back to begin my swing, but something was wrong and I started over.

I looked at Daddy, and nature was speaking to him through the songbirds and kissing him on the cheek with its breeze. I waited until the breeze slowed and then snapped my rod around. It was even more wrong than before, and I slapped my thumb on top of the reel. The line recoiled and the bait splashed just off the bank.

"Everything ok, Son?"

"Yeah, Daddy. I just — uh…"

"Forget it, Son. Just go again."

I reeled back in, leaving just a bit of lead in the line and closed my eyes. I thought about the days when a young boy was learning how to cast. And I thought about the days when a young man was bound and gagged and scared to death. I brought the rod into its backwards swing and paused to remember everything I now had and wondered how long it would last.

I lashed the rod around and the reel whined in distress. The line whipped and furled across the pond and the bait plunged on the other side of Daddy's. For the first time ever, Daddy's and my lines were crossed.

I turned to begin the walk of shame around Daddy to uncross our lines.

"Sit down, Son. If we get a bite, we'll reel it in together."

I sank more than I sat, and buried my face between my knees.

Daddy took off his hat and scratched his head. "Tell me again how everything's ok."

Daddy didn't push. He didn't say another word. He put his hat back on his head and pulled the brim over his eyes. He laid his pole on the bank and reclined with his hands behind his head and waited for me to surrender.

"Have you ever felt like things were too good, Daddy?"

Daddy didn't answer. He knew that more had to come.

"I mean — things change, right? They go from bad to good and from good to bad."

"That seems to be the way, Son."

"Well — Daddy. Things have been good for a long time now, the best I've ever known. And I'm thankful, Daddy. I really am."

"But?" Daddy advanced.

"But I've lost before," I carried on. "I've lost so very much. And now I have so much more to lose. I just can't bear to…"

Daddy's pole lurched and slid out of his reach. Daddy didn't flinch or pay any mind to the fish that was pulling his pole toward the brink of the murky water.

I reeled feverishly, trying to snag Daddy's line and save his cherished pole.

Daddy opened his knife and cut my line, and watched his pole vanish into its watery grave.

I was speechless, as Daddy had intended. "You cannot lose what you never had," Daddy explained. "And what you have had before can never be taken away."

"But, Daddy, your pole…"

"That was a damn good pole," Daddy conceded. "I caught a lot of fish with that pole, and I'm going to remember every one."

I understood so little, and I needed more. "But what about that fish, Daddy? That might have been the granddaddy of all the fish in this pond."

"That fish was never mine to have, Son. I guess he'll just have to be a hope and a dream for tomorrow."

The dawn was now upon us, and a new lesson was dawning in my mind. It was an old and simple lesson that I had never fully understood. Tomorrow is not yours. Live for today and make it your yesterday. Daddy had more yesterdays than tomorrows, and that was enough for him.

"Do you have enough line left for one more cast, Son?"

Daddy tied the swivel on my line and I attached the hook. Daddy baited and I cast.

The line trailed only inches above the surface of the pond and dipped into the water, leaving one, two ripples.

Daddy laid down, with his brim over his eyes. "That's the best cast I've ever seen. I'm going to remember that too."

I watched the sun rise, and Daddy slept. I thought about all the things that could never be taken away and dreamed of all the things that might come. Another hour passed without a bite, and Daddy slept. It was the most peaceful hour I had ever known.

I reeled my line in slowly to call it a day and felt a snag. I yanked to set the hook, and then reeled faster. I reeled and battled, and Daddy slept.

Out of the murky past, rod and reel emerged. "DADDY! Your pole! I got it!" And Daddy slept.

"Daddy? Daddy? DADDY!"

I pounded on Daddy's chest. I blew every breath of life he had left me into his lungs. Take a breath and BLOW! Take a breath and "HELP!" Take a breath and BLOW!

Help came from every corner of every acre. But no mortal effort and no helpless cry could hold Daddy back from his promised tomorrow.

They put him in an ambulance and Momma and Chappy rode along. Josie and Gene huddled with the kids and Cassie held me.

Life and love blurred in less than a heartbeat and the songbirds ceased their singing. There wasn't a ripple on the pond and I held tight to the pole that had caught a lot of fish.

They said it was an aneurism. They said it was quick and painless. They said sorry for your loss, but what did they know?

Did they know that you cannot lose what you never had? Did they know that what you already had can never be taken away? Someday I would have to try to explain that to the kids. For now, it would just have to hurt so damn much.

Chapter 30

Tommy sat next to me at the funeral and watched. He watched me set my jaw as I listened to Chappy extol Daddy's well-lived life. He watched the color drain out as I clenched Cassie's hand.

Momma reached into her purse and passed around a handful of Daddy's handkerchiefs. Gretchen held her handkerchief over her nose and sniffed to catch the slightest scent of Grandpa. Josh dabbed the tears from his eyes and folded them into his pocket. Ben unfolded his handkerchief and covered his face. Josie pressed her handkerchief against her mouth to muffle her sobs.

Tommy saw me refuse my handkerchief, and watched Cassie swipe a renegade tear from my cheek.

There was no flag draped over Daddy's coffin at the gravesite. He was a little too young for the first World War and a little too old for the second. There was no bugle and there were no weapons of war fired over his grave.

But a platoon of orphaned friends stood at attention in honor of the American they all wished to be. Chappy gave his last blessing and Tommy rose to command, "PRESENT ARMS!" Forty-two hands touched their brows, and Daddy was laid to rest.

The guests slowly departed and the platoon retreated to camp. Tents were pitched all around the farmhouse and watch fires were lit. Daddy's presence would glow through the night, and the kitchen light would burn bright.

Momma sat at the head of the table, the only one who would ever sit in Daddy's chair. She smiled as no one else would and spoke the wisdom that no one else could.

"First thing tomorrow, I'm going to start boxing up your father's things."

"Momma, don't move so fast," I tried to control. "Take some time to think about…"

"JAKE!" Momma silenced. Like so many times before, that's all it took for me to hush and listen.

"I'm going to need your help," Momma continued. "I've already stowed away everything I need. You kids will need to go through the rest of it to see what you might want to keep."

Momma reached into her quilted bag, and one-by-one, bestowed the most treasured gifts.

"Gretchen, this is the first bible your Grandpa ever read. You're the only one he would trust with its words."

Gretchen opened the pages to Matthew 28. *"And lo, I am with you always, even unto the end of the world."*

"Josh, this is your Grandpa's pocket knife," Momma willed. "He was never without it."

Josh clutched the knife in his hand and rubbed the spot that had been worn smooth by Grandpa's thumb. "I'll keep it sharp, Grandma. And I'll never be without it."

"Ben, this silver dollar was made the year that your Grandpa was born," Momma pointed out. "He always said that as long as he held on to this dollar, he would never be broke."

Ben studied the dollar with his mouth open in wonder. "Look, Josh, it says 1912. I'll always be rich now."

Momma waved a blue ribbon in front of Josie's face. "Do you remember this?"

"The father-daughter three-legged race!" Josie squealed. "He kept that?"

"You would be surprised at what he kept." Momma handed over the well-preserved program embossed with the number 1975. "He was so proud to see your name in here."

Josie opened the commencement program and Gretchen read out loud, "Josetta Ann Marshall, Valedictorian. What's inside that tissue paper, Auntie Jo?"

Josie unfolded the fragile leaf of tissue and strands of red hair tumbled into the light.

"When did he get this?" Josie whimpered.

"The day we cut the gum out of your hair," Momma chuckled.

Momma turned to Cassie next. "I took this snapshot, but I never got it into the album. Now it should go into yours."

I peered over Cassie's shoulder at the picture from not so long ago. Cassie's arms were wrapped around Daddy's neck, and I could hear him say, "I just might steal this girl away from you, Jake."

"Oh, Momma!" Cassie exclaimed. And I slipped quietly out of the room.

Voices called after me, but Momma directed, "Let him go. He won't go far."

Momma reached again into her quilted bag and slid the legal papers across the table. "Josie, Gene, this is your farm now. It was in your father's will. It's not paid for, you know. We mortgaged everything to get Eddie's Place started. But Jake and Cassie have a home of their own, and now this is your home."

"I don't know what to say, Momma," Gene humbled.

"Say you'll take care of Daddy's garden," Momma instructed. "And say that I can come visit anytime."

"Momma!" Josie gasped. "Where are you going?"

"Just down the road," Momma had decided. "My new home will be at Eddie's Place."

"No, Momma, NO!" Josie complained.

"JOSIE!" Momma silenced. Josie hushed and listened.

"I ran along and held on to your bicycle, until it was time to let go. You've pedaled far and you've spread your wings. It's time for me to let go and watch you fly. I have forty-two other children just down the road that need to learn how to fly."

Momma stood and tucked her quilted bag under her arm. "I need to go find Jake now."

Momma knew exactly where to find me. As she climbed the stairs, she heard the drawers in her room scrape open and slam shut. I was backing out of the closet when I heard Momma walk through the door. I spun around and the blood escaped from my face, like the pale of a young boy who was about to get a good whuppin.

Momma crossed her arms and squinted her eyes, and then gave way to a forgiving smile. "You're not going to find it in the closet, Jake. And you're not going to find it in his sock drawer."

Momma held out her quilted bag with one precious lump left nestled in its folds. I reached in and probed to the bottom, and my hand was filled with that perfect cylinder. The bag fell away and the letters on the tin can were brought back to life. "Ham and Lima Beans."

"Your father held that can every night, as he said his prayers. It was like a loose tooth that you can't resist pressing your tongue against until it hurts. There are some things that just hurt good."

I bolted for the door, but love pulled me back into Momma's arms. "Thank you, Momma."

"The best of your father is in you, Jake. Speak softly of his wisdom, walk proud, and run free."

I ran, down the stairs and through the kitchen. The back door banged out of my way, and I flew into the night. I buried my knees at the edge of Daddy's garden and held the can of ham and lima beans against my head.

I didn't cry. I struggled to pray. "Give me strength, Lord! Tell me what to do!"

Cassie was on her way out the door, but Tommy held her back. "Give me ten minutes with him, Darlin', then he's all yours."

Tommy approached and cleared his throat. He knew better than to sneak up on a guy who was ready to explode.

"You have to try that casserole your Aunt Margaret left for us."

Tommy sank his knees into the soil next to mine. "It's a damn sight better than that ham and lima beans you're holding."

Tommy wasn't hoping for a response. He was just warming up.

"What's the best ham and lima beans you remember?"

"When Rodrigues doused it with his hot sauce." I finally spoke. "Oh, God, Tommy, I miss him so much!"

"Yeah," Tommy agreed. "He was a damn good man. Do you remember what we did after we lost Rodrigues?"

"We regrouped on higher ground and you sent Borgelt and me back to get Rodrigues."

"Yeah," Tommy remembered. "We got him back home. I even saw his grave in San Antonio. But do you know what I did next?"

"You told us to get resupplied with more ammo and dry socks," I recalled. "Then you went to get briefed on our next mission."

"No, Jake. That wasn't the next thing I did. I wasn't fit for the next mission. Not until I cried out every tear for Rodrigues and pounded out every fear into my pillow."

Tommy remembered and I imagined.

"You have a long mission ahead of you, Jake, but you're not ready. You're in charge now and people are counting on you. Get yourself fit. That's an order."

Tommy didn't mince his words to soothe, and he made no attempt to excuse the way things are. He departed as quietly as he had approached, and left me in charge.

Cassie met Tommy at the door and he graced her with a kiss. "That's the second time I got to kiss the bride. Get yourself a pillow and run. He's all yours."

Cassie didn't question. She ran. She clutched a pillow in her arms and the back door banged out of her way. My eyes were fixed on the moon when Cassie snuggled next to me.

"One, two..." Cassie counted.

"Three stars to the right of the moon!" I screamed.

I buried my face in the pillow and screamed out every tear. I pounded every fear into that pillow until the feathers flew.

Chapter 31

For the next fourteen years, I took charge. I didn't concern myself with crops or livestock. Sam kept those well under control. I didn't worry about money. Josie knew where every penny came from and went. Chappy tended the souls and Momma tended the hearts.

I took charge of teaching how to fish, and I fished most every day.

Timmy learned to turn over any pile of manure and find a bounty of fishing worms. Brenda learned how to thread a worm securely on the hook, leaving just a little wiggle. Andrew learned how to smooth out his cast and keep his eye on the perfect spot to fish.

I pulled the brim of my hat over my eyes and learned how to listen.

"Maybe I should cast to a different spot," Andrew guessed. "I haven't had even a nibble."

"How long have you been at Eddie's Place?" I shifted the attention.

"Almost two years," Andrew answered with a hint of pride.

"Maybe it is time to reel in and cast to a new spot," I advised.

Andrew reeled in and thought and wondered. "Have I been here too long?" he asked.

Andrew's tackle slipped out of the water and the hook dangled clean and bare.

"No," I answered. "You haven't been here too long. You've just been fishing without any bait."

I handed Andrew another worm and pulled the brim over my eyes.

Andrew cast the fresh bait, and let it fly wherever it might. He let it drift and then sink, it didn't matter where.

"I've been thinking about getting into auto body repair," Andrew divulged. "I think I'd be pretty good at it."

"Uh-huh," I agreed. "I'd bet you would be. I wonder where that would take you. Maybe to the east coast, maybe the west coast. Where did you say you were from?"

"Florida," Andrew boasted. "Maybe someday I'll work on a Daytona 500 car!"

Andrew's line drew taut and he felt the tug. He reeled and shouted, "It's a big one!" He reeled in his prize and held it in his hand. "I've never caught a fish this big!"

I laughed and cheered and slapped my young fishing buddy on the back. "You're going to catch a lot of fish in your time, Brother."

Andrew and I fished until the stringer was full. Then we packed up our gear and headed up the path.

"Isn't this the biggest catfish you ever saw?" Andrew hoped.

"No, not quite," I had to admit. "But I've never seen a perch that big."

"Which one is the perch?" Andrew wanted to learn.

"The one with the color of the sun on his belly." I taught.

"And what's this, Jake?"

"That's my favorite," I pointed out. "That's the bass that gave you a hell of a fight."

I opened the trunk on the 54 Ford and spread the old blanket that had seen better days. Andrew laid the fish on the blanket in a tidy row.

"Hop in, Brother. We're going to town," I instructed.

The sun had not quite reached its highest arc, and it struck its glare across the windshield. The gravel was pinging on the chassis, and I turned the radio up louder.

Oh, how I loved that Marty Robbins. *"Out in the West Texas town of El Paso, I fell in love with a Mexican girl."*

"Where are we going, Jake?"

I didn't answer. I just sang along with Marty. *"Night time would find me in Rosa's cantina. Music would play and Feleena would whirl."*

"You know, Jake, I could fix those rust spots on your wheel well," Andrew assured.

Marty and I sang louder. *"In anger I challenged his right for this maiden. Down went his hand for the gun that he wore."*

"And I could slap a coat of paint on this baby and make it a classic," Andrew persisted.

I really bellowed out this part of the song. *"My challenge was answered in less than a heartbeat. The handsome young stranger lay dead on the floor."*

"Jake, are you hearing me?"

"Back in El Paso my life would be worthless..." "Help me finish this song, Brother," I demanded.

Andrew gave in. He put his feet on the dash, threw his head back and chimed in, *"Cradled by two loving arms that I'll die for. One little kiss and Feleena goooood – byeeee."*

We laughed at the awfulness of our voices and the sun warmed the hearts of two warriors who were now fishing buddies and two brothers who were joined in song.

I turned off the road just outside of town and pulled up to the bait shop that had been there as long as I could remember. We stepped into the shop and the smell of the holding tank full of minnows flooded my memory.

Old Jackson withdrew his hands from the minnow tank and wiped them dry on a smelly old towel. His weather-beaten face creased at the sight of Roy Marshall's little boy Jake.

Andrew and I held each end of the stringer of fish, and Old Jackson clicked a Polaroid. He tacked the snapshot on the wall, right under the picture of Roy and Jake Marshall and the biggest catfish I ever saw.

I shook Old Jackson's hand that smelled of fish and earth. We parted with a nod that said more than words could convey.

Our next stop was at Bobby's Auto Repair. Bobby spotted the old Ford and came out to greet us. I popped the trunk open and Bobby exclaimed, "Whoo-ee! Somebody's going to be eating good tonight."

"You and your family are, Bobby," I offered. "Get this mess of fish in a bucket of water."

Bobby carried the stringer of fish away and Andrew stood with his mouth agape. "But we caught those fish, Jake."

"Yes," I appeased. "They were our fish. Now they're our bait. Never forget to bait your hook, Andrew, and never be afraid to cast your bait into deeper water."

"Gee, thanks, Jake," Bobby returned.

"Thank Andrew here," I redirected. "He caught most of those fish."

Bobby reached for Andrew's hand. "Thanks, Buddy. You must be one of those Vietnam vets at Eddie's Place."

"Yes, Sir, 1st Cavalry," Andrew shook on.

"I was with the 1st Cavalry in Korea!" Bobby boomed.

"You two have a lot to talk about," I interrupted. "But I have some business to attend to."

I handed the car keys to Bobby and said, "That old Ford has some rust spots that need taken care of, and I'd like a new coat of paint. I'm going to hitch a ride home and leave Andrew here to show you how he can turn that jalopy into a classic."

I walked away, just like that. I didn't look back and Andrew didn't either.

Andrew was one of many who passed our way. He was one of many that escaped a legacy of war and cast his bait into the wind of tomorrow.

Chapter 32

I taught everyone how to fish, and everyone learned how to follow a dream.

We lived for letters from those who followed their dreams, and Momma was challenged each year to find enough places to display all the Christmas cards. For nearly twenty years, broken hearts and daunted spirits had been healed around the fire pit and Eddie's Place said, "so long" to future doctors and lawyers, butchers, bakers, and candlestick makers. It was not a bad legacy for the man who taught me how to fish.

I taught my kids how to fish, but they taught me more.

Gretchen didn't care whether a fish grabbed her bait. She was determined to be a fisher of souls. "I'm going to be a Navy chaplain, Daddy."

"Oh?" I responded from under the brim of my hat.

"The Navy was the first to let women spread the gospel, and that's where I'm going to cast my lot," Gretchen committed.

I raised the brim from my eyes and stroked Gretchen's cheek. *"And He will raise you up on eagles' wings, bear you on the breath of dawn, make you to shine like the sun, and hold you in the palm of his hand."*

I pulled the brim back over my eyes and advised, "Just remember your way home."

"I will, Daddy. I will."

Josh was the hunter, always in search of the prize. But he never fished without his brother Ben by his side. Ben baited the hook and always shed a tear. He knew that the worm had no brain, but he knew it could feel. If there was anything Ben understood, it was how to feel.

Josh cast with a purpose and his aim was sure and true. He always knew where his cast would take him, and it would never be where Ben couldn't go.

"Your sister plans on joining the Navy," I muttered from under my brim.

"Yeah," Josh already knew. "All I can say is that nobody better get in her way."

"Have you had any thoughts about the military?" I had to ask.

"I've thought a lot about it," Josh was clear. "But I'm not going anywhere unless Ben can come along."

Ben grinned from ear to ear. I nodded off in peace, and the years passed as if in a dream.

Gretchen rushed back from college to watch her brothers walk across the stage. Josh received his high school diploma and Ben did not. But Ben walked across the stage with his brother. Josh wouldn't have it any other way.

It would be three more years before a diploma bore Ben's name, and his brother would be with him when he walked across that stage. Ben wouldn't have it any other way.

Gretchen went on to seminary school, and the boys worked the farm. There was less and less for me to do. The boys were taking over and I felt the reins slipping from my hands. But I had learned from Daddy how to let go of the reins. I kept fishing and speaking softly of Daddy's wisdom.

Our family of five piled in the car and the crowd watched the dust in our trail settle behind us.

Josh drove and he knew the way to Kansas City. Ben counted telephone poles and made sure that Josh didn't miss any exits. Cassie and I hummed along as Gretchen sang. *"And He will raise you up, on eagles' wings..."*

Daddy was right. "Happiness is when right now is the best time of your life."

We cried our farewells in Kansas City, when we heard Gretchen's boarding call. She was on her way to officer training at Fort Jackson, South Carolina. There was no question that troops in war zones all over the world would someday be comforted by Chaplain Gretchen Marshall's faith. But with all her faith and all her determination, she cried the tears that I knew so well.

"Read ten verses every night, Ben, and I'll be reading along with you. Let's start tonight with the Gospel of John, *"And God so loved the world..."*

"I will, Gretch."

"Stay out of trouble, Josh."

"I can't promise that, Sis, but I'll try."

"Am I doing the right thing, Momma?"

"You've always done the right thing, Baby."

"I'm kinda scared, Daddy."

"Being scared will keep you safe," I assured. "Just do something for me."

"Anything, Daddy."

"Buckle your seatbelt," I ordered. "Then start writing, Dear Mom and Dad."

I didn't wipe the tears from my eyes. I let them dry in the wrinkles of my cheeks. What had been mine would never be taken away.

Chapter 33

The boys came bursting in as if the house was on fire. Their faces had the look of someone who had just discovered gold.

"Momma! Daddy!" Ben yowled. "We found a truck!"

We had no idea what this was all about, but we were excited. Ben's exuberance about anything always made our hearts leap.

"Calm down, Ben," Josh stilled. "Let me explain."

The boys sat at the table, and Ben laced his fingers together just like Josh.

"Ben and I have been thinking a long time about…" Josh drawled.

Cassie and I leaned in with our full attention.

"We've been talking about hitting the road, like you two did," Josh gambled. "We want to see all the places and things you've told us about. We want to taste those Omaha steaks and that Louisiana gumbo. We want to dip our toes in both oceans."

"I'll make sure Josh doesn't miss any exits, Daddy," Ben swore. "And I'll write you every day, Momma."

"We'll take care of each other," Josh guaranteed.

Cassie wiped her eyes and sighed, "I always knew this day would come. I just didn't think it would come so darn soon."

I stood and loomed over the boys. "Show me this truck."

Josh drove and Ben rode shotgun. Cassie and I clung to each other in the back seat. Cassie laid her head on my shoulder and sang softly. *Where are you going, my little one, little one? Where are you going, my baby, my own?*

Josh turned into Bobby's Auto Repair, and Andrew came running. Before we were out of the car, Andrew was buffing the chrome on the old 54 Ford.

"I'll take this old jalopy off your hands, Jake," Andrew joked.

"You can't afford it, brother," I retorted. "It's a classic."

"Come on!" Josh urged. "The truck's out back."

The boys raced ahead and Cassie and I sauntered behind.

"Andrew?" I questioned. "What's up?"

Andrew savored the moment. "Well, Jake. I got this old truck dirt cheap. Bobby and I have been working on it for months. It's a sweet ride, now, Jake. It'll carry your boys a lot of miles, and I'll give them a good price."

Cassie gasped at the sight of eighteen wheels and a big shiny cab. Josh was sitting in the driver's seat, chomping at the bit. Ben was thumping the tires and dancing in sheer glee.

"Do you have any idea how to drive this thing?" I shouted up to Josh.

"Not a clue, Daddy, but I'm going to learn."

"Climb down out of there, Son. We need to talk."

I laid my hands on Josh's shoulders. "You're biting off a lot to chew here, Son. Are you sure about this?"

Josh met my eyes with the sincerity he always did and smiled with the confidence he always had. "Is that what Grandpa asked you, Daddy?"

I was on the other side of the mirror now, and my own eyes were looking back at me. "That's exactly what he asked me, Son."

"And I'll bet you told Grandpa that you had never been so sure about anything in your life."

"Yes, Josh, that's what I told him."

"I'll bet Grandpa was really worried. But I guess he knew that you would remember everything he taught you."

Josh recited the lessons of generations and pledged from his heart. "I'll always take care of my family, and I'll never leave my brother behind. I'll work hard and I'll never give up. I won't take unfair advantage of another man, and no man will ever take unfair advantage of me or my brother. We'll remember who created us, and we'll remember our way home."

I couldn't speak. I could barely stand. Joy is stronger than sorrow and hope is stronger than fear. But my knees were about to buckle.

"The only difference between you and me, Daddy, is that I don't have a down payment."

I grabbed that young man like a sack of potatoes. I hugged with all my might and whispered in his ear. "Give me the car keys."

I took the keys and turned to Cassie. We didn't need to talk. We just needed to see eye-to-eye. I was still watching the flutter in Cassie's eyes when I dealt with Andrew. "Can you deliver this truck tomorrow with the fuel tanks full?"

"Sure thing, Jake, and I'll throw in five or so quarts of oil."

"We're going to need a ride home, Andrew."

Cassie's eyes welled up in tears and her lips pursed. I reached out with the car keys and dangled the bait. "Here's your down payment, Andrew."

Andrew snatched the bait. The boys whooped and hollered. Cassie and I stood, locked eye-to-eye.

I had traded baseball cards and marbles with the toughest of opponents. I had traded C-Rations and jokes with the best of friends. I had traded cattle for seed money and fish for favors. I had traded a shit-load of fear and regret for a glimmer of hope. This — was the best deal I had ever made.

Josh enrolled in driver's school the next day, and Ben kept thumping the tires. We talked into the wee hours night after night. Cassie and I remembered and taught. The boys listened and dreamed.

"What's the capitol of Utah?" Cassie tested.

"Salt Lake City," Ben snapped back.

"How do I get from Salt Lake City to Denver?" Cassie pushed on.

"Interstate 80 East," Ben had memorized.

Ben knew that it took him longer than most folks to learn, so Ben worked harder than most folks. Everything he learned, he locked away in a memory that would not fail him.

"Truck stop checklist, Buddy," Cassie prompted.

Ben shut his eyes tight and tapped into that steadfast memory. "Headlights, tail lights, turn signals, air pressure, oil, water, windshield, mirrors — and — uh — oh yeah, go to the bathroom."

Cassie traced her fingers around Ben's face from his hair to his chin and cooed, "Three eggs plus two eggs equals..."

Ben had that memory locked away too. It was a memory of the simplest of beginnings and limitless promise. It was a witness to a mother's assurance on the first day of school. "The world will one day understand how special you are."

It was a moment too profound to hold back the tears. "Five eggs, Momma."

Josh and I burned the fuel and ground out the miles in that old but sturdy truck.

"DEER!" I shouted.

There was no deer, but Josh methodically moved his foot to the brake and geared down.

Josh entered the curve at the perfect speed, but I yelled, "You're going to lose your load! POWER THROUGH IT!"

Josh put the pedal to the metal, gripped the wheel with fists of iron, and the smoke stacks plumed.

I threw everything at that boy, but he never flinched and never wavered. I tested him with every distraction and Josh kept his eyes glued to the road.

I taught Josh every song Marty Robbins ever wrote, and he taught me how to really sing.

We sat the boys down for our final lecture. "So, you passed the test and got your license, Josh. I suppose you think you're ready now."

"Yes, sir, I do," Josh boldly affirmed. "But not because I passed the licensing exam. I'm ready because I passed your tests, Daddy."

"Yes you did, Son. I'd ride with you anywhere."

"And Ben passed every test," Cassie announced. "You don't need a map when Ben's riding along."

Cassie bowed her head and shivered. "I have every confidence in you boys."

I detected a slight sniffle in her voice. "And I'm scared to death to let you go."

"Momma, please don't cry."

"Momma, don't be scared."

Cassie daubed her tears and got down to business. "Here are your medical records and Ben's prescriptions. I'll expect to see you come home at least every three months for doctor visits."

"Yes Ma'am," Ben obeyed.

"Here is a list of all the shippers we knew. Your Dad has called all of them and updated the information."

"Thank you, Momma," Josh accepted.

"Here is a list of the best truck stops and diners we knew. If you ever run into a waitress in Minneapolis, named Mabel, say hi for me."

Ben began immediately cementing a new memory. "Minneapolis Mabel – Minneapolis Mabel – Minneapolis Mabel."

Cassie's voice began to falter. "And you boys — you — pack lots of clean underwear."

Cassie dashed from the room with her face in her hands. The boys darted to pursue, but I stopped them in their tracks. "Have a seat, boys."

The boys sat on the edge of their chairs and stared at their mother's bedroom door.

"She's stronger than you know guys. Just give her a few minutes. Then you can go kiss her goodnight."

"There's no such thing as loving too much. But if there was, that would be your Mom."

"There's no such thing as an easy goodbye, and your Mom has said a lot of them. So have I."

"This will be our toughest goodbye, but it has to be. It's time for us to watch you chase your dreams."

I leaned forward and motioned for the boys to join me in a secret pact. Our heads were mere inches apart as I laid out my plan. We whispered and we plotted.

"That sounds great, Daddy. What can we do to help?" Josh volunteered.

"You talk to Auntie Jo and ask her to pack your Mom's bag."

"Ben, you ask Grandma to pack us a lunch."

Two days of secrecy passed. For two days, Cassie wondered what everyone was smiling about.

The cock crowed at about 5 a.m. on July 15, 1998. Twenty-seven years to the day, I rolled over and said, "Happy Anniversary. Get your overalls on. I'll see you downstairs."

Momma was flipping the eggs over easy. Josh was buttering the toast, and Ben was pouring the coffee when Cassie walked in.

"HAPPY ANNIVERSARY!"

Cassie sat at the table with a girlish grin. "Oh, my goodness!"

Momma served Cassie's eggs. "Eat up, Dear. You have a long day ahead of you."

I avoided Cassie's quizzical look and sipped my coffee.

Ben served the toast. "Wait until you see what Grandma packed for your lunch."

"Jake?" Cassie suspected.

I stuffed a whole slice of toast in my mouth and sealed my lips.

Josie and Gene walked in the door, and Josie planted a straw hat on Cassie's head. "Got to keep the sun out of your eyes and your eyes on the road."

"JAKE!" Cassie grew more frantic.

I washed down the toast and explained. "I found a load out of Wichita. Well — it's only half a load. But it should pay for the fuel to Fort Worth."

"FORT WORTH?" Cassie screamed.

Cassie danced from Grandma to Sister to Son and to Son.

I chased her out the door and the whole clan followed.

Cassie scrambled into the driver's seat of the truck and fired up the engine. I climbed into the passenger seat and warned, "I'm not one of those easy Texas boys you can have for a smile and a flashy truck. You're going to have to buy me dinner in Wichita."

Cassie gave a blast of the horn and threw in the clutch. We pulled slowly out of the drive and onto the road. It was a gentle ride the first two miles, and then we turned the corner. The engine revved louder and the breath of dawn passed through the windows.

I smelled my love of twenty-seven years and proposed, "PUNCH IT!"

Cassie threw her head back and laughed, "YOU'VE GOT IT COWBOY!"

View other Black Rose Writing titles at www.blackrosewriting.com/books
and use promo code **PRINT** to receive a **20% discount** when purchasing.

BLACK ROSE
writing™

CPSIA information can be obtained
at www.ICGtesting.com
Printed in the USA
FFOW02n0511190518
46768668-48921FF